Dear Dalia

A Simple Love Story: Book 6

Dana LeCheminant

First Printing: November 2020

ISBN: 978-1-951753-06-1

To my future husband:
may you be as dreamy as Colin—otherwise, we're going to have a problem

Dear Dalia,

I'm so excited for the first day of camp tomorrow that I can't sleep, so I figured I'd get a head start on this week's letter. I know you think I'm silly for getting so anxious every year, but there's just so much to look forward to and worry about that I can't hold it all in! What will the girls be like? Will my cabin be full of spiders like it was last year? Are the counselors going to push me into the lake again if I complain it's too hot? Every year is always so different, and no matter how many times I go, something new happens. Something unexpected.

And I feel like there's something big coming this year. I don't know what it might be or why I have those extra butterflies in my stomach, but I haven't been this nervous since I sang the National Anthem in that middle school assembly. You know the one where I forgot half the words partway through and had to start over?

This is worse.

But even though I'm so nervous, I'm still excited. You'll be proud of me for that, because you know how I get when I'm nervous. I promise I won't overthink things this time, and I won't end up bleaching my hair blonde like I did that summer before I started high school so I could fit in with the cool crowd.

OMG, it's almost midnight! I should really try to get some sleep, and I'll write again next week, as always.

Love and kisses!
Beck

P.S. Don't you dare say "I told you so" when everything turns out fine like it always does.

P.P.S. I learned today that the mice in the kitchen are no longer afraid of Buckles the Cat because he's too lazy. That could make things interesting this summer.

P.P.P.S. Is it weird for a counselor to still write letters home?

CHAPTER ONE

June 2020

"We've got a good crop of girls this year," Linda said as she scanned the list of camp attendees during our morning meeting. "A few more than we're used to, but that was why we hired Annabeth, so that shouldn't be a problem. She has a lot of energy, and—"

"And we just spent the last month training with her," Yasmine said loudly. Smart move, seeing as our camp director was about to launch into a monologue if someone didn't interrupt her. The rest of us head counselors shot her a grateful look. "We know Annabeth will be fine. And you say that about the girls every year."

Linda looked like she'd just tripped on an exposed tree root mid-stride and had to catch her footing, her mouth working through the words coming out of her head as she searched for her place. Yes, she could ramble, but she was the most organized person I knew and would have to mentally scroll through her list of agenda items and find her place again. "Right," she finally said, and she gave Yasmine a genuine smile. "The girls are always wonderful."

Sofie slapped her hand on the list in front of her, drawing all eyes to her end of the pool table around which we held our staff meetings. "You gave me the Connelly twins? *Again?*"

Linda's smile didn't change. "Yes, but I also gave you Lucy Pickery, so it evens out."

"Last year the Connellys dyed my hair blue."

Ah, yes, I had almost forgotten about that. She'd woken up in the cabin on Departure Day, when the girls were heading home at the end of the summer, and her scream had carried across the entire camp. Personally, I thought she'd rocked the blue, but clearly she hadn't appreciated it as much as she could have.

"Their parents agreed to let us search their luggage before they come through the gates," Linda assured Sofie.

I caught Gabby's eye across the table from me, and we both ducked our heads before we laughed. My best friend and I had worked at Camp Rockwood long enough to know a simple luggage search wouldn't stop Gigi and Nina Connelly from pulling their pranks. They were nightmares but geniuses, and not a single one of us had outsmarted them yet.

Neither of us, however, would point this out to Linda, and especially not to Sofie.

"Looks like Bailey Summerland is back in California," Gabby said, probably to get the subject off the Connellys. "She'll be fun to have."

"And we don't have to deal with Hattie VanDerman this year," Yasmine added as she ran her finger down the list.

For the first time all morning, Linda's smile faltered. "Yes, well, Miss VanDerman has, um…"

"She's in Juvie," Sofie said with a smirk. "I saw it on the internet a few weeks ago. The little brat finally got caught stealing."

I could see Linda's gears whirring, searching for the function in her mind that deflected touchy subjects we probably weren't supposed to discuss openly anyway, but I was curious and jumped in before our fearless leader could swing conversation back to business.

"What'd she steal this time?" I asked.

Sofie's grin was triumphant. "Her daddy's Mercedes."

"That explains the juvenile detention," Yasmine said and whistled low.

"Ladies," Linda said.

"I bet she crashed it too," Gabby added.

"I think we should—"

"Hopefully she actually learns her lesson this time," Sofie said.

"If we could—"

"I doubt it," I laughed.

Linda grabbed a billiard ball and slammed it down so hard on the table that all of us jumped in alarm. And then, as if nothing had happened, she put her smile back on and looked at each of us in turn. "You are my head counselors," she said, and there was only the slightest strain in her voice. Impressive. "I expect you to show a mode of decorum when the girls arrive. As always."

She didn't have to say specifically what that meant, and she knew she didn't have to worry. Not really. Here on our own, away from the girls and the other counselors, we tended to let out our frustrations and be completely ourselves. But once we stepped out of the rec room and onto the grass in front of the flagpole, we would be professionals. We always were.

Besides, summer was my favorite time of the year, and there was no way I would ever jeopardize my chance to spend two months doing something I absolutely loved. None of us would.

Sensing our return to seriousness, Linda let out a little sigh that would only be the first of many as the new year at Camp Rockwood began. "Let's make this summer a good one, shall we?" she asked.

The cheer from the four of us was so full of energy and enthusiasm, it could have been the voices of hundreds.

"Beck, could I have a quick word?" The Stomp would begin in less than ten minutes, but Linda pulled me aside just outside the mess hall, a bit of a frown on her face.

Frowns from Linda made me nervous. "What's up?" I asked. When she didn't immediately answer, I tried to guess. "I'll keep an eye on the Connelly girls."

Nope, not that.

"Sorry I jumped into the VanDerman conversation. I know you hate when we gossip."

Linda's frown increased.

"I'm out of assumptions," I said finally. "Is something wrong?"

"Did you look at your cabin list?"

"Uh." I wasn't even sure where I'd put it, but I was pretty sure Linda would have remembered that I never looked at my list. The surprise was more fun. "No. I didn't. Should I have?"

Linda nodded, but it was more of an absent nod. On the other side of the mess hall, a buzz of voices and shouts was growing as busload after busload of girls swarmed to the field. "We have a new girl joining your cabin this year."

That happened all the time, but I had a feeling this one was different. I was tempted to remind Linda that I had handled everything from wheelchairs to rebels to girls so shy they couldn't speak, but the look on her face made me pause. Now was not the time to show off.

"Who is she?" I asked.

"Macy Donovan."

"Never heard of her."

"You've probably heard of her father. Colin Donovan."

I searched my rather small database of names that didn't belong to preteen girls, but the name didn't strike any bells. Unless the guy was as famous as the likes of Ryan Reynolds, I'd never heard of him. "Who?"

Yasmine blew the whistle, the signal for the counselors to gather up and start catching the attention of the crowd of girls waiting on the field. We only had a couple of minutes before Linda was supposed to give her welcoming speech.

Linda sighed a little. "Honestly, Rebecka, you need to get out more. Colin Donovan only owns one of the most successful new tech businesses in San Francisco. He's been all over the internet for months!"

"He may have been on the internet," I replied, "but I haven't. And while I know we're not exactly rich kid central, what makes Macy any different from the rest of the girls?"

"Oh," Linda said, clearly distracted by the upcoming speech, "she shouldn't cause any problems, though I don't actually know her personality. I have full faith in your abilities."

I'd never seen our Head of Camp so distracted, and I had a sinking feeling in the pit of my stomach. It took a lot to truly ruffle her, and now she was entirely thrown off her programming.

"Thanks?" I said. "So what's the problem?"

"The problem is—"

Stomp stomp clap.

Linda's face drained of color. "Oh!" she said squeakily. "We need to go!"

Stomp stomp clap.

I so did not want to leave this conversation hanging like that, but I knew there would be no stopping Linda now that the chant had started.

Stomp stomp clap.

Taking her by the arm—she still looked horribly pale—I dragged Linda with me around the mess hall and tried to ignore the hundred pairs of eyes watching us as we raced to the little stage under the flag-pole, where the other counselors were gathered in a line for the stomp.

Stomp stomp clap. "We are, we are, Rockwood!" *Stomp stomp clap.* "We are, we are, Rockwood!"

Though still a little flustered, Linda took a deep breath and seemed to flip a switch in her brain, turning on her spunky side. "Are you ready?" she shouted.

"Yeah!" the girls shouted back as they continued to stomp and clap along with the counselors.

"I can't hear you!" Linda cried. "ARE YOU READY!"

"YEAH!"

"We are Camp Rockwood!" Linda shouted. As cheers rang out among the girls, she grabbed the megaphone from Yasmine and launched straight into her usual start-of-camp speech, though it took a moment for the girls to calm down enough to be able to hear her.

I knew I should be paying attention, but I was still a little on edge from the conversation we hadn't been able to finish. I had dealt with pretty much everything while working at this camp, but clearly this was something Linda thought was outside of my expertise if she was so nervous about it. What was it about this Macy Donovan that had Linda dropping her list as she prepared to read out the cabin assignments?

"You good, Beck?" Gabby asked as the rest of the counselors scattered to the edges of the field so the girls could start gathering.

I hardly knew, but I nodded and put on my best smile. "Always," I said then broke into a run until I reached my designated spot to wait for my girls.

I knew I wasn't supposed to play favorites, but I couldn't help but grin as my cabin assembled around me. Linda had been especially kind this year, and as girls like Julia Chambers and Brielle Beau gathered, I started planning out the rest of the summer. Each and every one of these girls was adventurous and energetic. Most of them were older as well, ranging from ten to thirteen, which meant we wouldn't have any activity restrictions like Annabeth across the field, who had what looked like three first graders clinging to her legs as their nerves got the better of them. Based on the fact that Willow and Brielle were talking a million miles a minute about how great the summer was going to be, our cabin was going to be amazing.

Then Macy showed up. I knew her immediately because I didn't recognize her, but there were also hints of a wealthy upbringing surrounding her, like her penny loafers and the way she shrunk away from a fly buzzing past as if it might attack. She was probably eight or nine, so a little younger than the rest of my girls, but I didn't doubt the rest of the cabin would welcome her with open arms. With this crop of campers, I wasn't worried about anyone being excluded.

As if brought on the breeze, trepidation filled my stomach with a churning that wasn't going to go away easily. Linda *never* divided the girls like this. I had *never* had such an easy group. I stared at Macy for a second, trying to figure out what about her was going to cause me problems, but she looked like an average rich girl trying not to look scared as she clung to the backpack that weighed down her shoulders.

Glancing out over the chaotic field then counting my girls—eight, as it should be—I took a deep breath and pushed my nerves down before they showed on my face. If something was going to go wrong, there was no point stressing myself out about it until I had all the info.

"Okay, ladies," I said, putting on my biggest smile. Immediately, I had the attention of seven girls. Macy stared at her feet. "Who's ready to make Cabin Three the best cabin this camp has ever seen?"

The shrieks that answered my question were loud enough to make a bird fly out of the bushes by the mess hall. I saw Gabby glance my way, and a second later, her own girls had a scream to match, followed by Sofie's and Chelsea's, each one louder than the last as our competition began.

"I'm sorry," I said. "I'm not sure I heard you. Who's the best cabin here?"

"Cabin Three!"

"Cabin Two!" came the response.

"Cabin Nine!"

On and on until the whole camp was alive with energy. Exactly how it should be.

Just before I was about to lead the girls off to our cabin, a wave from the flagpole caught my eye. Linda gestured me over, looking flustered. Man, she was really starting to cramp my style.

"Hey Julia," I said quickly, "lead the way, will you? I'll be right behind you."

Julia stood straight and proud, her grin infectious. "Aye aye, Captain!" she said with a flourished salute. "This way to Cabin Three, you scalawags!" And she marched off, a trail of girls following close behind.

I watched Macy Donovan for just a moment as she took up the rear, but only a few seconds after the march began, Kristy Kane took her by the arm and started chatting with her as they went.

Good girl.

Linda had gone into the rec room, which meant she was probably in her office. As girls around me said their last goodbyes to parents and hurried off after their counselors, I slipped across the field and hurried inside, determined to make this chat last as short a time as possible so I didn't miss too much of the start of summer bonding between my girls. It was one of my favorite parts of the year!

I started talking before I stepped through Linda's door, deciding I had best remind her how much I loved the first day of camp. "You really need to stop killing my buzz, Linda, or I swear I will toss you into the lake and—"

Linda coughed her *very important* cough, killing my threat immediately, and then she nodded her head to the chair in the corner behind me.

I was almost too afraid to look. The last time we'd had someone in that chair, it had been a police officer here to tell us there was a fugitive on the loose in the nearby forest. It was the *bad news* chair and always complicated things. The fact that someone sat in that chair on the very first day of camp had to be a bad omen.

Turning slowly, I saw the cell phone first, pressed to his ear as if he were in the middle of a conversation and had only stopped because of my interruption. I saw his suit next, well-tailored and the blackest of blacks. It fit over a slim but strong body, the kind I'd expect to see on someone who went to the gym often but didn't live there. His shoes were the shiniest I'd ever seen, though there was already a patch of dust on the left one. I had a feeling he hadn't noticed yet. I looked at his face last, not on purpose, but it seemed appropriate when I took in features that most definitely equaled Ryan Reynolds's. He had a sharp jaw, sharp haircut, sharp gaze. Handsome though he was, everything about him was sharp, as if he thought smooth edges were a weakness.

"Colin Donovan," I guessed. "Macy's dad." That last part I wasn't sure about, mostly because he neither looked old enough to have a nine-year-old nor had the countenance of a father who would personally bring his daughter to a summer camp in Northern California. He looked like the sort to stuff her into a car and send her on her way, glad to be rid of her for the summer. Plenty of parents dropped their girls off every June, but none of them looked a thing like this guy.

Realizing he still held his phone, Mr. Donovan glanced at the screen then decided to hang up, though I heard a voice on the other end start asking if he was still there. He kept the phone in his hand, ready to jump right back to it when he'd finished conducting his business.

"Her?" That one word filled the air with his disgust and disapproval.

I'm sorry, what? I knew the question was for Linda, but I stepped in between her and this guy who was starting to get on my every nerve. I had campers to go welcome, his daughter among them, and I did not need some high and mighty bigwig thinking me incompetent. "I'm Beck Alvarez," I said and held out my hand, though I would have rather hit him with it than let him shake it. "One of the head counselors here at Camp Rockwood. Is there a concern I can help you resolve while I'm here?"

He didn't even consider reaching for my hand, instead leaning around me to fix Linda with a stare that, honestly, I was glad wasn't for me. "I thought I made myself clear in my emails, Mrs. Young."

Behind me, Linda sputtered a little, which was uncharacteristic. Organized as she was, she always had the perfect responses for irate parents, no matter their grievances. "Of course, Mr. Donovan. I assure you, I was incredibly diligent in choosing which cabin your daughter should spend her stay here at—"

"My concern is not for the cabin," Donovan said, and he fixed that stare on me.

I wasn't usually intimidated, but geez, the guy knew how to scowl. I felt myself withering, which was not a feeling I enjoyed experiencing. What right did this jerk have to step into my world and assume he knew everything? How could he possibly think a couple of sentences—spoken in jest, no less—were enough to gauge my entire character?

"Beck," Linda said, her voice thick with warning. She knew me well. "I called you in here so we could discuss expectations for the next two months. If you could take a seat." It was not a request.

This is fine, I told myself as I sank into the chair closer to Linda's desk. *We'll just have a little chat, he'll leave, and I can get back to my girls.* Sitting there with my back to Colin Donovan, though, I was finding it hard to focus on positivity. I could practically feel his disapproval searing the back of my head.

"Like I started telling you this morning," Linda said to me, "Mr. Donovan's daughter will be attending our camp this year. Macy. I've put her in your cabin because I feel you're one of our best counselors, and—"

Mr. Donovan cleared his throat. "And I happen to disagree with her choice," he said.

Linda tensed, but I pretended I didn't notice and turned instead to face the guy behind me. There were a lot of things I thought about saying to him, but I kept my words civil. For now. He thought he had some kind of power here? He didn't, and I would make sure he knew that.

"I'm sorry you feel that way," I said calmly.

His jaw tightened.

"I truly believe Rebecka here is our best counselor," Linda added, and I had to turn and give her a warm smile because I knew she wouldn't say it if she didn't mean it. There was no room in that organized head of hers for lies. "I understand your concerns, Mr. Donovan, but there really is no way for us to change things now that camp has begun."

He narrowed his eyes, and his hand seemed to tighten around his phone. "Just switch her with another girl," he suggested. "How hard can that be?"

I snorted a laugh before I could hold it back, and his surprise made it all too easy for me to ask, "Do you understand girls at all, Mr. Donovan?"

"Excuse me?"

"Beck," Linda sighed, but she had sat down in her chair, knowing full well it was dangerous to step between me and a challenge.

And Mr. Donovan was certainly a challenge. Whatever he thought of me, he seemed to think he could make whatever changes he wanted without any consequences, and I had to make sure he understood exactly why he couldn't do that. I had to protect my girls. *All* of them, whether in my cabin or not.

"Mr. Donovan," I said and stood to face him, "we're twenty minutes into the first day of camp."

"Which should make a change like this easy," he said. Jeez, did he know any expressions outside of that scowl of his? And he kept his voice so smooth and controlled that I wondered if he even had any emotion behind his thick skin.

"You mistake my meaning," I replied. "Two minutes, maybe, but by now those girls have picked their bunks, chosen their best friends, decided on their enemies, and elected a leader to follow. You try to upset that, and you'll have eighty girls out for blood. Yours, specifically."

Donovan tilted his head to the side a little, a bit of a wrinkle marring that smooth forehead of his. "You make them sound like a savage civilization with no law and order, Miss Alvarez."

"She's not wrong," Linda said, probably not as under her breath as she might have planned.

"My point," I continued, "is we can't have you upsetting the whole order of things just because you're a little worried. Mr. Donovan, I promise I will be looking after your daughter all summer."

He got to his feet, folding his arms as he towered above me. He was tall, but it was his powerful energy that made him loom over me like he did. "But you're not looking after her at the moment," he said.

"Yes, because I'm busy talking to you."

"Rebecka." Linda's voice was as sharp as Donovan's skinny black tie as she stood and put on her *I mean business* face. "Could I speak to you in private for a moment? Mr. Donovan, if you don't mind," and she gestured toward the door.

I couldn't decide if his expression meant he wanted to storm out or shout at me until his voice went hoarse, but he thankfully agreed to Linda's request and slipped out of the office, closing the door behind him.

I didn't waste a second. "Don't try to tell me I'm overreacting. That is classic control freak behavior, and honestly I bet his daughter's relieved to be here at camp where he can't get to her because a man like that couldn't possibly be fun to have for a dad when he can't even step away for a few minutes let alone a few months, and I'm surprised you haven't sent him packing now that the girls are settling in and—"

"Beck," Linda said.

I dropped into my chair, staring at her. I'd never heard her sound like that, like the world was on her shoulders and she wasn't sure she could hold it up any longer.

"We can't afford to anger Mr. Donovan."

"Can't afford—"

"He has made a generous donation—extremely generous—to Camp Rockwood, and without it, we wouldn't…"

I swallowed, though it felt like my throat was stuck shut. "What are you saying, Linda?" Camp Rockwood had been open for fifty years, and never once had there been any money problems. At least, not that I knew of. Linda would have told me if… Wouldn't she?

Collapsing into her chair, Linda let her breath out in a steady stream and deflated. "The city has decided to sell the land, Beck. Some developer wants to come in and create a high-end resort, and we don't have enough stored up to... Without Colin Donovan, we'll lose this place. We'll lose everything."

"Sell the land?" The words tasted bitter, like when Chuck put too much cilantro in the salad. "I thought we owned the land."

Linda shook her head. "We've been lucky for so many years," she said. "The city has allowed us to use this plot, since we take on the girls from Hargrave School every summer and give the foster families a bit of a break. But with this economy, they're hard-pressed to sell while it still gets a good price."

"And Colin Donovan's money can buy it," I surmised. "But only if he stays happy and doesn't pull his donation." My heart ached at the thought, sitting heavy in my chest as my ears rang a bit. Lose Camp Rockwood? I couldn't even imagine the idea. I'd been coming to this camp since I was six years old, and I'd been a counselor since I turned eighteen. For more than twenty years, this place had been my home every summer, and I barely remembered a time before it. If all that went away...

Linda uttered a word I'd never heard her use here at Rockwood, and I raised my eyebrows. But she waved my reaction away and said, "I'm sorry to spring all this on you, Beck. I should have told you sooner, but I was hoping to find a way around it before I worried anyone. But you of all people... You deserved to know, and I'm sorry."

It'll be fine. I didn't believe that. *We can make it work.* That sounded better. *We'll find a way.* Reasonable. "I can be nice," I assured Linda, though the idea of facing Mr. Donovan again, especially now that my energy seemed to have been sucked out of my chest with a plunger, was making me a little nauseous. "I promise."

If Linda believed me, it didn't show on her face. She had been head of Camp Rockwood for six summers now, so she and I knew each other as well as we knew our own families. She could read me easily, but I could also read her.

"What?" I asked warily.

"I'm not sure you can last that long," she admitted.

I didn't realize she had such little faith in me. "It'll only be a few minutes," I reasoned. "An hour at most, and then he'll be gone."

Linda's face turned as white as the marshmallows we had prepped for tonight's campfire. "About that…"

CHAPTER TWO

"Absolutely not!"

Linda dropped her head into her hands, apparently giving up when she of all people should have been the one backing me up on this. "Beck, *please*."

"I am not okay with some strange bigshot from San Francisco lurking around my girls," I snarled as I paced the room. "I'm not."

Mr. Donovan, who had rejoined us at the same time Linda explained his plans to remain at the camp for the duration of the summer, probably should have been insulted by the unspoken accusation I very much intended to make, but he just stood there in the corner, his eyes on the opposite wall and his jaw muscles clenching tight. Honestly, his expression hadn't changed once since the moment I stepped inside Linda's office, and that was really starting to bug me. At the very least he could roll his eyes or something.

Prove you're actually human!

"He is not going to lurk," Linda said. "Are you, Mr. Donovan?"

"Of course he's going to say no," I complained, and then I paused and stared at the guy. Was he *smiling?* Barely, but yes. "This is not a good idea, Linda, and you know it. It's just not safe."

Taking a slow breath, Linda sat up straight and was doing her best to go back to the calm and collected woman that ran a perfect camp. "Beck," she said, "do you really think I would have agreed if I had any hesitation about letting him be nearby? He won't be here at night, and he'll stay out of the way during activities. You won't even notice he's here."

"The girls will notice," I argued and jumped back into my pacing. "They're going to wonder why there's a strange man wandering around their girls-only camp, and it's going to make them nervous! Besides, I really don't think Macy needs—"

Something grabbed my arm, and I found myself in the strong grip of a suddenly angry Mr. Donovan. "Don't pretend to know what my daughter does or doesn't NEED," he said, his voice dropping into an icy rumble. "Your job is to make sure she has a good summer here at Camp Rockwood. Nothing more."

"My *job*," I said as I ripped my arm free, "is to teach these girls that they are strong, and beautiful, and unique. My job is to make sure that when they go out into the world, they know they are capable of anything and everything, no matter who might tell them differently. Now if you'll excuse me, I have to check on my girls before they think they've been abandoned, like they clearly have before."

Just before I stepped through the door, Mr. Donovan threw his arm across the doorway and gripped the opposite frame so I couldn't pass. There was a fire in his eyes now, blazing as he glared at me from only a few inches away. "You're walking on thin ice, Miss Alvarez," he said slowly. "I am well aware of the trouble your little camp is in, and if I think for even a second my daughter is unsafe, physically *or* emotionally, I will take her and my money and never look back at this place. Is that clear?"

"Perfectly," I whispered, staring at him. He was hiding something about his daughter or their relationship, using his power to make sure it stayed hidden. But I would find out one way or another, and I had every intention of keeping Macy Donovan as happy as possible. Whether or not that happiness involved her father, I couldn't decide yet. "I would appreciate it if you let me pass," I said.

Mr. Donovan dropped his arm, but his threat lingered as I escaped the stifling rec room and hurried back onto the field where I could breathe again.

That was terrible. But no, it could have been worse. At least he hadn't followed through with his threat. The camp wasn't doomed just yet. *We'll be fine.*

But man, how was a girl supposed to lead camp initiation after an encounter like that? I felt drained, sick, and I honestly wasn't sure if I was capable of even putting on a fake smile. I needed to make sure I gave Linda an earful without the insipid man present, but I honestly wasn't even sure what had just happened.

Was this guy really determined to stay at the camp all summer? What did he expect to do? Sing campfire songs and braid hair with the girls? Absolutely not. And if he was going to spend the whole time watching my every move to make sure nothing happened to his precious little girl, this was going to be the longest summer of my life.

But now was not the time for moaning about something I clearly couldn't control. Now I had to check on my girls and make sure they were just as in sync with each other as I hoped they would be.

Passing two cabins full of screaming and laughing girls, I paused just outside Cabin Three, which was suspiciously silent. What were they up to? I rose up on my toes and peeked into the window that was mostly hidden from view by one of the bunk beds and cracked open just enough for me to hear what was happening inside.

Based on the way she was sitting at attention and scribbling on a sheet of paper, Julia had apparently seceded her role as first mate to Kristy, which was a smart move, in my opinion. Second mate was in charge of keeping the cabin clean, and Julia excelled at delegating. First Mate was my right-hand woman, and Kristy would be in charge from midnight to seven a.m., exactly how she liked it. Kristy was standing near the door reciting the camp rules to the rest. And unless I was mistaken, ten-year-old Lila had claimed the post of lookout and was already stretched out on her top bunk by the window, the cabin binoculars pressed to her eyes as she scoped out Cabin Six, Gabby's cabin.

"They've got Bailey," she muttered to herself, already planning for war.

The rest of the girls sat on bunks and sprawled on the floor next to half-open rucksacks and suitcases, listening carefully to their new leader.

Well, time to put my game face on.

"What are you doing, Miss Alvarez?"

I shrieked, and eight little heads swiveled around to the window where I stood. I ignored them, however, and turned to glare at Mr. Donovan, who stood right behind me and raised an eyebrow in concern. "Mr. Donovan," I gasped. "Don't you know it's rude to sneak up on people like that?"

"Just like it's rude to spy?" he countered, and one side of his mouth quirked up in a smile.

Oh, he thought he was clever, did he? Two could play at that game. "I thought we agreed you wouldn't lurk, Mr. Donovan."

"Technically I didn't agree to that. You spoke for me."

"Well…" Dang. I didn't have a response for that. *You win this round.* "If you must know, I like watching the girls when there are no adults around. They're completely themselves."

His dark eyebrows lifted a fraction of an inch. "Interesting," he said.

"Why are you lurking, Mr. Donovan?" I replied.

He lifted a little stuffed dog, its ears tattered and floppy and parts of its body well-worn from years of hugs. "Macy left this in the car," he said. It was the first time he'd spoken without any sharpness in his voice, and it caught me off guard.

"Oh," was all I could get out as I stared at the stuffed animal in his fingers. "Right. Well, I'll be sure to give it to her." But as I reached for it, he pulled it out of range.

"I'd rather…" He frowned. "I just want to make sure she's settling in."

I could not even begin to tell him how much that was a bad idea. It was bad enough he wasn't willing to leave camp and come back in two months, but Macy had been here for less than an hour. How could he possibly think anything had gone wrong already?

"Are you Macy's dad?" a young voice said behind me. Kristy stood at the other end of the cabin and had her hands on her hips in an impressive imitation of Linda when she was trying to make a point about something. "Parents are *not* allowed."

I highly doubted Colin Donovan had ever been told off by a thirteen-year-old, and he looked like he wasn't entirely sure how to react. His mouth hung open slightly, and he glanced at me as if looking for advice on how to respond.

I used the distraction to snatch the little dog out of his hands. "This is Macy's," I said as I passed it off to Kristy. "I'll come in in just a second, okay?"

She nodded, her eyes traveling between us adults. She'd grown a lot over the last year, I realized. She still had her trademark cornrows, though, and in my mind, she would always be the little eight-year-old I'd known her first year here. "Are we doing the usual initiation?" she asked after a moment.

I smiled. "Like I would break from tradition," I said with a scoff. "Give me two minutes." When I turned back to Mr. Donovan to tell him he could come back to the cabin at lights out to say goodnight to Macy if he insisted, the words got stuck in my throat. How could the man possibly be angry again?

"Initiation?" he growled. "That isn't—"

"For crying out loud." I folded my arms and said a silent prayer for patience. "Mr. Donovan, do you really think I would do anything that would hurt these girls? *Really?* We don't allow hazing any more than we allow boys from the camp a few miles down the road, so calm down. Don't take everything out of context and assume you know everything."

His jaw muscle flexed. "Miss Alvarez, I—"

"You need to let your daughter experience this camp properly, or else what's the point? Now, is there anything else you need from me, or can I go do my job?"

Finally, he couldn't find something to say that didn't injure himself more than me, so he kept quiet.

"Thank you," I said, letting out my breath in a large sigh. "Now, this may kill you, but could you leave Macy alone for a few hours? Just until lights out tonight. If you don't give her a chance to feel what it's like to be on her own and rely on the girls around her, she's going to get very homesick very fast. None of us want that."

He coughed, probably choking on his instinct to argue. "Fine," he said, and it seemed to cost him a good deal to say. "I'll expect a full report from you after the girls are in bed."

You've got to be kidding me. "Of course, Mr. Donovan."

To my utter relief, he turned and strode back toward the rec room, waving away a fly as if it had personally attacked him. *Thank goodness.*

But now I was completely thrown off my groove, and my usual enthusiasm for initiation was practically nonexistent thanks to the charming Colin Donovan. *You're fine!* Except I wasn't. The fate of the entire camp rested on my shoulders. *You know what you're doing.* Sure, but Mr. Donovan had so far managed to knock me off balance with his every word. *Be a professional and get over yourself.*

"Right," I said and took a deep breath. "For the girls."

After taking only a few more seconds to compose myself and put on a smile, I grabbed the pirate hat that hung on a nail by the door and stuffed it onto my head with a determination to forget Donovan and focus on what I loved most: this camp and these girls. I pulled the door open and jumped inside the cabin, shouting, "Avast ye!" and scaring at least half the girls, though most of them smiled a second later. "What be these grins on yer faces? Ye ain't been initiated yet!" I paused to take in their reactions and gauge the group dynamic now that there was an adult present.

Two of the girls—Madison and Zoey—had never been in my cabin before and weren't completely sure what to do with my ridiculousness, though they had to have seen my antics over the last few summers they were here. They looked at each other then at the other girls around them for cues. Julia and Kristy both jumped to their feet and saluted, followed by Lila and Brielle. I imagined Willow would have done the same, only she'd gotten her foot stuck between the bed and her suitcase and was trying to free herself. That left Macy, who hugged her little stuffed dog and kept her eyes on her feet.

She's nervous. Or maybe she was shy. Maybe she had never spent an hour without her nightmare of a father lurking just behind her. It was impossible to know.

I twisted my face into a ridiculous scowl and pointed at Kristy. "First mate?"

She grinned. "Aye, Captain."

"Do ye have the treasure?"

Kristy nudged Julia, who hurried to her bunk and grabbed the little chest I'd kept in Cabin Three since my first week as a counselor. She held it out to me as if it contained the wealth of the universe, and I matched her grin.

"I thank ye, second mate," I said as I took the chest from her. Jeez, she'd grown up too and looked an awful lot like her older sister, who had been one of my very first girls at Rockwood.

"What's in the box?" Madison whispered to Willow.

I took that opportunity to jump forward and claim center stage in the cabin, spinning in a slow circle to take in all eight girls. "This box," I said with as much mystery as I could manage, "holds everything you need to be a proper Cabin Three Pirate. Are ye ready to sail the savage seas, or are ye all a bunch of landlubbers?"

"What's a landlubber?"

Goodness, she sounds just like her dad. Momentarily caught off guard, I turned around and stared at Macy, trying to figure out how such a shy little girl could sound so completely terrified and disapproving at the same time. She had Donovan's same expression too, watching me as if I were the stupidest person she'd ever seen.

"A landlubber is someone who's bad at being on boats," Lila said from her bunk. "Open the treasure chest, Beck!"

A few other girls chimed in with, "Open it!" so I did, grinning as I revealed the wondrous trove inside.

Macy leaned forward in interest, and then her eyebrows pulled together in consternation. "It's nail polish," she said.

"Aye," I replied and was pleased to see her relax a little. "No pirate is complete until she has her colors. Now into pairs, all of ye!"

Thank goodness for Brielle, who immediately grabbed Macy's hand and asked if they could be partners. The other girls quickly did the same, and as soon as they'd grabbed their desired colors, I had the chance to step back and really get a good look at my group of girls.

Linda had seriously spoiled me this year, and I knew it was because of the curly-haired girl who was letting Brielle paint shimmering gold onto her fingernails. No, that wasn't quite right. Linda had given me such a good cabin because she knew I would have to spend a whole lot of energy dealing with the handsome man who seemed to think I was completely incompetent. Thanks to Linda, at least I didn't have to worry about my girls getting along. They were clearly all going to do well together. Even Macy, from the looks of it, though I had a feeling she didn't have many friends back home. She was too shy to be in a big group, and she kept glancing around the cabin as if waiting for someone to tell her she was doing something wrong. I'd seen the look before, and I hoped it wouldn't last. I needed Macy to enjoy her time here at Rockwood.

The camp needed her to have a good time.

The girls finished their painting right as dinnertime rolled around, though when we arrived at the mess hall, I realized we were the last cabin there. Everyone else had already loaded up their plates with cheesy pasta and found seats around the massive, enclosed pavilion. I directed my girls to get some food before finding their seats, but I was a bit distracted by the sheer silence of the room.

Well, not quite silent. Every girl seemed to be whispering to her neighbor, but compared to the usual cacophony of dinnertime, the place was almost eerie. I'd never seen it like this, and my stomach twisted itself into a knot as I searched the room for one of the other counselors so I could ask if I'd missed something.

That was when I saw him.

There, pacing in the back corner by the garbage cans and deep in conversation on his phone, was Colin Donovan. Apparently oblivious to the several dozen stares he was receiving, he followed the same path across the wood planks of the floor, back and forth, again and again, drawing more attention to himself every second he was there.

"He is so handsome," a soft voice said behind me.

I glanced back, horrified to see a few fifteen-year-olds watching Donovan with more dedication than they'd ever put into arts and crafts. One of them even sighed as if she'd found the man of her dreams and whispered, "He's an angel from heaven."

Okay, sure, he was a good-looking dude. I would never deny that. But he was the father of one of their fellow campers, not to mention at least twice their age. They were supposed to be obsessing over fellow teenagers, not sharp businessmen from San Francisco.

"I could watch that all day," a third girl said.

I turned to tell her how completely inappropriate a thought like that was for camp, only to find Annabeth the new counselor joining in on the ogling just behind the girls. "Annabeth," I scolded.

She simply shrugged and kept watching.

My girls had caught sight of the distraction as well, and though most of them simply looked confused, Macy was absolutely horrified. Her eyes wide, she practically shook as she stared at the other end of the room and seemed to put all of her effort into ignoring everyone around her.

I had to put a stop to this before things got out of hand. Instead of having to navigate the usual chaos of the mess hall, since the girls were so enthralled by the strange addition to the camp, I walked easily to the other side and approached Mr. Donovan warily. I couldn't stop myself from being hesitant to interact with him, given our very short history so far, but if he really was planning to stick around all summer, I just had to grit my teeth and ignore my unsettled stomach. Otherwise it was going to be a long two months.

It took two circuits around the garbage cans before he noticed me. He stopped walking immediately and paused in the middle of a sentence, his phone still pressed to his ear. "Let me call you back, Jeff," he said, and then he slipped the phone into his pocket. "Miss Alvarez," he acknowledged. I couldn't quite read his demeanor at the moment, though he wasn't glaring daggers at me, which was nice.

"Mr. Donovan," I greeted.

Silence.

Donovan coughed and folded his arms. "Is there something you needed, Miss Alvarez?"

"I need you to leave," I said without thinking. When his neutral expression shifted into a scowl, I realized my mistake and shook my head. "I mean leave the mess hall. You're distracting the girls from eating ridiculous amounts of mac and cheese."

He seemed to realize for the first time he wasn't alone in the building, his eyes going wide as he took in the scene of unusually quiet girls pretending to eat while they watched our exchange. "Oh," he said. "I didn't mean… I was hoping to stay out of the way and blend in."

Well, he walked right into this one: "Mr. Donovan," I replied, "we have exactly three men employed here at Camp Rockwood. One of them makes the food. One of them does the gardening and maintenance. And one of them does the laundry. If you want to blend in, you'd better grab yourself a broom and start sweeping."

Was that a smile from the ever-annoyed Colin Donovan? If it was, he wasn't very good at it. "If you think that would help," he said. Yep, he was definitely smiling, probably because attractive men like him were always aware of the effect they had on women, no matter their age.

"I don't think it will," I replied and gestured for the door. When he didn't move, I put my hand on his shoulder and gave him a push, which thankfully worked as the pair of us stepped out together and stopped just outside the door. And though I knew it was probably dangerous for me to speak around the guy, I couldn't hold it in: "I'm aware I can't keep you from spending your days here at Camp Rockwood, but is it really so much for me to ask you to keep your distance from the girls? Particularly when they're all together like this?"

He clenched his jaw and turned his head, his eyes fixed on the window through which I could see my cabin of girls finally settling in and attacking their plates of pasta. But then he relaxed and let his arms fall to his sides. "I didn't realize it was already dinnertime," he admitted as he turned back to me. "I was putting out some fires at work, and…"

I raised an eyebrow. "You're telling me you didn't notice eighty chattering girls filling the room around you?"

"I'm good at shutting out distractions," he replied.

"Incredibly good, apparently."

He glanced in the window again. "Macy looks worried," he said, and his smile disappeared, replaced with his signature scowl. "I hope your little initiation wasn't too alienating."

Well, so much for civil conversation. I couldn't pretend to know every little nuance of his daughter's emotions, but, looking in at the mess hall, I was pretty sure she was absolutely fine. In fact, I had a feeling the attention her dad had unintentionally brought her was probably to blame for the little frown on her face as she played with her mac and cheese rather than eating it. But I couldn't say that to him, not if I wanted to avoid getting into another argument with the guy, so I took a slow breath and forced myself to stay calm.

You can do this. "It's only the first day, Mr. Donovan," I said quietly. "A lot of the girls take a little time to settle in. Give it a few days before you start jumping to conclusions."

His gaze, as always, was sharp as he examined me as if searching for any signs that I was lying. Before he could say whatever clever thought probably came to his head, he pulled his phone out of his pocket and lifted it to his ear. "Donovan," he said and wandered off.

I watched him cross the field, batting away bugs as he went, and had to wonder if he was going to be working the whole time he was here at camp. If his job was so important, why not go back to the city?

"Please tell me that phone call is why Mr. Donovan looks angry," Linda said behind me.

I jumped and turned to her. "What? Oh, no, I don't think he's angry." At least, I hoped he wasn't. I had tried very hard not to give him a reason to be.

"He looks angry," Linda argued, though she probably couldn't see much of his expression now that he'd wandered to the other side of the field. "Please don't make me remind you to be nice to him. This is the most important job you have this summer, and—"

"More important than our girls?" I asked.

She sighed. "If we lose Donovan, we lose our girls. I hope you understand how crucial he is to the future of Rockwood, Beck."

Did she really think so little of my self-control? "Of course I understand," I said.

"Then show me." Without another word, she stepped back inside the mess hall and left me alone.

Dear Dalia,

This year has certainly been interesting so far, and we're only a week in! That thing I was dreading? I'm pretty sure I've figured out what it is, and it's not something that will be going away anytime soon. Yay. We have a parent at camp this year that is so much worse than anyone I've had to deal with in the last nine years, and that's because I can't just send him off until the end of summer and use all that time to figure out how to handle him. He won't leave! I know it's only been a week, but I can already see him falling into a routine that is going to make things miserable if he keeps it up.

He shows up every morning before breakfast, always chatting away on his phone—I swear I can hear him talking no matter where I go—and he wanders around the camp, following my girls and pretending we can't see him, even though he's not very good at hiding. He keeps distracting the older girls—gag me—and the counselors—somehow this is worse—and seems to have no idea what he's doing to the status quo of Rockwood. He hangs around until lights out and lingers at our cabin until Macy comes outside to say goodnight, and then he vanishes to who knows where. I'm half convinced he just disappears into midair, only to pop right back into existence the next morning because there's no way the man is actually human.

But him being around isn't the worst part! I swear he's trying to make my life miserable. It's like from the minute he met me, he decided I needed to be put into my place because clearly I have no idea what I'm doing, and he has this vendetta against me because he doesn't think I'm good enough for his precious little girl. The only time he speaks to me is when he has some criticism about something I've done or some advice on how to do things better, as if he has any idea how to run a girl's camp! He doesn't even know how to take care of his own daughter, and I can only imagine the horrors that would pop up if he had more than one kid. Sure, he tells her goodnight every day, but I know she hates it and would rather stay inside the cabin with the rest of the girls than go outside to talk to him. Either she's scared of him, or… I don't know if there's an or. From what I can tell, she really doesn't like him, and anytime he's within eyesight, she stops doing whatever she's doing and shuts down. I don't care how rich you are. If your own kid is too afraid to have a little fun when you're around, you've got a problem.

Most of the time Macy doesn't join in on activities, and she'll just sit off to the side and watch. Thank goodness for the other girls. If I can't sit with Macy, one of them does it for me instead of playing flag football or drawing with sidewalk chalk, so at least she's never sitting there alone. I'm sure if she was, Daddy would come swooping in to tell her she has to participate or he'll take her back home to her miserable life.

I don't actually know if she's miserable, but she certainly doesn't seem happy. I can't imagine Donovan is blame-free for that.

I don't mean to complain so much, but you're the only one who can really understand how this feels. I'm trying to be positive like you told me, but it's not exactly easy when you've got Sharp Suit breathing down your neck all day long. I'm hoping things will get better, but if this first week is any indication, I've got a long summer ahead of me.

Wish me luck!

Love,
    Beck

P.S. I don't have any scientific evidence to support this, but I have decided that the more handsome and rich a person is, the more unattractive his personality has to be. Just to keep the balance of things.

P.P.S. What kind of guy wears a full suit in the middle of summer? I'm pretty sure the man doesn't own any normal clothes, and he's had to send everything out for dry cleaning because he keeps getting dirt on his perfect pants.

P.P.P.S. I wish you were here. You'd know what to do.

CHAPTER THREE

"Beck?" Kristy was the last one out of the cabin on the way to breakfast, and she paused next to me at the door, her eyebrows pulled together in concentration and worry. "Can I talk to you for a sec?"

A quick glance at the rest of the girls—and a salute from Julia at their head—told me they'd be fine on their way to the mess hall. Technically I was supposed to stay with them, but Kristy looked so serious that I knew this was probably more important. "What's up?"

Before she spoke, she made sure there wasn't anyone close enough to hear what she said. "It's about Macy."

Uh oh. I could imagine Dear Dad leaning against the wall of the rec room, on his phone as usual, and if he noticed I wasn't with my cabin of girls and had—according to him—abandoned his precious little girl, he wasn't going to be happy. "What about her?"

Kristy bit her lip. "She doesn't want to do the zipline."

Why hadn't Macy said as much to me when I asked the girls ten minutes ago? There was nothing wrong with not wanting to do an activity, which was why Macy had spent most of the last two weeks sitting in the grass talking to one of the other girls.

"But she was talking about how excited she was," I said, furrowing my eyebrows. I remembered that specifically because I was surprised how easily I could hear her over the lunchtime conversation in the mess hall yesterday. "I thought she was looking forward to today."

Shrugging, Kristy glanced around again, but the wooded area around the cabins was empty and silent aside from a few birds flitting around and calling to each other. "I thought so too," she admitted, "but she told me this morning she didn't want to do it, but she didn't want you to know."

"So why are you telling me?" I asked. "It's important to keep secrets when someone trusts you with them."

"I know," Kristy replied, and she looked a little irritated. "But I thought this was important for you to know."

Huh. Insightful. "Do you know why she changed her mind?" I asked.

Shaking her head, Kristy looked even more worried as she leaned a little closer to me. "I think it's because of her dad," she whispered.

I swore internally. I was right. Macy was miserable, and it was because she was afraid of her dad, who was probably just as overbearing the rest of the year as he was here at camp. Not for the first time I thought about how much I hated the guy for insisting he be around when it was in his daughter's best interest to have some time away from home so she could learn and grow.

"I think…" Kristy shrugged. "I think she's worried he won't approve."

"Well I—wait, what?" That wasn't what I expected, and I stared at the thirteen-year-old who suddenly looked a lot older than she had a moment ago. "What do you mean, he won't approve?"

If he didn't want her to do camp things, why the heck would he bring her to a camp for an entire summer?

"She told me he expects a lot from her, and she's worried he won't like it if she does something unladylike."

I gaped at her. Was she serious? "*Unladylike?* That's ridiculous. Girls can do anything they want!"

Kristy smiled finally and nodded. "I know that. But I don't think Macy knows that. She's always looking at her dad, and she talks about the school she goes to and how they don't have recess or anything. They're always learning to play the piano and read Latin and dance ballroom. She doesn't even know how to do *The Bonkadoo*, Beck."

I had no idea what *The Bonkadoo* was, but I gathered from Kristy's shocked tone that it was weird Macy didn't know it. So Donovan was a bit old-fashioned in his idea of how a girl should act? If that was the only reason for Macy's reticence, maybe things weren't quite as bad as I was picturing. But if Macy was going to spend the entire summer on the sidelines, there was really no point in her even being here, and I would be going through Donovan's scrutiny for nothing. That would have to change. Now.

"Thanks for telling me, Kristy," I said, and I meant that. It was hard to get the girls to open up, since I was one of the grownups, so it was absolutely necessary to have girls like Kristy step up and try to look out for the younger girls. "You did the right thing. Now, I bet I can beat you to the mess hall."

She perked up and took off running, shouting back, "I bet you can't!" as she left the trees and rounded the corner to get to the main part of camp.

"Cheater!" I cried, but she was already out of sight. The girl was *fast*, no doubt about that.

I moved more slowly, trying to figure out how exactly I was going to confront Mr. Donovan. He likely had no idea he was the reason his daughter wasn't having any fun—probably because he was too busy blaming me for that—but I couldn't just accuse him of ruining her life. I had to be delicate, or this would be the last summer I ever set foot in Camp Rockwood.

No pressure.

I found him exactly where I expected to, pacing near the flagpole while early morning chatter filtered out from the nearby mess hall. He was even more agitated than normal, which was worrying, and he didn't notice me approach until he said, "Just get it done," and hung up his phone. Then he caught sight of me and froze, his scowl firmly intact.

"What?" he asked, and the word came out almost as a sigh.

Good morning to you too. "Is something wrong with work?" I asked. With any luck, he would have to head back into the city and give me a few days of peace.

"Why would anything be wrong?" he snapped back.

Okay, touchy subject. "Well," I replied, "because you're so much more delightful to be around today."

"Is there something you needed, Miss Alvarez? I don't have time to…" He sighed, pinching the bridge of his nose before focusing on me again.

I definitely had to play this carefully. He was clearly on edge as well as tired, and those didn't seem like two things that would combine well in an uptight businessman like Colin Donovan. "First off," I said, "your daughter is perfectly safe."

He folded his arms. "That is not a reassuring way to begin a conversation, Miss Alvarez."

"Second," I replied, "please call me Beck. I feel like I'm in trouble every time you speak to me."

He gave me a look that said, quite clearly, he didn't disagree with that statement and would probably keep calling me by my last name.

"Third," I continued, trying not to match his scowl. The man was absolutely infuriating, and having to stay on his good side was proving to be more and more difficult the longer he was here. "I'm worried Macy isn't enjoying the full experience of camp. She spends a lot of time on the sidelines, no matter how much her friends try to convince her to join in."

"And why are you bringing this to my attention?" he asked, raising one eyebrow. "Isn't it your job to look after the girls and make sure they're having a good time?"

Touché. But this battle was far from over. "It's not just me who's noticed," I said. "Other counselors have tried to get her to have some fun when we combine with other cabins, but no one seems to have much success."

Finally he softened a bit, a little more worry filtering into his expression. Surely he'd noticed how little his daughter participated, with all his lurking about. Or was he so focused on his work that he had no idea? "Is there anything she does?" he asked, his voice soft as well as his stance. *Huh.* So maybe he wasn't entirely sharp all the time.

"She'll sing around the campfire," I admitted. "She has a spectacular voice."

"She does," he agreed.

"And she'll do all of the arts and crafts, plus she's very dutiful about helping clean the cabin and when we have kitchen duty."

"But she doesn't do any of the fun things," he finished for me, nodding a little. So he *had* noticed.

Time for the dangerous part: "I'm worried she... She might be afraid of what you'll think if she does anything that isn't the usual routine for her."

Mr. Donovan opened his mouth, probably to argue, but he stopped himself before any words came out. He suddenly looked different, less rigid and put together. "Why would she think that?" he asked, and I was pretty sure he genuinely wanted an answer.

"I won't pretend to know your parenting style, Mr. Donovan, but if I had to guess, you probably have some pretty high standards?"

"Doesn't everyone?" he said, but his frown deepened.

So far so good. "Sure. But it's hard enough to fit in when you live a fairly normal life," I said, "and I can't imagine it's any easier being born to privilege like she's been. Maybe she hasn't had much of a chance to be a kid."

He didn't like that comment, but this time his anger wasn't directed at me. He took to pacing again as he worked over that thought. Then, to my utter surprise, he smiled.

"I remember being a kid," he said, as if he had actually forgotten for a minute there. "I got into all sorts of trouble, something my parents were not especially pleased about. Maybe that was why they sent me off to boarding school."

Boarding school. If he really wanted to blend in here, he probably should have kept things like that to himself. "A lot of kids here at Rockwood come from families who can barely afford new shoes every year let alone send their children to a boarding school. Some don't have families at all. But when they come here, they're all equals, and they can just be themselves because they have nothing to prove."

"And Macy can't do that because I'm here," he said. Was it too much to hope he would take that as a sign that he should leave? "I know you don't like me here, Miss...Beck...but I can't leave."

My heart throbbed in my chest. "Even if it would help Macy?"

At least he seemed torn about the idea, glancing toward the camp entrance as if he were still debating the idea of sticking around. His thoughts seemed to be swirling around in his head, and though his eyes were on me, they weren't cold like they usually were. That was a new sensation.

"I know you don't want me here," he said again, and his lips twitched with a brief smile. "And I know you think I'm being ridiculous. But I need to be here. *That* is best for Macy. I just wish I knew a way to help her relax a little."

"You can always tell her you approve of ziplining," I suggested, and I couldn't keep my disappointment out of my voice. *As if that would work.*

There was that flash of a smile again. "If I thought that would help," he said, "I would do it in a heartbeat. But Macy… She has too much of her...her mother in her."

I had no idea how I could have gone two weeks with this guy here and not once wondered about Macy's mom. Mr. Donovan wore a ring, but he didn't seem to have any reason to go back home for an entire summer. Still, I had never questioned the absence of a woman in the picture. And though I was desperate for an answer, since it might offer up a piece of the Macy puzzle, I kept my mouth shut. If Donovan's expression was to be believed, there was a reason he hadn't talked about the girl's mom before now; it was too painful a subject.

"Do you have any ideas?" he asked.

I blinked. Did he know what I was thinking? "About?"

"How I can help Macy."

"Right. Macy." I took a deep breath and held it in my lungs for a second. *Get it together, Beck.* "So you really think talking to her wouldn't do anything at all?"

His shoulders lifted in a halfhearted shrug, and then he leaned against the rec room wall as he focused his gaze on the buzzing mess hall just east of us. "It might work for a morning, but I have a feeling she'd go right back to it. Even if I stay out of sight, she knows I'm here."

An idea sparked to life in my head, and though I was terrified to speak it out loud and risk the glare coming back, I had a feeling it was probably the only thing that might help Macy have a little fun. "You could always come zipline with us," I suggested quietly.

Donovan turned to me with an expression of such bewilderment that it was almost comical. "Zipline? Are you out of your mind?"

I held my fist to my mouth to hide my smile. It wasn't that Mr. Donovan thought himself above something like ziplining. No, based on the pure and utter fear in his eyes, the oh-so-great Colin Donovan was *afraid* of ziplining. And I was enjoying the look on his face way more than I should have. "Why not?" I asked, and my voice shook with barely restrained laughter. "Maybe if she sees you doing it, she'll realize she's allowed to do it too."

"But that's…" He stopped, folding his arms again, though this time it was less of a power move and more to protect himself from the idea. And then he groaned, for the first time looking frazzled instead of completely in control, and he kicked a pebble into the side of the rec room. "Dammit, Miss Alvarez, you had to go and find *that* solution."

"Language, Mr. Donovan," I replied, and I couldn't hold back my grin anymore. "I wash girls' mouths out with soap for less than that."

"Ziplining," he grumbled under his breath.

"I take it that means you'll be joining us after breakfast?"

He shot a glare at me, but it wasn't as sharp as his usual ones. This one was almost a plea for help. "I thought I wasn't *allowed* to be around the girls."

I grinned. "I think we can make an exception this one time."

I'd never seen anyone so completely terrified, and that included the six-year-olds. Mr. Donovan followed my girls and me at a far enough distance that they hadn't noticed him yet, but even from this far, I could see how pale he was. Some of my girls were nervous, sure, but they mostly looked excited. Even Macy, who still hadn't told me she didn't want to do the zipline, was biting her lip and staring at the platform ahead with wide, eager eyes.

It wasn't all that long of a zipline, only a hundred feet, but it was high enough that the girls with fears of heights often opted not to do it. It spanned the shortest part of the lake and ended on the other side, where another counselor waited to help my girls dismount and unharness. Truth be told, it was one of my favorite parts of the camp. There was something freeing about having the wind in my hair and nothing beneath my feet, and if given the chance, I would spend all day flying across the lake.

Mr. Donovan, on the other hand, looked like he would rather get a root canal as his eyes traced the length of the line.

When we reached the base of the platform, I turned to the girls and waited until they gathered around me.

Mr. Donovan kept his same distance, probably waiting to see if he was actually needed to convince his daughter to make the jump.

"Alrighty, mateys," I said in my pirate voice.

Donovan's eyes went wide.

"It's time to see if ye are true seawomen or the landlubbers I know ye are. Which among ye will climb the mast and ride the rigging?"

"I'm no landlubber," Willow said proudly and stepped forward. She immediately tripped, bumping into Zoey. "Sorry, Zo. I'll go, Captain Beck!"

But before I could direct her to climb to the platform with me, Lila happened to glance back and catch sight of Mr. Donovan, and when she nudged Macy in the side, all the girls wanted to see what she'd seen. Macy immediately hid her face in her hands, and Julia and Kristy exchanged glances before giving me looks that said, "I told you so."

Since when did those two get so insightful? They were only thirteen.

I quickly searched my thoughts for the best way to go about things as the girls started whispering to each other. "Listen up, you dogs," I said, though my plan was still forming. I had to make sure I kept their attention off of Macy as long as I could. "Looks like we've got ourselves a stowaway." I fixed my eyes on Mr. Donovan and prayed he could read my look from that far. *Get over here. Now.*

He seemed to understand, and though he only grew paler as he stuffed his hands into his pockets, he slowly made his way over until he was just a few feet away and under the intense stares of seven young girls. Macy still kept herself hidden. Donovan gave me a pained look, still unenthused by my idea, but he said nothing.

How refreshing.

"Now," I said, "I'm not a captain who tolerates stowaways, am I, first mate?"

Kristy was confused for a second, but then she caught on when she glanced up at the zipline platform. "No, Captain," she confirmed.

"And do you know what I do with stowaways?" I continued.

Mr. Donovan swallowed, likely regretting his decision to join us this morning.

"I make them walk the plank."

Three girls gasped, their eyes jumping up to the platform. "He's gonna zipline?" Madison whispered in awe.

Macy's head snapped up, and she turned to face her dad with shock and something akin to horror on her face.

"Aye," I said, though I probably shouldn't have been enjoying the look on Donovan's face as much as I was. "He'll walk the plank, alright."

He grit his teeth so hard a muscle pulsed in his jaw.

"Up with ye," I growled at him and pulled a harness from a box below the platform.

If his glare was any indication as he climbed after me, I was pretty sure he was ready to push me off the platform by the time he reached the top.

I had no actual knowledge of men's clothing, but as I helped Mr. Donovan into the harness, I could tell just by looking at it that his suit was probably worth more than my car. That wasn't saying much, but… With my very limited internet access, I had looked into the guy a little more over the last week, just to get a better idea of who I was dealing with, and his net worth had made me want to cry a little bit. No man should have as much money as this guy had, and I could barely fathom how he managed to use it all.

How did one person go from a little business idea to owning the biggest tech company in San Francisco in less than five years?

"You sure this is safe?" he asked, pulling my attention up to his face. A drop of sweat ran down his temple as he stared down the length of the zipline. "I mean, I'm heavier than the girls who…" He glanced toward the ground below us then seemed to instantly regret it, shutting his eyes as he leaned back onto the platform. "Maybe I shouldn't."

I tried not to look too smug. "Do my ears deceive me, or is the great Colin Donovan afraid of heights?"

He chuckled nervously and grabbed the railing of the platform while I worked on the harness. "I'm afraid of breaking the line and falling to my death," he countered.

"You'll land in the water," I said, grinning. "Or are you telling me you're afraid of a little water too?"

"Are you telling me there's a chance it'll break?" His voice cracked a little, though he put on a brave face and pretended it hadn't. *Poor guy.*

I cinched up the last strap then straightened up so I could look him in the eye. "Relax, Mr. Donovan. You don't weigh nearly enough to break the line. Now, if you weren't as fit as..." *Maybe don't finish that thought.* "We get the line inspected every year, so you'll be fine. Sofie is waiting for you at the other end, and she'll make sure you arrive safely. Now all you have to do is lean forward and let gravity do the rest."

The man literally gulped as he squinted toward the other side of the lake. "I'm sure I could find another way to help Macy," he mumbled.

One look at Macy told me she was waiting to see if her dad would actually go through with this, her skepticism as clear as day. If he didn't make the jump, I was pretty sure she wouldn't accept anything else as proof that she was allowed to have some fun.

"Look," I said, and he did, though I could tell he was tempted to shut his eyes again, maybe even hug the rail. "Macy thinks things like ziplining aren't appropriate. But if fabulous Dad enjoys himself a little bit, maybe she will too. I suggest you try closing your eyes and pretend you're in the crow's nest of a pirate ship, feeling the wind in your hair as you sail across the sea."

"Not helping," he said through clenched teeth.

Don't say it, Beck. "Do you need a push?"

He glared at me, but it was a different glare from the one I'd gotten used to. This wasn't anger. No, this was defiance, as if my little jab were enough to push him over the edge and no longer make this a suggestion. I'd issued a challenge, and I had a feeling Colin Donovan was not one to shy away from a challenge.

"Time to walk the plank, you bilge rat!" I said, loud enough for the girls to hear.

"I'll find a way to repay you for this," he replied, and then he was flying, fancy suit and all, and shouting as if he were running from an angry bear he'd just woken from hibernation.

Twenty minutes later, Macy was screaming with delight as she crossed the lake and looked to be having the time of her life, and I had just a little more respect for Mr. Donovan. Maybe he wasn't so bad after all.

Dear Dalia,

Is there a word for being constantly surprised and never once feeling like your feet are underneath you? Because I'm starting to think I have that. And unless this feeling in the pit of my stomach is just some new allergy I've developed, I'm not sure I'm going to like whatever's coming. Three weeks down, and something tells me this anxiety is only just beginning.

I just wish I knew what was causing it.

I have a feeling it has to do with Colin Donovan, but I haven't been able to prove that yet. Besides, he's lurking less and working more, so I haven't noticed him as much. It's been nice, and his daughter has been having all sorts of fun this week.

I wish I could just spend a few hours at our waterfall so I could figure all this out. It's been too long since I was there last, and maybe that would help.

I'll try to keep my chin up, but please send your prayers my way. I think I'm going to need them.

Lots of love,
Beck

P.S. There's a raccoon who's taken up residence in the attic of Cabin Six, and they've turned him into their mascot and sneak him leftovers. He's very happy.

P.P.S. You know that song you used to sing to me when I got scared during thunderstorms? I can't remember the last line. I wish you were here so you could sing it again.

CHAPTER FOUR

The storm broke in a flash of lightning and a crash of thunder, right in the middle of freeze tag. Rain wasn't an uncommon thing, but this storm was a doozy, and I didn't blame the girls for shrieking and making a mad dash for the mess hall. It was like the sky, which had been overcast and threatening for two days, had suddenly decided it couldn't hold anymore and chose to dump everything it had all at once. I helped shepherd everyone into the mess hall and was immensely grateful we'd been doing a camp-wide activity instead of being spread out across the property. I was especially glad no one had been on the lake.

"Everyone split into your cabin groups!" Gabby yelled once everyone had gotten to safety inside the giant pavilion.

It took a bit of repeat instructions to be heard over the pounding of rain and the rumbling of thunder, but eventually the girls managed to obey, and I quickly counted them to make sure I had all of mine. "Eight!" I shouted and held my hand in the air.

Within a few seconds, each of the other counselors had done the same, which meant all of our girls were safe.

Able to breathe easily again, I hurried into the back closet near the kitchen and grabbed as many board games as I could carry. Gabby joined me, and together we brought out enough games that we could easily outlast the storm.

"Maybe some snacks?" Gabby suggested after we'd set everything on the tables, and she led the way into the kitchen. The moment the door closed behind us, though, she bumped my shoulder to get my attention. "Did you see who's trapped in here with us?" she asked.

I immediately pictured some horrified squirrel who was deeply regretting his decisions, but I had a feeling that wasn't what she meant. "No," I said, "who?"

Pulling me toward the circular windows in the kitchen doors, she directed my gaze to the farthest end of the building. There, looking a bit like a half-drowned rat who'd been cornered by some hungry cats, stood Colin Donovan. The cats were four alarmingly interested teenage girls who had decided it was a great idea to talk to the handsome man who lurked in the distance.

Gabby snorted a soft laugh as she watched. "He looks terrified," she said, and she wasn't wrong. Donovan looked almost as afraid of the girls as he had the zipline. That, at least, I saw as a good thing.

"I should go rescue him," I grumbled and hurried out before one of the girls thought it was a good idea to touch the guy.

By the time I managed to navigate the chaos that was evolving around the board games, they had pretty much pushed him up against the wall as he tried to keep a respectable distance.

"So what is it like living downtown?" one of them asked him as I approached.

"Do you go to a lot of parties?" asked another.

"My dad works for Google. Do you know him? You should be friends."

"Hi, ladies," I said loudly. "Did you see we're playing games? Maybe you should go find one to join." I tried to ignore the relief in Donovan's expression and keep my focus on the disappointed girls. "Mr. Donovan has work to do, and he doesn't need you girls giving up your precious summer time asking silly questions."

Though a couple of them looked ready to argue my point, all four of them turned and joined the rest of the girls, leaving me alone with Donovan.

He let out his breath as if he'd been holding it the whole time. "I'm sorry," he said, and he ran a hand through his wet hair, pushing it out of his face. "I've been trying to keep my distance, but then the rain…"

I fought against a smile, but I definitely had to address that hair situation. "Mr. Donovan," I said, and to my alarm my cheeks blossomed with heat before I'd even said anything else. *How annoying.* "I don't think you realize how distracting you are."

He had started running his fingers through his brown locks again and paused, his thick eyebrows pulled down low. "What?"

He was genuinely confused. *Huh.* "You've got a bit of a Mr. Darcy, *The Notebook*, 'showing up on the doorstep begging for forgiveness' kind of vibe going on," I said, "and that's not helping anything."

Honestly, maybe it was the rain, but with how little I'd seen him since the ziplining incident, I had almost forgotten just how handsome the guy was. His hair was usually moussed and perfectly styled, but now that it was more natural, I realized just how much of it he had. It was almost like he focused so much on work that he sometimes forgot to get a haircut, and it just kept getting longer. Plus he'd gotten some sun over the last couple of weeks, and there was a bit of color in his cheeks from his run from the rain. In a weird way, he looked more alive than I expected.

Or maybe that was just the bewildered expression he gave me, as if I were talking complete nonsense.

"I hope your suit isn't ruined," I said and frowned because of all the things I could have said, I had to go with that?

He glanced down, his own frown matching mine. "I have plenty." He seemed just as confused by his response as I was by my question.

Clearly we did not talk well if our conversation didn't have some bite to it or involved his daughter or my competence.

"So." I turned to stand at his side rather than in front of him. It gave me an excuse to look out over the girls and also not see his attractive face, which was turning out to be rather distracting this close up. There was something about his jawline I'd never seen in a guy before, though I couldn't quite place what it was. Or maybe it was the green of his eyes, which were softer than I'd thought originally.

"I've noticed you're not hovering as much," I said eventually.

Though I didn't look directly at him to see, I was pretty sure he glanced at me as if trying to judge my thoughts on the subject from my face. "I haven't felt as needed," he said slowly. Was he upset about that?

"Macy seems to be having fun," I said. "She even waded in the lake yesterday, though I haven't been able to get her in a canoe yet."

He dropped his head a bit. "She doesn't like water. I'm not sure why. Ever since she was a toddler—bath time was a nightmare. At least she'll take showers, but…" When he paused, I chanced a glance at him, and he'd turned pretty red. "Sorry," he said, "I probably shouldn't… I just worry about her, you know?"

"That's not something to be ashamed of," I replied.

"Even if it results in me lurking?"

Oh goodness, had I known Donovan had a smile like *that*? I was pretty sure I'd never seen it, at least not in full force or up this close, because I would have definitely remembered it. Apparently the rain really had worked hard to make him more attractive than before, because it had loosened him up enough to get him to smile.

In the weirdest way, I wanted to see more of it.

"After I started dating my wife," he said, "she told me I had had a tendency to stand off in the distance and watch her, and she almost didn't agree to our first date because she thought I was creepy. Apparently I haven't grown out of that one."

Wife. So that answered that question, though I wondered why she would be okay to let him spend the whole summer off in a girls camp. Coughing, I surreptitiously moved myself a little farther away from him, not because I really thought I was standing too close but simply out of respect for his wife. "At least you're aware of your flaws," I said. *That sounded stupid.*

Donovan chuckled.

Okay, not completely stupid. "They say once you know there's a problem," I added, "it's easier to fix it. Take me for example."

He cocked his head, and his eyes took me in with just a little too much scrutiny, so I moved another couple of inches away. "And what are your flaws, Miss Alvarez?" he asked.

Oh, there were so many ways I could go with that one, but this civil Donovan was starting to weird me out. I went with the sharpest approach in the hopes it would bring back his sharp personality, the one that gave me a chance to work out my frustrations because he was an easy target.

"I thought you had them all catalogued for me already," I said. "Otherwise, why else would you object so strongly to me as your daughter's counselor?"

His face flushed red again, and he ran a hand through that luscious hair of his, likely without realizing it. "Miss Alvarez."

"Beck."

"Beck, I may have been a bit…short. With you. The day we met."

I raised my eyebrows. "A bit?"

He paused, accepting my response with a nod, and then he said, "There is nothing in the world I want more than my daughter's happiness, and this was the first year we…" He took a deep breath. Whatever he was trying to say, it wasn't easy. "We always do our summer vacations together, and this was the first year we haven't been attached at the hip. It's hard not to wonder if I made a poor decision."

I really had no clue about his background or family traditions or whether or not he was a good father, but I had to believe he was telling the truth. He loved his daughter almost to a fault, and his doubt was weighing him down.

"Mr. Donovan, I know I've only known your daughter for three weeks, but you would not believe the change I've seen in her. Wading in the lake, for one, but it's more than that. Do you see her over there, sitting next to Willow and Madison?"

He raised an eyebrow. "I don't exactly know the names of the others," he said, "but yes, I see Macy."

Joking, huh? Rolling my eyes, I kept talking instead of taking the teasing avenue that was so tempting. "Well, do you see what game she's playing? Or rather, do you hear it?"

There was a lot of noise in the room, what with the rain and the girls competing to be the loudest, but it was impossible not to catch the shouting happening at Macy's table.

Donovan's eyes went wide. "Is that Pit?"

"That is Pit," I confirmed. And Macy was shouting louder than any of the others as she tried to trade her cards and win the game. It was not a game for the faint of heart. "She wouldn't have done that a week ago, so we're doing something right here at Rockwood."

"Clearly." Though he was still paying attention to our conversation, Donovan stood transfixed by his daughter's transformation, his eyes full of what I could only describe as wonder as he watched her ring the bell and laugh as the other girls groaned at having lost.

"So don't let yourself worry too much," I said and patted his arm. *Whew, he really does have muscle under that suit coat of his.* "From what I can tell, you're a great father."

And before I let my hand rest too long on that impressive tricep, I pulled myself away and went back up to the kitchen to help Gabby and Yasmine chop up the apples to distribute to the girls.

I had made only one slice before Gabby slid up against me, her head right up against mine. "What was that?" she whispered.

I was used to her invasion of my personal bubble, but this time felt like she had moved in just a little too close for comfort, even though she had definitely been closer before.

"What was what?" I asked.

"You and Gene Kelly out there."

I raised an eyebrow. "Singing in the Rain? That's your go-to?"

"You don't get more classic rain than that," Yasmine offered, though she returned to her apple slicing when I gave her a playful glare for not being on my side.

"Answer the question, Rebecka," Gabby pressed.

Though I was tempted to play along and give her something to freak out about, I went with the truth, mostly because I had no idea what Donovan would do if word somehow circulated back to him that supposedly I had felt something happen between us. "You're making stuff up, Gabs," I said. "He's married, for one, and for another, he's the father of one of my campers. That's just gross."

"It might be gross," she replied, "and maybe he's wearing a ring, but those were not the glances of a man happily married. And you weren't innocent either."

She's gone crazy. "Did you get struck by lightning?" I asked.

Gabby rolled her eyes and grabbed my hand, once again dragging me to the window to look out at Donovan. He had his phone out, but for once he wasn't talking on it. It looked like he was reading something, or maybe scrolling through pictures. "You've ruffled his feathers," she said, like that was supposed to mean something.

"I haven't ruffled anything," I disagreed.

"Yas, back me up here."

But Yasmine lifted her hands in the air and said, "I haven't talked to the guy once, so I don't have an opinion." She grabbed a tray of apple slices and came toward us. But just before she pushed through the swinging doors, she turned to me and said, "But I haven't seen you that red in maybe ever, Beck, so maybe Gabby's right."

Gabby lifted her eyebrows in triumph, but she definitely hadn't won anything yet. I had a feeling I was only scratching the surface of Colin Donovan, and there was no telling what I'd find underneath.

The rain continued the rest of the day. We kept the girls in the mess hall until dinner, but we decided it was probably best to get everyone back to their cabins before it got too late. One cabin at a time, we all made a break for it, counselors going with their girls to make sure everyone got back safely.

Luckily, most of my girls seemed to enjoy the rain and laughed as they piled into Cabin Three, flicking water on each other and sliding around in their wet shoes. Only one seemed thoroughly peeved by the soaking, and she immediately went to her suitcase to grab dry clothes.

Apparently Macy's aversion of water extended to the rain.

"Ahoy, mateys," I said to calm the rest down. "Seems we have a hurricane on our hands. Batten down the hatches and secure the hold!"

"Make sure the windows are closed," Julia translated when I got a couple of blank looks, and they all quickly checked to make sure everything was sealed up tight.

Thank goodness the roof isn't leaking like last year. But now I had to find a way to entertain eight pre-teens until it got late enough that I could make them go to bed. A game, perhaps? Or maybe Ridiculous Theater. But before I could make any suggestions, Kristy hopped to her feet.

"Sing us a story, Beck!" she said, catching me off guard.

My cheeks blossomed with heat as the thought of singing brought a bit of anxiety to the back of my mind. "What?" I hadn't sung anything on my own like this in almost a year, and I wasn't even sure if I could remember any lyrics completely. But I couldn't ignore the excitement of a few of the other girls who knew me well. Maybe if I had some time to prepare. "Oh, I don't—"

"Please sing a story," Brielle begged.

"Please, Beck!"

"You're so good at it!"

And one little voice added, "You can't sing a story, can you?"

I smiled at Macy. She didn't know it, but her question was enough of a challenge that I couldn't help but rise to face it. "Sure you can," I said. "Haven't you ever sung 'Love Story'? Or any song, for that matter?"

Macy frowned. "Well yeah, but that's different from telling a story."

"Just sing one and show her, Beck," said Julia with an eager smile.

I matched her grin. "Which one?"

"'La Adelita,'" Willow suggested from her bunk.

It was by far one of my favorites, so I nodded and grabbed my chair from where it sat in the corner. "I'll start singing as soon as you're all in dry clothes," I said.

By the time everyone had changed into pajamas, the rain had stopped, leaving the cabin quiet and peaceful. The girls were all tucked in their beds, and the sky had lightened just enough that there was a sort of warm glow coming in from the windows. It was the perfect setting for the song, and any doubts I might have had vanished. These were my girls, and there was no reason to be afraid of them.

I cleared my throat, took a deep breath, and then began to sing:

> *En lo alto de la abrupta serranía*
> *Acampado se encontraba un regimiento*
> *Y una moza que valiente los seguía*
> *Locamente enamorada del sargento.*

I rarely spoke Spanish, and I sang it even less, but every time I sang this Mexican ballad, it felt like something came to life inside of me. It was a reminder of my childhood and all the good things I had in my life, and it had a way of reaching the girls, even if they didn't understand all the words.

> *Popular entre la tropa era Adelita*
> *La mujer que el sargento idolatraba…*

I never sang the song quite right, but I didn't care. I liked it better slow and emotional, and the girls hunkered down in their beds as I kept singing, all of them starry-eyed and transfixed. It brought a smile to my face as I sang. I loved these girls. Even if I only got to see them for a couple of months a year, I felt like they were a part of me, and I wanted them to have every happiness in life. Moments like these, when things were calm and quiet, I couldn't help but imagine a better world for them, where they could be strong and beautiful and brave and gentle and all the things they wanted to be.

The end of the song came far too quickly, leaving me feeling full and peaceful as I sang the last few lines.

> *Y se oía que decía aquel que tanto se moría…*

> *Y si acaso yo muero en la guerra,*
> *Y mi cadáver lo van a sepultar,*
> *Adelita, por Dios te lo ruego…*

But I stopped before the last line because I could not for the life of me remember what it was, which was almost horrifying. How many times had I heard this song? More times than I could count. And that last line felt important, but it just wouldn't come to me. So I hummed the last few notes and let the song hang in the air in front of me, unfinished. I had tears in my eyes, but the girls didn't seem to notice. Most of them had their eyes closed, smiles on their faces.

Macy, however, was looking at me, and she was crying too. "But what does it mean?" she asked quietly.

"It's about a soldier," Kristy murmured.

"And the woman he loves," Willow added.

Some of them had heard the song enough to remember the translation from Spanish, but I knew the rest would be confused if I didn't help out. "It's the story of a girl named Adelita," I said. "She was in love with a soldier who went off to war, and she followed him because they couldn't stand to be apart. The soldier wanted to marry her, but he went off to battle and was wounded, and he sang of his love with his dying breath."

Zoey sniffed from a top bunk, tears streaming down her cheeks. "That's so sad," she whispered and hugged Lila, who lay next to her.

"But what happened to Adelita?" Macy asked.

That wasn't part of the song, and I wasn't sure if there was a real answer to that question. But based on the way Macy was staring at me with those dark brown eyes of hers, she desperately needed one.

What kind of thing did a little girl like her need to hear? "Adelita went on with her life," I decided. "She fell in love again and got married, and she had lots of beautiful little children."

"She just forgot about her soldier?" Macy whispered.

Uh oh. She looked like she was on the verge of more tears, so I shook my head. "She didn't forget about him," I said. "It's okay to miss someone, even if you move on."

Boy, did I know it. And while it wasn't even eight o'clock yet, I was suddenly exhausted. What was it about that song that seemed to drain me more and more every time I sang it?

"Well," I said, getting to my feet, "maybe we should call tonight an early night. Tomorrow we start practice for the canoe races, and I want you all in ship-shape so we can beat Cabin Six!"

"Bailey's going down," Lila muttered just loud enough for me to hear it.

I raised an eyebrow but said nothing, mostly because I wanted to beat Gabby as much as my girls wanted to beat her girls, apparently. It was the one activity she constantly whipped my butt in. "Anybody need anything before I head out?"

"We got it covered," Kristy replied, which probably meant she would take care of it if anything came up. Man, Linda had seriously spoiled me this year.

Only when I pushed the door open did I have the sudden horrifying thought that it could be my last year. Was Linda more worried than she let on? It wasn't like I had argued with Mr. Donovan in a while, so I couldn't imagine him pulling his funding. At least not for now. *It was probably just in case things went sour*, I told myself. Otherwise why would Linda give me such an amazing group of girls?

I stepped out onto the tiny front porch with the intent to pause for a moment and take a couple of calming breaths before I joined the other counselors in our shared cabin, but I stepped into something more solid than I expected and would have fallen backward if an arm hadn't wrapped around me.

"Miss Alvarez!"

Pulling myself out of his hold and ignoring the fact that he smelled ridiculously good for being half-soaked with rain, I looked up at him. "Mr. Donovan," I replied. "What are—"

"I wanted to check on Macy—"

"—you doing here?"

"—before I headed out."

He coughed and took a step back to increase the distance between us. "I figured I should take off early," he said again, now that I wasn't talking at the same time. "So I thought I would tell Macy goodnight."

"Oh." *Why am I so surprised? He does this every night.* But as I stood there, weirdly at a loss for words, I could hear Julia teaching the others the words to the song. "Actually, it might not be the best time," I said. "They're singing."

He lifted his eyes to the cabin instead of looking down at his muddy shoes, which must have been fascinating with how intently he'd been staring at them. "I can hear that," he said. "But I don't hear Macy."

I could hardly distinguish between the girls myself, and I would have been impressed if he had heard his quiet daughter. "She doesn't know the song yet," I said when I realized he was worried. "She'll get there."

"Spanish?" he asked.

Whether or not he meant me to, I read more into his question than just wondering about the language. "My mom grew up in Mexico," I said. "She taught me all the folk songs she learned as a girl."

He nodded but said nothing, still listening to the girls sing.

Feeling awkward, which wasn't something I experienced often—thank goodness—I looked around at the still-dripping woods now glittering in the growing evening sunlight. It was beautiful, and I couldn't understand how Donovan could be in a place like this every day and still pay so much attention to his phone.

Which begged the question: "Where do you stay at night, Mr. Donovan?"

He glanced at me. "In a hotel."

"I figured as much. You don't strike me as the camping type."

That quirk of a smile played at his lips again, and he looked down at his mud-splattered suit. "What gave me away?"

"The nearest hotel is at least thirty miles away," I said. "Aren't you going to get tired of driving that far every day?"

He cocked his head. "Are you trying to get rid of me again, Miss Alvarez?"

"If I thought it would be that easy, maybe I would be, but you're stubborn." As soon as I spoke, I bit my lip, worried I had overstepped.

But Donovan's smile grew. "Yes, I am stubborn," he admitted. "It's a trait you and I apparently share. But the drive isn't too bad, and my driver probably enjoys having the middle of his day free for once. Usually he's taking me all over the city." He caught sight of my face and frowned. "What?"

"You have no idea how strange the concept of having a driver is, do you?" I said. "At least in the real world."

His frown deepened, but he seemed more confused than angry. "My world isn't the real world?" he asked.

I shook my head. "In the real world, we hope our cars actually start when we turn the key, and then we drive them ourselves." I probably sounded too sarcastic, but I couldn't help myself.

After growing up fighting and clawing for a place in the world, it was hard to look at guys like Colin Donovan and not resent the fact that they had everything handed to them. Hopefully staying here at camp for two months would help Macy see the other side of the coin from the one she knew, but Donovan himself was probably a lost cause.

"I know it probably won't change what you think of me," he said, "but I do occasionally drive my own car. I would rather maximize the time I can spend with Macy, so I employ Emil so I can work more before I get home."

Well now I feel mean. "I'm sorry," I said, though I wished I didn't have to. It was a lot easier to tease the guy than try to be genuine and nice. Our first interaction still left a bad taste in my mouth, even though it had been a few weeks since, and I couldn't really imagine us actually becoming friends over the next month or so. But he deserved some humility from me. "That's a good reason to have a driver."

His eyebrows rose higher on his forehead, so he probably hadn't expected an apology. "Uh, thank you."

And there we were again, standing in an awkward silence because we hadn't figured out this whole civil thing.

"I owe you an apology as well," he said finally, sliding his hands into his pockets. "I wasn't… I didn't treat you fairly at the beginning of the summer. I had no right to question your abilities when I had no basis for them."

Wow. Return humility from Mr. Bigshot himself? That was not even remotely what I expected, and I had no idea how to respond to that. "Uh," I said, because I had to say something. "Thanks."

As silence yet again surrounded us, broken only by the patter of rainwater dripping from the trees, my thoughts strayed to Macy. Everything I thought I knew about her life was probably wrong, since I was clearly wrong about most of my assumptions about her dad. From what I could tell, he was a really excellent father who wanted the best for his child, and her home was, I hoped, a happy one. But she was still so afraid to try things, and I wasn't sure if all of that was because she worried Mr. Donovan wouldn't approve. Maybe there was something more to it than that.

She was missing so much, and I knew without a doubt the rest of the girls would want her on the team for the canoe races in two weeks, as well as joining in on the rest of the fun here at camp. If she kept being so afraid, what was the point of her even being here? I knew how it felt to be afraid, but I also knew how to overcome it. I had learned early on that being afraid didn't do anyone any good, and maybe I could pass that on to Macy, starting with the canoe races.

But if I wanted to get Macy into a canoe, I had a feeling I would have to get her dad in one as well.

Just as I opened my mouth to see if he would be interested in helping again, he spoke first: "You have an incredible singing voice, Beck," he said quickly, and then he was gone, tramping through the mud and shaking his head as he returned to the camp entrance.

"What in the…?" Bewildered, I stood there longer than I probably should have and tried to understand why he would choose something like that as his parting words. And did that mean he had been outside the cabin long enough to hear me singing? *That's concerning.* But more importantly, his sudden departure hadn't given me time to ask for his help, which was kind of a big deal because Macy's camp experience likely depended on it.

Oh well.

I would ask him in the morning, since if it would ever have a chance of working, it would have to be sooner rather than later. I had no idea if he would even be open to the idea, but he *had* gone with the zipline suggestion despite his serious fear of heights. Canoeing would be a walk in the park compared to that, and it wasn't like he could complain about not knowing how to do it.

Any idiot could paddle a canoe.

Dear Dalia,

Turns out not every idiot can paddle a canoe. What do they even teach people at those fancy boarding schools if not how to row a boat?

Missing you,
Beck

P.S. Why do they say women are confusing when men are even worse?

CHAPTER FIVE

"Mr. Donovan?"

I had a feeling he had been expecting me to waltz up to him while the girls ate breakfast, because for once he didn't have his phone pressed against his ear. Also for the first time, he had a plate of food and was fiddling with a bunch of grapes as he stood in the corner of the mess hall. In the few weeks I'd known the guy, I had never once seen him eat. Part of me had been slightly convinced he was actually a robot. But I supposed camp food would have done a bit of damage to that physique of his, so it made sense why he wouldn't eat it.

"Miss Alvarez." He pinched a grape from the stem, rolling it around in his fingers but not eating it. There was a bit of pink in his face, which I figured was because of the few girls who were giggling to each other at the nearest table while they ate their breakfasts and tried to sneak looks at him.

Not a robot, I decided. That was nice. I had dreamed the night before that he didn't have actual human emotion and was simply programmed to be the way he was.

"Was there something I could help you with?" he asked after a moment.

Right. I had come with a question. "I have a proposition for you."

"I get a lot of propositions," he replied gruffly. "Most people generally try to give them to me quickly."

Being at the top of the tech industry probably made his time incredibly valuable, which once again made me wonder why he was even here when he could probably do much more work in the city instead of telecommuting like he was. Time in the car or no, he couldn't possibly be getting much done. But I couldn't exactly tell him that, since he didn't seem to be in the best of moods to begin with, so I had to tread carefully.

I swallowed my instinctive response—"You think you're high and mighty, don't you?"—and replied, "It's about Macy and the lake."

The color in his cheeks disappeared almost immediately. "What about her?"

You don't have to freak out about every little thing. "We have our canoe races coming up, and it's usually the most popular part of the summer. Everyone loves them, even the girls who aren't as athletic as others. And while there's nothing wrong with being a support from the sidelines, I think Macy would have more fun with the rest of her cabin."

As usual, Donovan's eyes sought out his daughter in the mess hall, and he watched her smile with her friends for a moment before bringing his gaze back to me. "You want me to talk to her?" But then he frowned as it hit him. "You want me to hop in a canoe."

I shrugged, still a little wary of pushing him too far this morning. I couldn't be sure of his exact mood, especially when he worked so hard to keep emotion out of his face. "It worked with the zipline," I said, "and now she's always first in line for it."

"But a zipline isn't a lake," he replied, reminding me that Macy was afraid of the water.

Did he really think I was stupid enough to forget something like that? "You'd be surprised how many girls are afraid of the lake their first time," I said. "Once they get that push to get in and see how fun it is, I can hardly get them out of the water for the rest of the summer."

Still rolling the grape between his fingers, Donovan seemed to be thinking hard about the situation. And then, to my complete and utter surprise, he tossed the grape in the air and caught it in his mouth.

The nearby teenagers cheered, and only then did Donovan seem to realize what he'd done. Swallowing the grape, he set his plate on the closest table and folded his arms. "I'm not sure—"

"You just caught a grape with your mouth," I said, as if he wasn't already aware of the fact and red-faced.

He clenched his jaw. "Is that really important enough to—"

"So you do know how to have some fun." I could hardly believe it!

"Miss Alvarez, I—"

"Call me that one more time, and you'll be finding a snake in that fancy car of yours on your ride home tonight. I've done it before, and I'll do it again."

The threat—a mistake, I knew—did something strange to Donovan. Instead of aggravating his frustration, it almost seemed to calm him down and relax him. He dropped his arms back down to his sides and pulled his eyebrows together, once again more in consternation than anything. It was like he didn't know what to make of me and was hating that unknown. A man like him, who probably craved control—hence starting his own company—would hate me if I didn't have the ability to tone down my true self like I reluctantly did around him. I enjoyed the chaos that came from letting go, and he was probably terrified of it.

But when I threatened him, it was just enough of a slap in the face to bring him a little closer to my level.

"Are you afraid of nothing?" he asked, and his voice seemed to carry a sense of awe. For the first time, I didn't feel like he was looking down on me. "You know I hold the fate of your little camp in my hands, right?"

I grinned, though I wasn't sure why his comment didn't worry me like it should have. "Why be afraid when you can be alive? Besides, I think my little camp might be growing on you. So I'll see you at the docks in an hour?"

It was a challenge, and he knew it. His eyes narrowed, his jaw clenched tight again, and there was a spark of fire in his gaze that I hadn't seen there before. "Count on it," he said after a moment and left the building.

I felt like I'd won something, which was ridiculous because it hadn't even been a battle. Colin Donovan would do anything for his daughter. So why was I grinning like an idiot as I watched him through the mess hall windows?

The girls split half and half at the edge of the lake, each decked out in a life jacket and gripping a paddle. All but one. Macy had changed into a swimsuit like the others and had even slipped her life jacket over her shoulders, but she hadn't buckled it or reached for the paddle Madison had grabbed for her. She was eyeing the lake with worried eyes and her bottom lip between her teeth.

I desperately hoped her dad would show up, but so far he was nowhere in sight. And as much as I wanted to pull Macy aside and talk to her, I couldn't neglect the rest of my girls.

"Okay, crew!" I said, throwing as much enthusiasm into my words as I could. "I've been sailing the high seas for all my life, and never had I lost a ship until three years ago, when the Dread Pirate Gabby set sail for the first time. Do you remember that, first mate?"

Kristy looked positively fearsome as she replied, "I will never forget, Captain."

"What happened?" Zoey whispered, her eyes wide.

"Captain Gabby came up from behind," I said in a low voice. "We never even saw her coming, and then *bam*!"

Macy and Willow both jumped.

I put on a scowl. "They shot us straight out of the water," I said. "And every year since, that scurvy Captain Gabby has beaten me and my fine crew. But not this year. Right, mateys?"

"Right, Captain!" several shouted at once.

As I began pacing in front of them, I tried to judge Macy's expression. She looked excited, but she also looked terrified, and her eyes kept darting between the lake and direction of the rec room. Without her dad to prove he was okay with her trying something new, how was I supposed to convince her she could?

"Alrighty, you dogs," I said as I traced my path along their line, "if we want to beat Captain Gabby and her gang of ruffians, it'll take all of us. A canoe is more than just a hunk of wood and a few paddles. A canoe can sense your heart, and it can only reach its true potential when its occupants are one with each other. Are you feeling loyal?"

There were a few mumbles of yes.

"I said, are you feeling loyal to your fellow pirates?" I shouted.

"Yeah!" seven of them shouted back.

Macy looked a little green.

"You really get into this, don't you?" asked a voice behind me.

I shrieked and jumped a foot in the air. Though I normally didn't scare easily, he'd come out of nowhere! The girls immediately burst into giggles and lost their fearsome pirate stances, but I ignored the burning in my face and turned to greet Donovan.

"You came," I said, quiet enough that Macy wouldn't hear. I didn't want her to know I had a plan to convince her. She had to come to her decision on her own.

Donovan seemed to catch on to my secrecy and nodded. "I said I would." Then louder he added, "I've wanted to try canoeing since I was a kid, and you were making it sound so…exciting." That last word came out with a raised eyebrow and a bit of mocking in his voice.

I just smiled then turned back to my girls. I would find a way to get him back for that surprising bit of teasing. "Looks like you're in for a treat," I told them. "I won't be coaching from the sidelines this year, because now I have a landlubber to order around and row my boat for me!"

Julia and Brielle were the only two who didn't look completely confused, though Kristy caught on a second later and glanced at Macy. Macy, like the rest, was staring at her father as if she couldn't possibly comprehend what was about to happen.

"He's going on a canoe?" Lila asked after a moment of silence.

Her question, which was so full of disbelief, wasn't all that out of place, mainly because Donovan definitely was. Seriously, did the guy own anything other than a suit? At least he had taken off his jacket and rolled up his sleeves, but I didn't know how he expected to keep his pants dry or his leather shoes from getting ruined.

Donovan apparently didn't know what to say to the question, so I answered for him: "This here novice needs to be schooled in the ways of piratery, so I hope you all show him how it's done. Into the boats with ye!"

Seven girls rushed to the waiting canoes on the shore. I worried Macy was going to stand there in indecision until her fear won out, but then she picked up her paddle and followed the others.

"Don't say a word," I warned Donovan, as if he was really stupid enough to mess up something that was likely monumental. "And go grab yourself a life jacket. No one can go on the lake without one."

He didn't move, staring at me as if I'd said nonsense. "But she's getting in the canoe. Do I really have to…you know?"

I sighed. "Pineapple."

"What?"

"Stupid questions deserve stupid answers. Now get in the boat, Mr. Donovan."

I was pushing my luck, but it was seriously hard to be completely civil to the guy, even if he wasn't as bad as my first impression of him. Something about him just brought out the strongest side of me, which wasn't the side I needed to show to the guy who had the power to shut down the one place that still felt like home to me.

To my relief, he slipped on a life jacket and approached the canoe where I waited for him. He wasn't nearly as scared of this idea as he'd been of the zipline, but that didn't mean he looked at all comfortable. At my direction, he climbed into the little boat, and when I gave it a shove to push it into the water, he grabbed the sides as if afraid he was about to fall in. He may have been a handsome fella, but he was sure afraid of a lot of things.

Much like his daughter.

Before the momentum of my push took the boat out of my hands, I leapt in behind Donovan and settled into my seat. "Feel free to grab your paddle at any time," I said and rolled my eyes. The man was literally gripping the sides of the boat for dear life, and I could only imagine his expression.

To his credit, he let go and picked up the paddle sitting at his feet. "Go easy on me, Captain," he said. "This camp is a new frontier for me."

I suppose he deserves some pity. But that was easier said than done. "Have you really never spent any time in the outdoors? Who wears a suit while canoeing?"

"Someone who was caught off guard," he replied. He must have seen what the girls were doing, because he started dipping his paddle in the water to match. "I don't only own suits, you know. But my driver went into town for the day and won't be back until later, so I couldn't grab a change of clothes."

I didn't like not being able to see his face. Not like the guy was super expressive to begin with, but just his voice alone made it even harder to guess his mood. "Well," I said and began paddling opposite him so we didn't go in a circle, "just don't capsize the canoe, and you'll be fine."

"Comforting."

As we paddled after the girls, the sun glittered on the lake around us, hot and bright. The water was smooth and clear, and I couldn't have imagined a better first day of canoe practice, especially because all eight of my girls seemed to be having fun.

"So why pirates?" Donovan asked after a moment. "From what I can tell, you could have chosen anything."

That was true. Gabby went with a wildlife theme, and several others had chosen princess. Annabeth, with all her little girls, had quickly switched from ninjas to ponies after she saw her group the first day. But forever and always I would choose pirates.

"My mom used to read me *Treasure Island* when I was a little girl," I said. "She liked reading the classics because they helped her with her English, and that was always my favorite one. It felt like one I could relate to."

"I've been thinking you have some Jim Hawkins in you."

Well that was unexpected.

"What?" he asked when I didn't respond, and he tried to turn around to see me, though he could only manage partway. "You don't think I've read any books before?"

I narrowed my eyes at him. "You don't make any sense, Mr. Donovan."

"How do you mean?" At least he didn't sound upset about my comment. I was getting seriously lucky with some of the things I said, and I knew I shouldn't push it.

"I don't know, exactly," I said. "With the girls, it's pretty easy to figure them out, but I'm at a loss with you."

He tried to look at me again, only this time he was determined and got up just enough to turn completely around without tipping the canoe over. Once he was again safely situated, he locked his eyes onto my face and started paddling backward.

"You say that as if you're easy to understand yourself," he said.

Did that mean he'd been trying to figure me out? But he had already apologized and seemed to think I was a perfectly capable counselor for his daughter, so why would he need to understand who I was beyond that?

"Why?" I asked, though I knew it was a pretty loose question.

He scrutinized me for a moment, his gaze sharp, as usual. "What is it about this camp that you love so much?"

Out of all the questions he could have possibly asked, I had not even considered something like that, and I stopped paddling so I could properly stare at him and try to understand. "What?"

He stopped paddling too, so now we were just drifting slowly through the water while the girls practiced a little distance away under the capable hands of their two captains, Kristy and Lila. He rested his paddle on his lap and leaned a little closer. "You clearly don't like me," he explained, "and you would have personally tossed me out of the camp if given the chance."

He wasn't wrong, though it wasn't like I hated him. "So?"

"So why are you so loyal to a scrap of wilderness that you would work so hard to make a guy like me happy?"

I didn't really understand the point of his question. The answer should have been obvious. "I couldn't let myself be the one who made the camp shut down," I said. "The girls look forward to coming here every summer."

He leaned even closer, resting his elbows on his knees. "There are other camps out there," he replied. "Better-funded camps, I might add. No, this one is special to you personally." He fixed that sharp gaze on me so intently that I actually felt a little uncomfortable.

The last time I'd had a man stare at me for so long, I'd slapped him in the face and made him leave the club where Gabby and I had met for drinks early last spring. Donovan may not have had the same creepy vibe, but I still felt like he was seeing more than I was used to letting people see.

It was easy to hide from preteen girls. Not so much from adults.

"I started coming to this camp when I was six," I said. And he just kept staring at me, letting the silence grow until I felt the need to fill it before he discovered something embarrassing. "And my mom worked here every summer."

He finally softened and sat up again, a little smile lifting the corners of his mouth. "See?" he said. "Now you make a little more sense."

"Does that mean it's my turn?"

He paled a bit. "For what?"

Oh, so he could interrogate me no problem, but he had an issue with me doing the same thing? *Too bad, Mr. Donovan.* "Why are you here?" I asked.

He frowned. "You know—"

"I know why you said you're here," I interrupted, "but even the most overprotective parent can leave their child alone for a few weeks. Wouldn't you rather have some time to yourself for once?" *And what does your wife think about you being here?* I couldn't help but look at the ring on his finger and wonder what she was like. Macy was so much like her dad that I couldn't even guess at her mom's personality.

"We go on vacation every summer," he said, mumbling a bit.

"This isn't exactly a vacation," I replied.

"It is for Macy."

"But that still doesn't answer my question."

He looked ready to jump ship and simply swim away instead of answering, his eyes full of anxiety and his hands gripping his paddle. Was it really something so horrible?

A splash behind him pulled his attention away, and he froze. "Macy!" he gasped.

One of the canoes had tipped, knocking all four girls into the water. Macy was among them, and my heart kicked up a notch when I watched her bob to the surface with wide, horrified eyes.

"Macy!" Donovan shouted, and he grabbed his paddle and started swiping at the water.

"Wait!" I said, though the word got lost as Donovan's wild movement nearly knocked me out of the canoe. "I'm sure she's—"

Next thing I knew I swallowed a mouthful of water as I tumbled into the lake. I coughed and grabbed onto the overturned canoe just as Donovan himself came up spluttering. I latched onto his arm before he could start swimming, and I could tell he was about to start yelling at me when laughter caught my ears.

"Thar she blows!" Kristy called from her canoe. "You alright, Captain?"

Eight girls were laughing at us. *Eight.* Even Macy, who floated with tears of laughter in her eyes as she watched her always composed father grip the end of the canoe with near desperation.

"I think you need more practice, Dad," she called to him.

He froze again, still clinging to the bottom of the boat, and seemed to think he had heard his daughter wrong.

"She's fine," I said quietly. I was still holding his wrist, I realized, and I let go before he realized the same thing. "Sometimes you just have to let her face her fears on her own."

And Donovan turned his gaze back to me, the weirdest expression on his face. If I had to put a word to it, it would be utter and complete joy.

We spent the rest of the hour watching from the beach. Donovan helped me swim the canoe back to shore, and then he surprised me yet again by joining me in sitting in the sand, though I couldn't imagine he was all that comfortable in his sopping suit. But he just took off his shoes and plopped down next to me as I watched Kristy and Lila teach their cabin mates the most efficient paddling techniques.

After what felt like an eternity of silence, which I didn't plan to break considering how he'd been avoiding my last question, Donovan coughed a little and leaned his head in my direction, though he kept his gaze on Macy. "You might not realize how big a deal this is," he said softly, "but seeing Macy having fun with other girls her age, and in the water, no less, it's… It's almost a miracle."

Glistening water dripped from his hair onto his shoulders, and his wet white shirt clung to his body. I wondered if he had any idea how much more he was giving off a Mr. Darcy vibe than he had in the rain. He'd given Matthew Macfadyen a run for his money, but he was pretty much putting Colin Firth out of his job this time.

Pay attention, Beck. Shaking my head to rid myself of *Pride and Prejudice* fantasies, I returned my gaze to the lake and said, "Does Macy not have friends in school? She's such a sweet kid."

"I know that," he replied with a bit of bitterness, "but I'm not sure anyone else does. She's so quiet, and because of my…because my business does well, the kids at her school mistake her shyness for disgust and thinking herself better than them. It shouldn't be a problem, but the other parents know me well and pass it on to their kids."

"But here Macy can just be another one of the campers," I said. "Everyone is equal."

He smiled wistfully. "I'm starting to see why you love this place. I would have killed to be just like everyone else when I was a kid."

I was pretty sure, from my very limited research and conversation with the guy, Donovan had been rich his whole life. His tech company had simply made him even wealthier than before. If a guy like that was wishing he had lived a life like mine, he clearly had no idea how the real world worked. Even if he sometimes drove his own car.

And I had no idea how to comment on that thought, so I steered the conversation back to Macy and camp. "So you brought her here where there's no parental influence to prejudice the other girls. Smart move." The poor girl was probably starved for genuine friendship, and I was yet again grateful for the girls Linda had put into my cabin with her. Not a single one of them had a cruel bone in her body. "Brielle lives somewhere in Oakland, and I think Zoey is from somewhere in northern Sonoma county. If Macy wants to keep in touch after summer's over."

Donovan looked over at me and gave me a smile I hadn't seen before. It was warmer. Softer. "That's a good idea," he said. "Thank you, Beck."

"You're welcome, Mr. Donovan."

He let out a small laugh, shook his head, and leaned back on his hands, looking more at ease than I'd ever seen him. "I think at this point you've seen enough of my less than dignified moments, so I'm not sure I deserve Mr. Donovan. It's Colin."

I raised my eyebrows. "Really?"

"Is it that hard to believe I have a first name?"

"It's hard to believe you would let me use it."

There was a shriek on the lake, and we both looked up to find the two canoes having a splash battle. I couldn't tell who was winning, but the girls were definitely having fun.

"I really am sorry for the way I acted," Donovan—Colin—said. "That first day was... Well, I'm not trying to excuse my behavior, but sometimes the stress gets to me. Trying to balance work and Macy... It wears me down. And that first day of camp was right at the height of everything."

Where did his wife fit in with all that? It was nice seeing this softer side of him so I was too hesitant to ask, but that didn't mean I couldn't ask the many other questions that were rolling around in my head. "What is it you do for work, Mr., uh, Colin?"

His sideways grin was more alarmingly handsome than it had a right to be. "You mean to tell me you haven't already looked up my life story on the internet? All the juicy details are easy to find."

"Not when you have terrible Wi-Fi," I replied. "I'm basically outdoors most months of the year, so that doesn't leave a lot of time for stalking strangers."

"Huh. I didn't think it would hurt this much to not be known by someone."

I was tempted to throw some sand at him, but I refrained. Barely. "So what do you do?" I repeated.

"I do my very best to keep my company from imploding while keeping myself sane as much as possible." He laughed when I raised an eyebrow. "Fine," he said, "though you can't blame me if you fall asleep. It's not particularly exciting."

I had a feeling he could make anything sound exciting. "Try me."

He smiled. "I started my company when I was twenty-five," he said. "Our website and app essentially work with local companies and provide interactive digital travel brochures for tourists in some of the more popular cities around the country. It's grown beyond that in the last year or so and expanded to a sort of online marketplace and ad space, but the brochure is still the heart of it." Then he looked at me and said, "What about you?" as if his life sounded perfectly normal. *Everyone creates a billion-dollar company in their twenties.* "I mean, what do you do when you're not at camp?"

Shrugging, I ran my hand through the sand and left a trail of ridges with my fingers. "Teach kids how to ski in the winter," I said with a little hesitation. My life was going to sound so boring next to his. "And I usually do corporate training seminars in the fall and spring."

"Corporate training seminars?"

"You know, like those team-building activities where you have to get everyone across a pit or up a wall?"

Colin shrugged, and clearly he hadn't worked for a company that required team-building exercises. Then I had to wonder how he ran his own company and if people liked working for him or if his employees resented him. At this point, though, I couldn't imagine them hating him unless he was constantly stressed. *Maybe that's the case. Maybe they only get the mean version of him.*

"Is it that terrible that I don't know what you're talking about?" he asked.

Whoops. Focus, Beck. "No, the seminars aren't very common, and it's mostly the boring companies who do it. To spice up work life or something."

He turned and leaned on one hand, which was a lot closer to mine than I thought he realized. "So let me get this straight," he said. "You take regular office workers out of their element and force them into situations where they are wildly uncomfortable, for the sake of the greater good?"

When he put it that way, it sounded a bit diabolical, but, "Yeah, that's pretty much how it goes."

"Well, that certainly sounds like you."

Did the man just make a joke? I snorted a laugh, and he gave me a crooked smile, and it felt like the whole world was out of balance because there was a chance I was starting to like this guy. And a friendship with him was all sorts of out of the question, for more reasons than I could count. Technically he shouldn't even be here, so warming up to him would only end in some sort of tragedy.

"Looks like the girls are coming back," he said after a glance out on the lake.

He was right, and the two canoes were speeding toward shore, each determined to beat the other. They were already off to a good start, and there was a chance we could actually win the races this year.

Getting to my feet, I brushed the sand off my legs and took half a second to examine Colin one more time before I had to get back to routine camp life again. It had been weirdly nice talking about normal things with a fellow adult for once. Even with the other counselors, we usually just talked about the girls, and my other jobs weren't much different. Was this how regular adults felt when they had conversations? I'd only really had the experience with one other person before now, and that wasn't exactly an avenue I wanted to go down again. But with Colin, it seemed different somehow.

"Thanks for teaching me how to canoe," he said and gave me another one of his staggering smiles. "Even if I'm clearly not good at it."

"It takes practice like anything else," I replied, though my voice shook a bit, which was ridiculous. It wasn't like I was scared of the guy.

As he stuffed his hands into his still wet pockets, he seemed almost nervous when he said, "If I decide to take it up, can I count on you to be my coach?"

My stomach did a weird sort of flip, and I couldn't seem to find my words before he turned and wandered up the beach, back toward the rec room and mess hall. He walked without a purpose, it seemed, his shoulders hunched and his steps slow, and I had to wonder why a man like Colin Donovan would be drawn to a lake he definitely didn't like.

CHAPTER SIX

At the campfire at the end of the week, every single girl seemed to be talking about the upcoming canoe races. Since each cabin had had a chance to have their first practice, it was definitely the most exciting thing coming up, though they still had almost two weeks to train and perfect their trash talk. Though not every cabin was as tight knit as mine, and some of the girls spread out to sit with other friends, most of them seemed content to stay with their teams now that loyalty and synchronization were important.

For the first time in years, however, I couldn't seem to focus on the upcoming races. They were usually one of my favorite parts of camp, and I was more competitive than most, but I couldn't seem to pay attention during our practices or while Kristy and Lila were talking strategy, which had always been something I absolutely loved to take part in. And I wasn't really sure why I was having such a hard time.

I was often the person the other counselors came to when they had problems, whether with the girls or with life, but I figured it was my turn to get some advice from people I trusted more than anyone. As our girls chatted and laughed around the massive bonfire we burned every Friday, I slid into a seat between Gabby and Sofie at the counselor table off to the side. Both of them were prepping s'more supplies, setting out graham crackers with chocolate sandwiched between so they would be ready for the fire-roasted marshmallows the girls would bring over.

I grabbed a box of grahams and joined in, but I kept breaking the crackers.

Sofie noticed first. "What's up with you, Beck?" she asked.

As I broke yet another cracker, I decided I should just sit and let the others do it. "I'm having a weird week," I said.

Across from me, Yasmine and Chelsea glanced at each other but said nothing. So they were listening but not inclined to participate in the conversation? *Great.* I liked all of the counselors Linda hired, but I wasn't sure I liked them enough to include them in my personal woes.

I spoke a little quieter. "I'm not sure what it is, but I just feel off, you know?"

"At least you didn't wake up to a snake in your boot," Sofie said with a sigh. "And I know the Connelly girls are only getting started."

I couldn't help but smile because I'd woken up to Sofie's screams, since all of us counselors shared a large cabin. "They only prank you because they like you," I assured her. "At least they're smart enough to distinguish which snakes are venomous, right?"

Sofie rolled her eyes. "Yes, that makes me feel so much better," she said, her sarcasm thick.

"So you don't know why you're off your game?" Gabby asked me. She, at least, seemed more invested than Sofie, and she took her role as my best friend seriously. *Thank goodness.* "When did it start?"

"A few days ago," I decided, though I couldn't be sure. "Sometime after our first canoe practice."

Gabby's little crooked smile was a bit concerning. "You mean after you sat side by side with a certain handsome multi-millionaire after falling into the lake with him?"

My stomach did that same flip again, the one it had been doing every time I caught sight of Colin. He'd been working most of the day the last week, so he had been lurking even less, but I always seemed to know where he was, even when I couldn't see him. I was just glad he had gone back to his hotel for the night so I could actually have this conversation without wondering if he would accidentally overhear. Yasmine and Chelsea, on the other hand…

I took Gabby's hand and pulled her away from the table. Once we were far enough from both the counselors and the girls, I decided it was safe to respond to her comment. "What are you talking about, Gabs?"

"Don't play stupid, Beck."

"I'm not."

She lifted one eyebrow. "Right. Because you have no idea how you look at the guy when you think no one is watching."

I really didn't. I mean, he was attractive, sure, but we had only just barely hit a point where we could talk civilly. There was nothing more to it than that. "I think you're grasping at straws, which never turns out well for you."

But Gabby wasn't deterred, and she leaned nice and close, which meant she was ready to drop what she considered a truth bomb. "I know what you'll say, Beck. You've barely talked to the guy and he was a pig at first and he's a camper's dad and—"

"Do I need more of a reason than that to tell you there's nothing there?" I interrupted. "Mr. Donovan is not the reason I'm off my game, Gabby. I promise you." At least, I was pretty sure he wasn't. Like Gabby said, I'd barely spoken to the guy unless it involved his daughter.

"Reason or not," she said, "you get a look in your eyes anytime someone says Colin Donovan."

I worked very hard to keep my expression neutral, just in case. I had to shut this down before she took it too far. "The guy's married, Gabs."

"No he isn't."

Of course he was. He'd told me about his wife. Not much, but still. And there was the matter of the ring he wore on his left hand, the one I could always see when he was on his phone because he most often held the phone with his left hand instead of his right. "What are you talking about?" I asked.

Something sparked in her eyes, as if she'd seen something important in my face. *Stop looking at me with those crazy eyes.* "Either I'm losing my mind," she said, "or you have a crush on Colin Donovan."

"No," I said back. "I really don't. You're definitely losing your mind."

"What if I told you his wife was dead?"

"Gabby!"

"But it's true!"

As much as I didn't want to think that, I couldn't really imagine Gabby lying about something like that. She was more inclined to browse the internet if given the chance, and she had a boyfriend back in Santa Rosa where she lived who might have searched things for her and given her all the details during one of their frequent phone conversations.

I felt awful asking, but for some reason I really wanted to know the details. "Tell me," I sighed. And I told myself that I wanted to know because maybe it would help me help Macy, even if that was only a minor part of why. Mostly I hoped it would help explain why Colin was the way he was.

Gabby gripped my hand and leaned close so no one would hear but me. "So it looks like it was a few years ago," she said. "Some kind of accident. There wasn't a lot of information online, so Mr. Donovan probably tried to keep it quiet."

I swallowed. "Please tell me you're not trying to make it out like some hushed up, suspicious thing."

Gabby rolled her eyes. "Of course I'm not saying that. I'm just saying Donovan probably didn't want the world to exploit the tragedy. But what's important about all of this is the fact that *he's not married.*"

That poor family. If what Gabby was saying was true, Colin's relationship with Macy suddenly made a lot more sense. Of course he would want to keep her close. Of course he would worry about her having fun. Especially if his wife's death had only been a few years ago, Macy would have been old enough to remember her but young enough to not understand why her mother suddenly stopped being there, and there were a lot of after-effects that probably still haunted her.

I knew that well.

"Why does it matter if he's not married?" I muttered, though I had a feeling I knew what Gabby would say.

"Because," she replied, "it means you don't have to feel guilty about flirting with him."

I stared at her. "I haven't flirted with him."

"Please."

"I'm not just saying that to be defensive," I argued. "I've barely talked to the guy, and I definitely haven't flirted. You've seen me flirt. I'm terrible at it."

Gabby rolled her eyes again. "Yeah, well, that's because you spend all summer with us and the rest of the year with the same hippie weirdos. You don't ever give yourself the chance to practice."

For good reason. "Gabs, remember the last time I actually flirted with someone?" I wasn't keen on thinking about it, but I needed her to understand she couldn't push this thing she apparently thought I had with Colin. Married or not, there were still so many reasons it wasn't a good idea to have any sort of relationship with the guy, romantic or otherwise.

At least my argument seemed to have worked, and Gabby frowned. "Okay," she mumbled, "Kurt was a bad one."

"He cheated on me," I replied, my voice low. "'Bad one' is a bit of an understatement, don't you think?"

I had met Kurt Hansen when his team came for a company retreat two years ago. He'd given me his email before he left, and we'd written back and forth until I was able to drive into Oakland to meet up with him for dinner. For the next three months we spent most weekends together, and things had seemed to be going well. He told me he loved me and didn't want to date anyone else, and I started picturing the life we could build together. I went into the city in the middle of the week to surprise him, since I'd been given a rare day off. He hadn't been alone in his apartment, and I had cried the whole way back to the wilderness, where I'd been ever since.

The city held nothing but heartache.

"I've given up on that sort of thing, Gabs," I said. "I just want to look after my girls."

Though she looked disappointed, Gabby gave my hand a squeeze and nodded. "Fine," she whispered. "You know yourself better than anyone, and you know what you need. But if you're really not going to let anything happen with Captain Handsome, you might want to tell *him* that." And she nodded her head behind me with a pointed look.

I felt the blood drain from my face, and I turned in alarm. There he stood, as attractive as ever, off to the side and just out of the firelight. But it was impossible not to see him when he stood out as much as he did. The only man under fifty inside camp boundaries. He wasn't wearing a suit for once, and I suddenly found it impossible to look away from the guy. Put him in jeans and a henley, and he looked almost normal.

Something pushed me forward, though I honestly had no idea if it was Gabby giving me a nudge or my own stupidity propelling me closer to the man. *What're you doing here?* Probably not the best way to phrase that question. *I thought you left for the night.* Still a bit blunt. What could I possibly say that wouldn't come across as belligerent?

"Linda invited me back for the campfire," he said as I approached. His eyes were wary as they reflected the firelight, as if he had anticipated me asking either of those slightly rude questions.

I tried to smile, but Gabby was in my head now. If I smiled at him, would it look flirtatious from the outside? "They'll probably start singing soon," I replied. "It's one of my favorite parts of camp."

He nodded, and for some reason he still looked nervous. "I think Linda wanted to show me some of the parts of camp I haven't seen yet."

That was probably a smart move on Linda's part, though I had a feeling she didn't need to worry about losing his money. He had seen enough improvement in Macy to know this place was good, hadn't he?

"You're not wearing a suit," I blurted out.

Smiling, he glanced down at his outfit. "That's because I'm not working."

It took me a moment to make sense of that comment, partly because I had to stop myself from saying, *No, that look is definitely working.* "So you wear the suit because you're working," I said, though I knew I was pretty much just repeating his own words. "Does it help you focus or something?"

His chuckle was almost adorable. "Something like that," he said. "Do you do this campfire every Friday?" He jumped back as a couple of girls rushed past with flaming marshmallows on sticks, eager to get their graham crackers and chocolate to complete the treat. "It's a bit dangerous, don't you think?"

I just laughed. "Clearly you haven't spent enough time around kids," I said. "They're always dangerous." And then I stiffened as I realized what I'd said and who I'd said it to. "Sorry, I didn't mean…"

Luckily, Colin shrugged one shoulder, but he folded his arms and returned his gaze to the fire instead of me. "No, it's fine. I don't get to spend as much time with Macy as I'd like, and it's my own fault for not working harder to be with her."

That wasn't at all what I'd meant for him to get out of my comment, but I wasn't sure how to fix it. "You're running a ridiculously successful company," I said. "There are always going to be sacrifices."

"Maybe," he agreed, "but I'm not sure they're always worth it."

Having spent most of life in summer camps and the like, I was not used to people being gloomy. And I didn't like it. I could comfort the deepest of teenage drama, but a father missing lost time with his child was more serious than I was equipped to handle. And while I knew I wasn't qualified to try to cheer the guy up, I couldn't just stand there and let him be miserable because he wasn't perfect at being a single parent.

So I would just have to use the skills I did have.

"How about a s'more?" I asked, doing my best to sound cheery.

He turned to me, one eyebrow raised. "Some more what?"

I was pretty sure my jaw dropped to the ground. "Are you kidding?" I said, and it felt like the world had just done a somersault. "Are you telling me you've never—"

Colin burst out laughing before I could finish my sentence, and it was the most musical sound in the world. "Relax," he said and put his hand on my arm.

For a second I was sure my heart had stopped.

"Technically," he said, "I've never had a s'more, but that doesn't mean I haven't seen the most iconic baseball movie of all time. *The Sandlot* is a classic." When I raised an eyebrow at him, he laughed again. "I was still a kid, even if I was a rich one."

I really had no idea what to say to that, and hearing a laugh like that was enough to disrupt any girl's thought process. Maybe Gabby was right. Maybe Colin Donovan really was the reason I was so off my groove.

And I had no idea what to do with that.

Shaking myself loose from his little spell, I tried to imagine he was just like any other camper who was new to the art of fire-roasted food. It wasn't easy, given he was twice their height and a million times more handsome, but if I tried not to look at him, I figured I could mostly manage it. "Well," I said, "I happen to be an expert at making s'mores, so maybe I can teach you. Maybe."

He bumped his shoulder into mine, which definitely wasn't something the campers ever did. "Are you saying I might be unteachable?" he asked.

"I'm saying you can't teach an old dog new tricks."

"Old? I'm only thirty, Miss Alvarez."

Geez Louise, that was younger than I expected. That put him at only a few years older than me. *Focus, Beck.* "I seem to recall telling you exactly what would happen if you called me that again," I said.

He didn't look the least bit chagrined. "I'm not actually afraid of snakes."

"I find that hard to believe. You're afraid of everything."

"You only think that because you're afraid of nothing."

"That part's true."

"Are you going to teach me how to make a s'more or not?"

"Get yourself a stick, Mr. Donovan."

A moment later, we were both crouched in front of the fire, and I could feel eighty pairs of eyes on me. Technically, they were probably on Colin, but since I was right next to him, I could feel those stares as easily as if I were looking back at the girls. They'd pretty much stopped chatting, leaving the crackle of the fire as the only sound in the night air. That was going to have to change.

"I don't know if you've noticed," I whispered to Colin, "but we have a bit of an audience."

He kept his gaze on the fire, and I couldn't tell if he was red or not in the orange light. "I am aware," he whispered back. "Maybe I should leave. I don't want to disrupt—"

"You deserve a s'more, Colin."

He gave me a sideways look that really didn't convey much emotion. He was back to hiding it, and I wasn't sure if that was good or bad. "What do we do?" he asked.

"Do you sing?"

He dropped his marshmallow in the dirt and quickly reached down to grab it. "Do I what?"

"Sing."

"No."

Then I'll do it myself. As much as I wanted to force him into joining me, I had a feeling it wouldn't be all that easy. Especially with the song choice that popped into my head. Leaving him down by the fire, I jumped to my feet and spun in a quick circle to make sure all the girls were now paying attention to me instead of him, and then I took a deep breath and shouted the first line of a Spice Girls song I knew they wouldn't be able to resist.

At first there was silence as the girls all looked around, wondering if they'd missed some instruction. But, as I knew they would, half the girls in my cabin jumped to their feet, led by Kristy, who shouted back the next line of the song.

I grinned and sang the third line.

And next thing I knew, the whole camp had joined in and were singing "Wannabe" at the top of their lungs. From there, someone would start a new song, and they'd be singing for the rest of the night.

"And that," I said as I sat down next to Colin again, "is how you distract a bunch of teenagers."

His eyebrows were high as he looked around us and watched the girls start dancing as they sang, fully engrossed in their song. Then he turned that wide-eyed gaze to me as if he'd never seen anything like me. "You're like some terrifying wizard," he said finally.

I raised an eyebrow. "Is that a compliment or an insult?"

"I haven't decided."

"That's a dangerous position to take when I'm the one who will decide whether or not that marshmallow of yours will end up delicious or burned to a crisp."

"That's a lot of power for one woman, don't you think?"

And as eighty girls—and a few of the counselors—sang their hearts out around us, I found myself grinning. Colin Donovan kept on surprising me, and it was hard not to wonder what it would be like to be his friend.

"Well," I said, "do you want to give me that power or not?"

He looked at the marshmallow on top of his stick then gave me a little bow as he sat there in the dirt. "Teach me your ways, oh wise wizard."

Dear Dalia,

I know time always goes by quickly here at camp, but this year seems different. It's like time has jumped into double time, and summer is coming to a close before I can even appreciate how wonderful it's been. Things have been so much better than I expected before summer began, and I think that's part of the problem. Time flies when you're having fun, and all that. I just don't want it to fly this fast.

My girls won the canoe race. Kristy got her team to block both of Gabby's canoes right at the end, and Lila's boat crossed the finish line without contest. My girls were thrilled, and it was especially nice to see Macy look proud of something she'd done. All the girls this year, in the whole camp, seem to be building each other up more than ever, and I'm pretty sure there are going to be lifelong friendships from this year, which is exactly what we like to see. We've even had some girls discover new talents, and we haven't had a single injury, unless you count the time Sofie went into her cabin to wake the girls up one morning and stepped in a puddle of honey. She wouldn't have gotten hurt if she hadn't scared herself so bad that she tripped into the wall and bruised her shoulder.

I still have that feeling of dread hanging over me, though, and I'm not sure why. When everything is going so well, it's like I know it can't last. I've had more fun the last few weeks than I think I've had in a long time, and I just know it all has to end sometime. Everything does. But what is going to go wrong? Are we going to lose the camp still? Or is there something more on the horizon, something I just can't see because I'm being blinded by all the good things. And there are so many good things to blind me.

I think that might be what scares me. The fact that he's been such a big part of those good things, and he's leaving along with the girls.

I don't know if I should protect my heart now, before it's too late, or if I should hold onto those good things as long as I possibly can.

Tell me what to do. You were always good at that.

Needing you,
Beck

P.S. I'm not supposed to be scared of anything, but I'm more scared than I've ever been in my life.

P.P.S. I still can't remember the last line of that song.

P.P.P.S. Tomorrow is the big hike, and Mr. Donovan is coming. I can't decide if I should be excited or worried.

P.P.P.P.S. At what point are there too many post-scripts in a letter?

P.P.P.P.P.S. Is it against the rules for a camp counselor to be homesick? Because I…

CHAPTER SEVEN

"Isn't it too early in the morning to be writing in your journal?"

I looked up in the middle of writing a sentence, and though I should have been proud of myself for not jumping out of my skin at the sound of a very unexpected voice, I was more surprised by Colin's appearance than anything.

"You look…"

He sipped at his cup of coffee and didn't even bother glancing at his outfit this time, though he'd started doing that any time I made a comment on his appearance. It had happened more often than I would have expected these last few weeks, but that was because I'd seen less of the suits and more of the sort of thing I was used to seeing out here in the wilderness. Jeans, t-shirts, flannel. Today, he wore cargo pants and a pair of hiking boots that looked like they had probably cost a couple hundred dollars. If I hadn't grown to recognize the way he couldn't seem to get the right side of his hair to cooperate completely, I might not have even recognized him at all because he had changed a lot over the summer.

"Different," I decided. "You look different."

"I look like I might actually fit in for once," he corrected. "But when one's daughter asks if one is going on the 'big hike,' one must prepare."

"One should probably also talk like a normal human," I replied. I scooted over on my little bench by the lake, and he sat next to me without hesitation.

It had become a sort of routine for us, if I wasn't busy with my girls. Sometimes we talked as we sat next to each other, and sometimes we didn't. He still worked a lot, so we hadn't had tons of time together, and when we did talk, it was usually about Macy or some feature of the camp he admired. And while it was nice to have a sort of comfort and familiarity with each other, I was quickly starting to realize that when the summer was over, there really wasn't any reason for us to keep in touch. Maybe Macy would come back to the camp the next year, but I doubted Colin would need to come with her. She had grown up a lot over the last couple of months and seemed well-suited to her new bit of independence.

"So what are you writing so early?" he asked again. "And why so early?"

It really wasn't that early, and the reveille would be waking the girls up in twenty minutes or so. "Says the guy who probably got up long before I did so he could do his hair for the big hike," I replied.

"Touché."

"It's a letter."

He glanced at the page under my hand, but not long enough to read any of it. That was one of the things I liked about Colin. He didn't pry into my personal life, and he was content to let me say as much or as little as I wanted. "To whom?" he asked, though I knew he wouldn't ask again if I chose not to answer. No matter how curious he might be, he rarely pushed me to answer his questions.

And maybe it was because I was feeling extra torn up about camp ending soon, or because I desperately needed someone to talk to about the anxiety building in my chest, but I wanted to tell him everything. "It's to my mom," I said. "I got in the habit of writing her letters every week when I would come here as a kid, and I never really stopped."

He gave me a soft smile. "I'm sure she loves getting them."

"I'm sure she would," I replied. "If she were still around to get them."

"Oh." He looked like he was about ready to launch into an apology, and that wasn't something I wanted him to do.

"It's okay," I said and put my hand on his arm. "She died a while ago, and it's not like it's something I put out in the open for everyone I meet, you know?"

He gripped his coffee cup a little tighter and stared down at my hand for a moment. Then he looked out over the lake, his expression as neutral as it had been back at the beginning of the summer. He'd dropped his mask so often over the last few weeks that I'd forgotten how empty he looked when he put it on.

"Yeah," he muttered, "I do know."

I hadn't been brave enough to ask about his wife after learning what had happened to her. I still wasn't brave enough. So I stuck with a topic I knew a lot about: "It was hard at first," I said quietly. "Growing up, it was just me and her, 'cause my dad didn't stick around, so I went to her with all of my problems. I could talk to her about anything, and she always had some magical solution. Just not for when she got sick."

"What was it?" he asked.

"Kidney disease. She was on a transplant list, but it took too long to find a match."

He was looking at me again, but I kept my eyes on my notebook. For some reason, I really didn't want him to see me cry.

"How old were you?" he asked next.

I brushed a tear away. I hadn't cried over my mom in almost a year, and doing it now made me feel like I'd lost some traction in my attempts to move on. I thought I'd been doing so well, but clearly it wasn't as well as I thought.

"I was twenty," I said. "But she'd been sick for a few years. It was one of the reasons I came to work here, because I thought maybe it would bring me closer to her before she was gone."

"I don't think anything makes losing people easier," he replied softly.

It was the perfect time to ask him about his wife, but I was still so afraid of what it might do to our tentative friendship. He rarely answered any personal questions I posed to him, so I wasn't sure how open he was to sharing. If I asked about her, would he even tell me? Or would he shut down and hide behind that wall of his again?

But he spoke before I could: "I actually came to camp a bit early because I, uh, I was hoping you could help me with something."

I raised my eyebrows. "I didn't know you were capable of asking for help."

It got a small smile out of him, which was nice. I liked things better when he was happy, because he didn't seem so weighed down by stress. "Trust me," he replied. "I surprise myself sometimes. But I'm not sure there's anyone better qualified for this particular problem."

Interesting. "You're saying I might be good at something? I'm intrigued."

Though he laughed a little, he still looked overly serious. "I'm, uh, worried about Macy."

That caught me off guard. We'd been talking about his daughter all summer, and we had both agreed she was doing well and would likely take her newfound courage back to school with her at the end of August. "What about Macy?" I asked.

His shrug was almost dejected. "She's just been… I don't know. I was honestly surprised she even invited me on the hike today. She barely looks at me and pretends I'm not even here, and it's been at least two weeks since she came out of the cabin to say goodnight to me. Honestly, I'd been considering going back into the city and just picking her up when camp is over."

I had a feeling he'd been wanting to say a lot of that for a while. It was like the pressure of it all had been building, and now he couldn't hold it back anymore.

"Colin," I said, and I surprised myself by taking his hand.

That was probably a bad idea. But I held him tight, and he squeezed back, and it felt so natural that I didn't want to let go. Especially when he looked up at me with an expression that said he was desperate for the comfort of human touch.

How long had he gone since the last time anyone really touched him?

"I don't think you have to worry," I said, trying not to imagine more physical contact with the guy than I already had. "Macy is hitting that age where she's learning who she is, and she probably knows she can't do that if she's always relying on you. She's spending her summer with her friends, and none of them have their parents here. She's just trying to fit in."

He frowned. "What if I've kept my distance too much? We've always been really close, but now…"

"Hey," I told him. "You will always be more of an expert on your own daughter than anyone else. But I've been around girls like her for my entire life, and from what I've seen her become this summer, you really don't have anything to worry about. She's growing up, and she'll start wanting more space, but that doesn't mean she loves you any less. She might not know how to show it, but she's glad you're here. As long as she knows you'll always be there for her, the two of you will be fine."

I really didn't know what else I could tell him. My mom and I had always been close, and even when I hit my teens, she'd been my best friend. I could try to imagine what it would have been like to grow up with a father, but I couldn't say how close I would really be to him. But I wished I had more to say to the guy who clearly needed reassurance.

Then, to my complete surprise, he set his coffee cup on the ground and pulled me into a hug. "Thanks, Beck," he said, and his voice wavered a bit in my ear. "I know I shouldn't have brought all my problems to you, but you're just so…"

Heat immediately spread across my face, and I was glad he couldn't see me as I tried to play it cool, shrugging as best I could while still wrapped in his tight hold. This was so not within the boundaries of parent and camp counselor. But neither was I complaining. "I'm approachable," I said and somehow managed to sound normal. "I know. I'm basically the camp therapist, which probably isn't always a good thing."

When he pulled away, his face was red all the way out to his ears, just like mine, and I had to wonder what that meant. Was he as affected by that hug as I apparently was?

He coughed and grabbed his coffee, and then he was on his feet. "Well, the girls are lucky to have you, at any rate." Then he hurried off toward the mess hall just as the trumpet call sounded in the camp speakers, signaling the girls to wake up and get ready for the day's hike.

"What is with this guy and running away the moment he gives me a compliment?" I wondered out loud. With only a couple of days left of camp, I was pretty sure I wouldn't get the chance to find out.

The "Big Hike" was our longest event of the year, and it was both loved and hated by the campers. Some of them were eager to make the twelve-mile trek, while many others faked illnesses and injuries to get out of doing it. When all was said and done, we generally only had half the girls go with those of us counselors who actually enjoyed hiking, while the rest stayed back and did arts and crafts most of the day.

Personally, I loved the hike. It gave me a chance to get even farther from civilization, and I never felt more comfortable than when I was out in the wilderness. Gabby was coming with me as always, and while we led the way up, Sofie and Annabeth (who was probably just eager to get away from her ridiculously young group of girls) would take the rear and made sure no one got lost.

Everyone from my cabin was making the trek except Willow, who had tripped too many times while hiking and knew it was better to stay on even ground, and they all pushed themselves to the front of the gathered crowd. I was overjoyed to see Macy looking as excited as the rest, even though she'd never done anything like it. She had her little backpack stuffed with snacks and water, and she was beaming from ear to ear as Brielle told her all about the baby deer they had seen last year.

"Who's ready to climb a mountain?" I asked the forty or so girls who were waiting.

Cheers of excitement replied to my question.

"I can't hear you!" I shouted.

Every girl cheered even louder than before, and the energy they gave off was infectious. Even Colin looked excited as he wandered up to the back of the group. His eyes were bright and warm, and I was pleased to see he wasn't nearly as dejected as he'd been an hour earlier. He nodded a greeting when he caught me looking at him, but he seemed content to hang out at the back.

"Alright, ladies," said Gabby next to me. "Before we head out, we have a couple of very important rules. Anyone know what they are?" She fixed her gaze on the Connelly twins to start.

They rolled their eyes in unison. "No pranks," one of them said. "We know."

"Exactly," I replied. "We want everyone to stay safe, so we don't want anything happening that could put anyone in danger, even if it's a harmless prank."

"How about another rule?" Gabby continued.

A girl named Rosa raised her hand. "Nobody goes in front of Beck," she said and grinned at me. I had had her in my cabin a couple of times, and I was pretty sure she was sixteen now. This would be her last year, and that was almost depressing to think about. She'd been one of my very first girls, and she would be saying goodbye to Rockwood.

"Even I don't go in front of Beck," Gabby replied. "Mostly because she's crazy fast, but yes. Beck leads the way, and everyone else has to stay behind her. What else?"

"Don't leave the trail," said Zoey.

"And don't go anywhere by yourself," Madison added next to her.

"I'm pretty sure Cabin Three is the smartest cabin," I said to Gabby, just loud enough for the whole group to hear but pretending it was a secret.

Gabby scowled at me then turned to the five girls she was bringing from her cabin. "Anyone?" she asked them.

They glanced at each other, then Bailey Summerland hesitantly said, "Drink lots of water and let you know if we're feeling sick or hurt in any way?"

"Yes!" Gabby threw me a look of triumph, and I just laughed. "Well," she continued, "that's all the rules, so let's get going!"

"Let's have some fun!" I added. And I smiled at Colin, hoping he knew I meant that for him too. He deserved to have some fun.

He smiled back.

The first hour of the hike was filled with singing and laughter, but after that we fell into an easy silence as we walked the forest trail. Birds chirped around us, squirrels chattered at us, and the sun shone through the leaves and filled the air with a greenish brilliance I hadn't found anywhere but the wilderness. As I walked, I could hear dozens of little feet crunching through the dirt and leaves, and I really couldn't imagine a more perfect sound than that.

"You look like you're in your element," a deep voice said just behind me.

I didn't turn around, mostly because I didn't want him to see how easily I lost my calm at the sound of his voice. "This is home for me," I agreed.

His heavy footsteps fell into pace behind me, like my own steps were suddenly amplified. "I can see why it would be, but I'm not sure I could ever survive out here for long," he said. "I don't know how you got so good at all this."

I glanced back enough to give him a smug smile. "Years of practice," I said, "combined with a natural inclination to be awesome." My glance back had told me Gabby and the girls were farther behind than I thought, which meant Colin had probably really had to hoof it to catch up to me. I slowed my pace a little, and to my surprise so did he. "Are you going to stay a step behind me the whole time, or…?"

"Well," he replied, "the rules were pretty clear. I may not be a camper, but I'd hate to have to face the consequences of passing the great Beck Alvarez."

I rolled my eyes at him. "I feel like you're some weird bodyguard when you're back there. I promise I won't tell anyone if you accidentally take a step in front of me."

His mock fear, combined with a surreptitious look around the forest, made me laugh, and then he pushed himself just fast enough to bring him to my side. "Yeah," he decided as he looked down at our feet while they moved in sync. "I like this better."

"So do I," I replied. "I'm glad to see you've been working on that lurking problem of yours."

"I've been told it's one of my lesser qualities. It has never gotten very good ratings, so I figured it would be best to get rid of it." He met my gaze, and his smile made my knees a little weak. But then it changed, shifting into something more along the lines of confusion. "What?" he asked.

"Huh?"

"You have this look on your face," he said. "Like you're trying to decipher a line of code that makes no sense." He put his hands into his pockets, and he looked so at ease that I wasn't afraid to say what was going through my mind.

I looked up at the trail ahead as I spoke. "I thought I had you figured out from day one," I said. "You were probably my least favorite person in the world—"

"Ouch."

"—and I couldn't even in my wildest imaginings see us being civil let alone…"

He leaned just a little closer so our elbows brushed as we walked. "Let alone friends?" he suggested.

"Is that what we are?" I asked and looked over at him. I wanted to think so, but it was hard to know what he was thinking. Maybe there was nothing to this relationship we'd been building. Maybe he thought there was more to it than I did. Maybe I didn't understand him at all, so whatever he said next was crucial to knowing what I could let myself feel.

He thought for a moment then nodded. "Friends," he said again. "I like to think we're friends."

"Me too," I said. "I don't talk to many adults, so it's been nice talking to you. Someone who, you know, understands what it feels like to lose someone."

I was pretty sure he didn't realize he was doing it, but he twisted his wedding ring with his thumb. "I've spent the last three years thinking I had to go through this alone," he said quietly. "You have no idea how much I've needed to meet someone like you, Beck. To help me remember the good parts of life."

His words left a ball of warmth inside me, and I was pretty sure it was important that I met him too. I didn't know how yet, but somehow knowing him would help me in the long run. But would that something happen in the next two days? Because after that, he was gone.

We walked the rest of the way up the little mountain in silence, and it was probably my most favorite time doing that hike ever.

The hike led to a little lake, and the girls all spread out with their lunches for some quiet time to themselves. Some of them stayed in pairs or trios, but most of them found their own little spot to hunker down for an hour or two and enjoy the quiet of the wilderness, something they couldn't get down at camp.

The other counselors sat together in the shade of a large oak to chat and keep an eye out on the girls, but I opted for a more solitary spot, my second favorite spot in all the world. It wasn't quite as nice as the waterfall my mom and I had fallen in love with when I was a kid, but it was still pretty great. There was a giant boulder along the water's edge, and it had the perfect place to sit and look out over the vista of trees and water. I'd found it when I was ten, and I'd been sitting there ever since.

Besides, it offered a pretty good view of all the girls, so I could make sure everyone was okay while we took this solo time.

This time, however, I wasn't alone. Colin hesitated at the base of the boulder, probably aware that everyone had gone off on their own, and it looked like he was trying to decide if it was a good idea to climb up and join me.

"You're lurking again," I told him with a small smile.

He matched my smile. "It's my default when I don't know the boundaries," he replied.

"Come on up before you relapse into stalker status."

He breathed a sigh of relief and scrambled up the rock face. "Thank you," he said as he settled himself next to me. Though he glanced down to the ground with a bit of a grimace, apparently he decided it wasn't so high that he had to be nervous, and he shifted himself until he got comfortable.

I wouldn't have thought I would like sharing this space as much as I did, but my rock had suddenly become the most comfortable place in the world. I could have sat there all day with no sounds but the breeze in the trees.

Colin, apparently, could not.

"I can see the appeal to it in certain situations," he said after a moment, "but I'm not a big fan of silence. After my wife was gone, the house was too quiet most of the time."

"It's the worst part," I replied. "There's a sort of emptiness there that's hard to fill."

We sat for a moment in silence, and I wondered if it was still bothering him. But he didn't look too unnerved as he looked out at the spectacular view, and he had the classic signs of someone discovering something new, something powerful. I'd seen it hundreds of times over the years, and I couldn't help but smile as I watched him take it all in.

"I know places like this have always existed," he said, a little breathlessly, "but I didn't think I would feel so…"

I could think of any number of words to put in there for him. *Overwhelmed. Free. Content.* But I wanted to hear what he had to say, so I kept quiet. What would a rich city boy call a place like this?

His word choice was far better than any of mine: "Alive." He turned to look at me. "I can see why you love all of this, Beck. I can't even remember the last time I just sat and took a deep breath of fresh air. Thank you."

I shook my head. "I didn't do anything," I said. "Nature does all the work. I just exist within it."

He leaned closer, and his hand brushed mine. But instead of pulling it away, he simply kept his fingers there against mine as he said, "You pushed me to be there for Macy, and if you hadn't done that, I definitely wouldn't have ended up here in such a beautiful place. Neither would she. We owe you so much. *I* owe you."

I could hear his words, but I wasn't sure I understood them. Not when he had somehow moved even closer, and he was looking at me in a way he hadn't before. In a way that didn't exactly fit with the idea of us being friends. And while my head was screaming that I needed to get out of there because it was a terrible idea and couldn't possibly end well, the rest of me stayed where I was. Even leaned into his touch as he lifted his fingers to touch my cheek.

Don't do it, my head said.

But there's something here, my heart argued.

Remember what happened last time you fell for a guy.

That guy wasn't Colin.

I closed my eyes, holding my breath as our noses brushed.

"Dad?"

We broke apart immediately, and I felt my stomach clench when I saw Macy just a few feet away, staring at us with tears in her eyes.

Colin let out his breath shakily. "Mace," he whispered. "I wasn't—"

"What about Mom?" she asked, and her tears slid down her cheeks. She was ready to bolt. I could see it in her eyes, and no matter what Colin said, it was only going to make things worse. *What was I thinking?*

Colin looked just as worried as I felt, his eyes wide. "Macy, let me—"

"You promised you wouldn't forget about her!" Macy whimpered. And then she ran.

"Macy!" Colin struggled to his feet and slid down the boulder, though he missed the landing and went sprawling in the dirt. "Macy, wait!"

I jumped down after him and grabbed his arm before he could run after her. "Let me get her," I said quickly. "You can't just—"

He tore himself free and darted into the trees after his daughter.

Gabby was already hurrying over to me, the emergency pack in her hands. "Do you need me to—"

"Get the rest of the girls back," I said as I slipped the pack on. It was heavy enough that it would slow me down, but there was no way I was going without it. "Keep your radio on, okay?"

She touched her hand to my shoulder. At least she understood how to stay calm, unlike Annabeth, who looked ready to run after them without a clue what she was doing. "Don't let them get too far, Beck," Gabby warned.

I nodded then ran off in the direction of Colin's desperate shouts. The forest wasn't huge, but it was big enough that Colin and Macy could easily get lost, which terrified me. If I let them get too far, it would end up getting dark before they found the trail again.

"Colin!" I shouted as I ran, dodging trees and thickets. "Colin, wait!"

"Macy!" He sounded desperate, so he had probably already lost her trail. "Macy, where are you?"

"Colin!" I could hear him fighting through the thick underbrush, so he wasn't too far. If I could just catch up to him… I pushed myself faster and finally caught sight of him. "Colin, stop!" He had to pause when he reached a ravine and couldn't keep running, just long enough that I was able to grab his arm. "Please wait," I said.

He was frantic, searching around him as his chest heaved. "Let go of me."

"You have to wait a second," I told him. "Think." Though he tried to pull his arm free, I held on with all my strength. "You don't even know if you're actually following her."

"If you don't let go of me, I swear to God," he growled and then he tugged again.

This time he was stronger, and though I held on tight, he pulled hard enough to knock me off balance. I tried to catch myself, but his foot slipped off the edge of the ravine and pulled me with him, and together we tumbled over the edge.

Crashing through branches and bushes, I slid and rolled until I came to a painful halt at the bottom, right in the middle of a freezing stream. I forced myself to ignore the pain and scrambled to my feet, though the heavy pack on my shoulders made that difficult. Colin lay a few feet away, groaning as he pushed himself up onto his hands.

"Are you okay?" I asked him breathlessly.

He glared at me and rolled over so he could sit against the bank and assess the gash on his arm that had already started bleeding.

"I'm sorry," I said, though I didn't really mean it. "I had to stop you before you got yourself completely lost."

"Macy," he croaked.

"I'll find her," I assured him. "Go back to the trail, and I'll bring her back to the camp."

But he shook his head, pushing himself up to his feet. "I'm not going anywhere."

I didn't have to know the guy well to know there was no point in arguing with him. "Fine," I said, "but remember the rules. Nobody goes in front of Beck."

He gripped his injured arm, still fuming a little, but he nodded. "You have to find my little girl."

"I will."

I backtracked the way we'd come until I got to a point where I knew I'd seen Macy. She could have gone any number of directions, but to my relief the ground was still damp from the last rain we'd gotten last night. It only took me a minute to find a little footprint heading north.

"Come on," I said to Colin and hurried forward.

Macy's path was easy enough to follow, and if ever I lost sight of her tracks, I just had to slow down and look around for a moment. Colin was pretty quiet behind me, only occasionally calling out his daughter's name, and I told myself not to imagine what he was feeling because then I would start to panic. We still had a few hours of daylight left, and Macy would get tired before she could get too far on her own.

Everything will be okay.

But it was hard to believe that thought, no matter how many times I said it in my head. All of this was my fault. I had a million and a half reasons why I should have kept my distance from Colin, and I had ignored them all and let myself think there was a chance this thing we had between us could be something more than casual acquaintances. *You're a fool, Beck Alvarez.*

"Wait," Colin said suddenly, and he grabbed my arm. "Listen."

I did. At first I didn't hear anything, but then I caught a whimper.

"Macy?" I called as my heart kicked up a notch.

"Macy!"

"Dad?"

Colin's strength seemed to leave him for a second, and he had to lean against a tree, but as soon as I started running, he was right on my tail. We didn't have to go far; Macy called out again, and the sound brought us to the edge of another ravine.

And there at the bottom was Macy, covered in dirt and scratches and holding her ankle as she sobbed.

"Macy!" Colin practically leapt down the steep slope, sliding down until he reached her and scooped her up into his arms. I couldn't tell what he was saying, but he murmured into her ear over and over until she wrapped her arms around his neck and returned his embrace.

I dropped the soaking pack off my shoulders and rummaged around until I found a length of rope. "Here," I said, tossing one end down. "I'll pull you up."

With Macy still in his arms, Colin wrapped the rope around one hand a few times then gave me a nod. It wasn't easy, but I managed to give Colin just enough leverage to walk back up the bank with Macy in tow.

"She hurt her ankle," he said when he reached the top. He could barely breathe, and his fingers shook as he set her on the ground.

I knelt in front of her, and though I could tell she wasn't happy to see me, she was too scared to push me away. "Did you hurt anything else?" I asked her gently.

She shook her head, still crying.

"May I?" I touched a finger to her swelling foot. When she nodded, I carefully removed her shoe and took hold of her foot. "I'm going to make sure it isn't broken," I told her, and I gently rotated her ankle a little. She squirmed, but the pain didn't seem to get any worse. This time I spoke to Colin: "I don't think it's broken, but I can't say for sure. I'll brace her foot, and we'll have to carry her back, just in case."

Though Colin nodded, he was seriously pale as he sat just behind Macy and supported her back. I would have to take a look at the gash on his arm too, and I had a feeling he wasn't going to be strong enough to carry either his daughter or the pack of supplies. Not for a while. Not unless I convinced him.

I had to make a decision.

"Here's what we're going to do," I said, trying to sound confident. I didn't know if this was the best choice, but my gut said it might be the only choice. "I'm going to wrap your foot, Macy, and we're going to give you a piggyback back to camp. Think that'll be okay?"

Macy glanced at her dad, who was staring blankly into the trees, and then she nodded.

"Great," I replied. "Colin."

He looked over at the sound of his name, and I worried he was close to falling into a catatonic state that would be difficult to get him out of. "I'm going to need your help," I told him.

It took him a moment, but when he understood what I said, he nodded and slowly got to his feet. "What do you need?" he asked, his voice weak but determined. There was a look in his eyes that went beyond fear or relief or pleading, and I'd never seen anything like it. It was like his expression was telling me that he needed me more right now than he'd ever needed anyone. If I didn't stay calm and collected, he was going to fall apart.

You can do this, Beck. You've been trained for this.

I took a deep breath and held it for a moment, letting my thoughts still until I could set aside whatever feelings I might have for the man standing nearby and focus only on what needed to happen right this moment. At this moment, I didn't matter. What mattered was getting Macy and her father back to the camp in one piece before it got too dark to see the way home. I took another breath and made a list in my head.

First: radio back to Gabby and let her know I'd found Macy.

I reached for the radio where it sat on my belt, only to discover it wasn't there. It must have been knocked loose when we fell down the ravine.

New plan: "Colin, do you have your phone?"

His fingers trembling, he reached into his pocket and held it out to me. There was barely a signal, but I hoped it would be enough to contact Linda's office. I dialed the number and prayed it connected. To my relief the phone started ringing, and though it rang multiple times, I was overjoyed to hear Linda's voicemail on the other end. "Linda, it's Beck," I said. "I'm with Mr. Donovan and Macy, and everyone is fine. We'll make it back to camp before it gets dark, and tell Gabby not to freak out."

The phone ended the call for me, having lost its signal at the perfect moment, and I handed it back to Colin.

Next task: "Colin, there's an emergency blanket in the pack. Macy might want it."

He nodded and slowly moved over to where I'd left the pack, pulling it open and digging around inside.

Now: "Okay, Macy, this might hurt a little, but it's going to make it feel better when I'm done. Can you be brave?"

Tears filled her eyes again, and I wanted so badly to pull her into a hug. But I had to focus, so I kept my distance until she nodded and whispered, "I'm scared, Beck."

"It's okay to be scared sometimes," I replied. "But you don't have to worry. Not with your dad here to keep you safe."

Colin was still limply searching for the blanket. I had to grab the ankle wrap anyway, so I stepped over to him and put my hand on his arm. "You okay?" I whispered.

He seemed to lose the last of his strength and sank to his knees, the pack falling to the ground in front of him. "What have I done?" he whispered back. "Something could have happened to her, and I…"

"This isn't your fault," I told him. *It's mine.* "She's going to be fine." Grabbing both the blanket and the compression wrap, I gripped his shoulder then returned to Macy. "So," I said to her, "I always find that it's easier to ignore the pain if I have something distracting me. Do you want me to sing you a song, or tell you a story, or—"

"How could he forget her?"

I blinked, staring at the girl who couldn't seem to look away from her father. I wasn't even sure if Colin was able to hear her, because he looked like he'd lost all control of his faculties as he slumped in the dirt. "You think he forgot about your mom?" I asked her. Yes, I had to focus on her ankle, but I couldn't just ignore the desperation in her question.

Macy swallowed as tears filled her eyes again. "He promised," she said. "He promised he would always love her, and then…" Only then did she seem to remember who she was talking to, and her expression hardened. "He promised," she repeated, this time to make sure I knew what that meant.

No number of deep breaths would make this conversation easier. I had to distract *myself* now, so I started wrapping her foot and being as gentle as I could. "Did you know," I said quietly, "that my mama died too?" I couldn't bring myself to look into Macy's face, but I assumed she shook her head. "It was seven years ago, which sounds like a long time but doesn't feel like it. She was the only family I had, and I thought there was no way I could ever replace her and get a new family. But you know what?"

"What?" she said.

I glanced up and found her hanging on my every word. I brushed her cheek free of tears and smiled. "Families change," I said. "That's what makes them so wonderful. Sometimes you lose people, sometimes you get new ones. My new family is everyone here at camp, and I can still miss my mom and love my new family too. And I think you can be the same way. You have so much love in that heart of yours that you will never run out of it."

Macy sniffed, looking down at her foot as I finished wrapping it. "Do you really think so?" she asked.

"I know so."

"I'm sorry I ran away."

My smile grew, and I knew the worst part was over. We could keep going from here, and I could finish my goal and get these two back to safety. At least, I was pretty sure I could. That all depended on whether or not Colin could find the strength.

"Tell you what," I said to Macy, keeping my voice low. "I think your dad is going to need some help getting down the mountain."

"What's wrong with him?"

"He loves you so much that he got too scared by all the things that could go wrong. I think we'll have to work hard to let him know that he's brave enough to make it back. Brave like you."

Her smile was small, but it was there nonetheless. "Dad?"

He immediately turned, holding his breath as he waited to hear what she said.

"Can you carry me back?"

He was on his feet so fast that I was afraid he was going to get dizzy and fall over. But amazingly, he stood steady, and he clenched his jaw tight as if determined to prove that he could do anything for his little girl.

I was pretty sure he could.

CHAPTER EIGHT

We made it back to Camp Rockwood just as dusk was leading into twilight. One of the campers must have seen us and run to tell the others, because before we'd even reached the edge of the trees by the mess hall, we were suddenly swarmed by counselors and campers alike. Yasmine took Macy from my shoulders, where she'd been for the last two miles, and Gabby grabbed the pack from Colin, who had been pretty much silent the whole hike back. Outside of exchanging Macy for the pack, the only interaction I'd had with him was just a brief touch of his hand to mine as we started walking. It wasn't much, but he'd said a lot with it.

Linda was, to no surprise, freaking out. She shoved little campers aside and started pelting questions at Macy, asking how much pain she was in and if she was cold and if she needed to have Chuck fire up the ovens and make her a souffle. Poor Macy looked more overwhelmed than she had all evening and didn't seem to know what to say to the woman she'd probably never spoken to.

I decided to step in before Linda scared the girl out of her wits. "I think she just needs to get some rest," I said.

Linda glanced at me then froze when she caught sight of Colin. "Mr. Donovan," she breathed, utter terror in her quivering words. "I am so sorry something like this happened. I assure you, nothing has ever—"

"It's fine," Colin said. He looked exhausted, but thankfully he didn't look angry. "It wasn't the camp's fault."

"You're bleeding!" Linda almost screamed. "Sofie, can you—"

"On it," Sofie said, putting her hand on Linda's shoulder before the director started hyperventilating. "Mr. Donovan, I can help you with that cut, if you want to follow us to the rec room. We have a full first aid kit in there, and Yas is an EMT. She'll look at Macy's ankle too."

"That's…" Colin took a slow breath. "Thank you." And though he glanced at me, he didn't offer me a word before he followed Sofie across the field and disappeared.

"Okay, girls," Gabby said loudly just as whispers started growing among the campers surrounding us. "Sun's gone, so you know what that means."

They probably had tons of questions for me, and I could see everyone from my cabin glancing between me and the rec room where Macy was, not sure who they were more concerned about.

"Bed," I said, and I put enough force into the word that even the most curious of campers turned and trudged back to the cabins, leaving me alone with Gabby while the other counselors followed after the girls to make sure everyone was where they were supposed to be.

"Beck?" Gabby asked and touched my arm.

My strength immediately vanished, and I sank to the ground in an exhausted heap. "I did something bad, Gabs," I moaned.

She crouched next to me. "You mean when you almost kissed Colin Donovan?"

Oh goodness, had the whole camp seen that? "Why did I do that?"

"Because he almost kissed you first," she said simply. "It's no big deal, Beck."

"It *is* a big deal. You saw what happened to Macy."

"What I saw was a girl who was realizing her dad was healing faster than she was. That's not your fault, and nobody got seriously hurt."

I wasn't so sure about that. Tomorrow was the last day of camp, and at three o'clock, less than fifteen hours away, I would get my last look of Colin and never see him again. It was bad enough having to think that I wouldn't have his simple friendship anymore. If I let myself think of him any more than that, the separation was going to hurt a lot more than a fling was worth.

"FYI," Gabby added, "you look like crap. Maybe you should take a shower."

"Thanks," I grumbled and let her pull me back to my feet.

But before I could go do as she suggested, she grabbed my hand and added, "Don't cut the flower before it's had a chance to bloom."

"What is that supposed to mean?"

"You know exactly what that means. Goodnight, Beck!"

She was right about the shower, though the hot water stung when it hit the little cuts and scrapes I'd gotten on my arms and legs. I hadn't even noticed any of the pain until now, but I was more bruised and battered than I'd thought. Rolling down a ravine was one thing I didn't need to experience again, that was for sure.

I stayed in the shower so long that it felt like I'd rinsed the whole day away, something I badly needed. I'd messed up. No matter what Gabby thought, I shouldn't have even let myself talk to Colin too often. It had only led to trouble, and even a friendship with him couldn't go anywhere beyond tomorrow. At three in the afternoon, he would leave with Macy, and that would be that.

I hated it.

For the first time since I started working at the camp, I didn't want to join the other counselors for the last night celebration we always had. They would swap stories about their girls, laugh at whatever antics the Connelly girls might have concocted while they were on the hike, and they'd mourn the girls we were losing because they were too old. And while it made me feel like I'd forgotten a part of myself, I didn't want to do any of that.

So instead of going into the counselor cabin after I showered, I climbed the ladder on the side of the mess hall and settled into my favorite spot in the whole camp, a little nook on the roof where I could sit with my back against a wall and gaze up at the stars.

Another summer was over. Another year without my mom. And I couldn't help but think about what I'd said to Macy just that afternoon. *The people at camp are my new family.* It was true, but only to an extent.

The people I loved most were in this camp, but they weren't my family. Not really. My family vanished when my mom died, and I was alone like always.

I'd only been up on the roof for twenty minutes when I heard someone climbing the metal ladder, and I sighed. "I'm not really in the mood, Gabby," I said.

"Can we talk?" Colin replied.

My stomach did a sort of flip, but I nodded. "This isn't too high for you, is it?"

He grunted a response but pretty much crawled over to me instead of walking, which told me it *was* rather high for the man who was scared of heights. But that didn't stop him. As usual, he sat at my side without hesitation, though he was closer than he'd ever been before. Part of that was because my secret space wasn't large, but he could have put an inch between us if he really wanted to.

"How's Macy's foot?" I asked when I decided he wasn't going to start whatever conversation we were about to have. This was his time to talk, and I would let him do it when he was ready.

"It's not broken," he said, lifting his eyes to the sky. He seemed fascinated by the stars, as if he'd never really seen them before. Maybe he hadn't. "But I have a feeling she'll pretend like it is for the extra sympathy. And she's already figured out that it will make a great story to tell the other kids at school in a couple weeks, especially now that she's going to a new school."

New school? *Interesting.* I wondered what kind of school that was, and whether or not she would still be expected to excel at so much. But I didn't need to know those things, so I held my questions back and simply smiled.

"When I broke my arm when I was eight," I said, "I felt like I was queen of the world at school. Everyone wanted to sign my cast."

Still gazing at the stars, Colin matched my grin. "I tore my ACL during football practice in high school, and everyone just tried to steal my pain meds."

"Yikes."

"I went to a classy school," he said and turned that grin of his to me. Then his amusement faded. "Beck, I'm…"

"I'm sorry," I blurted out. So much for letting him talk. "I shouldn't have—"

"If there's anyone to blame here, it's me," he said. "I shouldn't have stayed at the camp in the first place, and I shouldn't have…" Pausing, he looked down at my hand where it rested on my lap then grabbed hold of it, though he seemed just as confused by the action as I was. *Talk about mixed signals.* "I don't…"

I needed something to ease the tension rapidly building between us, something to keep that emotional distance I should have kept in the first place before it got me into trouble. "Tell me about your wife, Colin." *What in the world am I thinking?*

His eyes met mine, searching for some sort of understanding. But he must not have found any, because he frowned and said, "Why would you want that?"

Good question. "Because I want to know why you're hurting so much," I said.

He still held fast to my hand, and I didn't fight him. I needed something to hold onto, and he was a strong, sturdy option, for a lot of different reasons.

Colin took a slow, strengthening breath. "Jada," he said, and he couldn't help but smile at the sound of her name. "I met her when I was fourteen, but we didn't become friends until we were sixteen."

"I seem to recall there was some lurking involved," I said.

He laughed softly. "Once I worked up the courage, I asked her out eight times before she finally said yes, during our last semester of high school. Three months after graduation, we were married. Two years after that, we got Macy."

I didn't want to hear any of this, but at the same time I felt like I absolutely had to. "What was she like?" I asked.

"She was the kindest person I've ever met," he said immediately. "She was friends with everyone, never thought about herself, and she just had this glow about her. It was like she had come down from Heaven to bless the lives of the people she met, and I fell in love with her the minute I saw her." Tears filled his eyes, and his hand tightened even more around mine. He was looking at the stars again, but I wondered if maybe he was looking for her up there. "I can't count the number of times I've wondered how I got so lucky to have her in my life. Of all the people in the world she could have picked, she picked me."

She sounded amazing, and it made sense why he would miss her as much as he did. I couldn't even imagine losing someone as close to me as a spouse; it was hard enough with my mom.

"Macy was staying at her grandparents' when Jada died," Colin said, and his voice had grown infinitely softer. "I got the call about the accident while I was off on a work trip, and it felt like the world just disappeared around me. And all I could think about the whole way home was how I was going to tell Macy that her mom was gone."

His shoulders slumped, and—I didn't think he even meant to—he fell into my arms. And while it hurt more than I thought something could hurt, I held him. I held him because I knew he would fall apart without me.

"I've been so lost without her," he said, almost sobbing. "And Macy—she's all I have left. I can't lose her. I can't."

Suddenly I was crying, and though I fought it, I couldn't stop. I didn't have anything left to remind me of my mom except this camp. Rockwood was my last tie to my family, and even though I knew Colin wasn't going to let it die this year, I couldn't count on the place still existing after next summer. I couldn't count on Linda keeping things the same. Familiar. Home.

I cried with Colin, because I had a feeling nothing was going to be the same after tomorrow came and went, and I wouldn't have him to hold me like I was here to hold him.

CHAPTER NINE

I woke the next morning in Gabby's bunk, with absolutely no idea how I'd gotten there. It was still early enough that the sun hadn't crested the east hill, and all around me the deep breaths of the other counselors filled the room with comfortable whispers.

I glanced up and could see Gabby's weight bowing my bunk overhead, which probably meant she could fill in the details of how I had ended up in her bed instead of mine.

I kicked the center of the bulge in the mattress above me, and Gabby snorted awake. "Outside," I whispered then rolled off the bunk and crept out of the cabin.

Nearly five minutes passed before Gabby finally came outside, yawning as she did. I'd spent those minutes pacing and trying desperately to remember, and the fact that my memories were so dim was rather concerning. Just how exhausted had I been that I couldn't even remember walking to my own cabin?

"What's up?" she asked, still mid-yawn.

I grabbed her wrist. "What happened?"

Though it took her a second, the moment she realized what I was asking, her tired expression morphed into one of absolute delight. "I was wondering if you'd remember," she said.

"Start talking, Gabs."

"About what, Becks?"

I groaned and kicked at a rock in the dirt near my foot, though I regretted it as soon as my bare toe collided with it. It was small, but it was solid. "I'm freaking out a little bit," I warned her.

Her grin was seriously over the top, but at least she was willing to talk. "I was just about to go to bed after doing my last check on the girls," she said. "Everyone else was already asleep. And I figured you were still up on the roof with Mr. Donovan, so I—"

"You told him I was up there, didn't you?" I said. It wasn't like I was angry that she had, but still. I didn't need her getting in the middle of the complication that was Colin Donovan and me.

She shrugged and continued her little tale. "I figured you'd come in on your own sometime, but then there was a tap at the door. And when I opened it…" She sighed as if remembering something magical. "He was carrying you, Beck," she said, and she grabbed my shoulder to emphasize the impact of that fact. "You'd fallen asleep in his arms, and he carried you back here, all the way from the mess hall."

Colin had carried me? How could I have possibly been so tired that I didn't remember something like *that*? I remembered climbing down the ladder after he suggested we should go to bed, but beyond that… The ground swayed a bit beneath me, so I touched my palm to the side of the cabin as I tried to comprehend what had happened last night. I must have been half asleep already by that point. "We were talking," I said, hoping that getting it out in the open would help things make sense. "Then we stopped talking."

Gabby wiggled her eyebrows. "What did you do then?" she asked, way too much insinuation in her tone.

"We sat there in silence," I said with a scowl. "But it was nice. We just watched the stars for a while, and I finally felt like I could breathe again after everything that happened yesterday. I got a little tired, so we decided to come back, and…" And apparently the man freaking carried me back like some damsel in distress because I couldn't walk a hundred yards to my cabin. "Gabs, I'm falling apart."

She laughed and took both my hands, pulling me close to her until I basically had to look into her face. "Then this isn't going to help anything, but I'm going to tell you anyway."

Oh, I definitely didn't like the sound of that. "What?"

"Donovan told me to tell you goodbye."

For a second, I was pretty sure the ground disappeared beneath my feet, and when I tried to say something, no sound came out of my mouth. I coughed and tried again. "Goodbye? But today's the last day of camp. What about Macy? Is she already—"

"He said he has a conference call or something today, so he's just sending his driver to pick up Macy."

"Goodbye?" I repeated. But I was supposed to have all of today to figure out what I could possibly say to the guy before I would never see him again, because I hadn't wanted to leave things how they were last night, with the pair of us crying all over each other because clearly we had been bottling it up for a while. I had, at least. And now I was out of time, and there was nothing I could say. Nothing I could do to make the pain of losing my friend any easier.

"Breathe, Beck," Gabby said and gave my hands a squeeze. "It's not like he lives in Dublin. San Francisco is just a few hours away."

"Just a few hours," I said, and I was pretty sure she didn't realize how large a distance that really was. I never had any reason to go into San Francisco. I had nowhere to stay. I didn't know anyone. And the last time I had driven into a big city to see a guy, I'd had my heart broken. That wasn't something I could do again.

The trumpet reveille suddenly blasted over the camp speakers, making me jump, and I wasn't sure how I was going to survive the day feeling like a chunk of me had just gone missing. How had Colin become such a prominent fixture in my life that I noticed almost immediately when he was gone?

"Breathe," Gabby said again. "Think about the girls. It's their last day too."

Right. "The girls," I repeated, and thinking about my cabin of eight beautiful faces brought a sense of order back into my mind. This summer wasn't about me. How many times would I have to tell myself that? However many it took to remind myself that Colin was gone, and I had to move on, and there was no point in mourning the loss of something that was never going to happen anyway.

Macy wasn't writing. There could have been any number of reasons, but she was, as far as I could tell, the only girl out of eighty who wasn't scribbling at the sheet of paper in front of her. It was a camp tradition, and all of the girls were writing letters to their parents to tell them about what had happened over the summer at camp. Some of them did it grudgingly, I knew, and some of them didn't even have parents. But every single girl had at least one person in their life, be it guardian or friend, who would be happy to read what they wrote.

Apparently Macy didn't think so.

Without drawing attention to myself, I slowly moved through the mess hall to where she was sitting with her wrapped foot on the bench next to her. "Hey," I said gently and nudged the pencil a little closer to where her hand rested on the table. "You don't want to write a letter to your dad?"

She huffed a sigh, her dark eyes fixed on the blank paper. "What's the point?" she asked. "He was here the whole time." And though she tried very hard to look annoyed, there was something else in her expression, though I couldn't put a finger to it.

"Well," I said, "what if you tell me about your favorite parts of camp, and I can write it all down for you? That way you won't forget. In case you want to write a letter later."

She folded her arms, that mystery emotion growing. "I liked the canoe race," she said.

"Was that it?"

"And singing around the campfire."

"And?"

"Getting new friends. And I liked the zipline. That was my favorite." She hunched in on herself a little, a movement that reminded me a lot of Colin, though I had to make myself ignore that thought. "I'm glad I came," she said quietly.

I kept myself from saying anything, knowing there was probably more to her comment. If she wanted to talk, she would talk.

"I didn't want to at first," she said after a few seconds. "I don't like going far away from home. But then Dad said he would come with me, so I…"

My heart seemed to sink into my stomach as the missing piece fell into place to explain the look of utter fear hiding just behind her eyes. She hadn't been home when her mom died. The poor girl was probably so worried that if she went somewhere without her dad, she would never see him again.

"Do you wanna know what I think?" I said softly. "I think there is nothing in the world your dad would want more than to read a letter from you. You don't have to give it to him today, or next week, or ever if you don't want to. But I think you'll regret it if you don't. I write letters to my mom all the time."

Macy furrowed her eyebrows and frowned at me. "But you said she's—"

"She's gone," I said before she could use a harsher word. "But I still write to her and tell her all the things I wish I could say to her, because it makes me feel like she's reading them up in Heaven."

Reaching for the pencil I held out to her, Macy tapped it against her lips and got a thoughtful look on her face. "Maybe I can write to my mom," she said, and I deflated a little. Colin would just have to go without a letter this time around, since if that was what she wanted to do, I wasn't about to stop her.

"That sounds like a great idea," I said and did my best to smile.

What is wrong with me? I had barely spent any real time with Colin Donovan, and there I was, sitting next to his daughter and trying not to notice how she lifted one eyebrow when she was concentrating, just like he did, and how her nose was angular, like his, and she was left-handed like him. Why hadn't he told me goodbye himself? I would have woken up if he tried, and I could have said… Could have said what? I didn't know.

What I did know was I only had a few more hours to spend with his darling little girl, and then there was basically nothing that could bring us together again any time soon. Maybe I would see him next

summer when he brought Macy to camp again. By then he would probably have found someone better equipped to help him work through
his pain, and it wouldn't matter.

I'd lost my friend forever.

After what felt like thousands of hugs and millions of tears, the last bus
drove beneath the arch of Camp Rockwood. We counselors breathed a
collective sigh that was both relief and sadness, but as soon as that last
bus rounded the corner, our summer together was over. A few of us
would stay a couple of days to help clean up and store everything until
June, and then we would part ways.

I sent Macy off with the Donovan driver, Emil, who was a lot
younger than I expected and hardly seemed like someone who would
be content to drive a guy around all day, but he was cheery and even
greeted Macy with a high five before he helped her limp to the car. She
waved at me as the car crunched across the gravel road, and that was
that.

"What a year," Gabby said, watching the last yellow bus disappear
around a corner of the winding lane.

I folded my arms because it felt like I was missing something and I
wanted to hold it again. "Tell me about it."

"My hair is still blonde," Sofie breathed with relief.

"And now it's back to real life," Yasmine added.

The other counselors muttered things I didn't care to listen to because I was just trying to breathe. When the summer started, I never
could have guessed where it was going, and now I wasn't sure I could
go back to the way things were.

What I needed most was a distraction. But before I could turn to
Gabby and suggest one more canoe race, a true test of who was better,
Linda touched my arm and gave me a look that told me to follow.

She waited until I had stepped into her office then jumped right
into it: "This came for you," she said and held out a letter.

I rarely got mail, which must have been why Linda decided she
needed to hand it to me personally instead of putting it in my box in

the back of the rec room. Still, I found it strange that she would feel the need to give it to me *now*.

I took the letter and glanced at the return address. "*Davenport and Iyer?*" I read out loud.

Linda shrugged. "They made me sign to verify it had been delivered, so I figured it was something important."

The address listed was in San Francisco, and just the sight of the city made my pulse beat a little faster. Had it come from Colin somehow? But no, he wouldn't have made it back to the city yet, since Macy had just barely left. Fingers trembling, I tore open the rather short letter and read it quickly. All I got was a jumble of words, so I forced myself to slow down and focus.

But even after I'd gone through the letter several times, I still couldn't make sense of it.

It was a joke. A prank. Some mistake. And yet the neatly written note was addressed to me and had come directly to the camp. It contained phone numbers and hotel information. And a twisting feeling in my gut, which was almost always right, told me that all of this was real, and I was about to lose all sense of control over my life.

To Miss Rebecka Alvarez,

> *While this may come as a bit of a surprise, you are the sole beneficiary of one of my clients, who recently passed. In most cases, there would be no need for me to write to you myself, but the property is extensive, and my client was very specific in her terms and required I personally administer the benefits to you should she not have the opportunity to approach you herself. As this seems to be the unfortunate case, I must therefore ask you to come by my office here in San Francisco at your earliest convenience. Said client has arranged for lodging and transportation should you require it, and my assistant is available at all hours to arrange anything else you may need.*

> *Yours,*

> *Harris M. Davenport, Esq.*

Dear Dalia,

I don't know what to do. My life is spinning out of control. I'm all alone.

Help.

Beck

CHAPTER TEN

I stepped into the lobby of the *Davenport and Iyer* law firm almost two weeks after receiving the letter. I told myself that it took me so long because I had a lot of camp things to do, but really, as much as I hated to admit it, I was simply terrified because I had no idea what this meant for my future life.

Being this afraid of something had only added frustration to my anxiety, so by the time I got out of my car (the cost of parking in San Francisco was ridiculous) and found the right building (*Why are there so many people in this stupid city?*), I was pretty much falling apart. Linda had tried multiple times to tell me the letter was a good thing, that a mysterious inheritance could mean any number of exciting things, that I shouldn't start to freak out until I knew exactly what was in store, but her reassurances hadn't done much.

As a girl whose whole life had been spent in the same place, apparently I wasn't great with unexpected change.

I stood in that fancy lobby, clutching my worn-out messenger bag that contained most of my possessions that weren't clothes, and I desperately wished I had someone with me who could tell me everything would be fine.

"Can I help you, honey?" asked a kind-looking receptionist, though she did eye my tattered jeans with some misgivings. I didn't blame her for being unsure if I were in the right place, since, as I'd learned,

Davenport and Iyer were a corporate law firm, something that had only worried me more. I certainly didn't look like the sort who would use their services.

I grabbed Mr. Davenport's letter and held it out to her. I figured that was easier than trying to explain.

"Ah," she said as she caught sight of it. "We were wondering when you would show up, Miss Alvarez. I was worried the letter didn't reach you."

"Is…" I took a deep breath so my voice wouldn't shake. "Can you tell me what's going on?"

She smiled and typed something into her computer. "I'll have someone out here right away to explain things until Mr. Davenport is free."

Within seconds, it seemed, a frazzled-looking young woman with an armful of files came from the hallway behind the receptionist's desk. "You Alvarez?" she asked me by way of greeting. "Great. Follow me. I've got about five minutes to get this info across before I have to be in a meeting that I'm not remotely prepared for thanks to the big guys deciding they don't want to do the small stuff so they pile it all into us paralegals even though we're already busier than them, and they get all the credit! Have a seat."

I did, though most of the chair was covered with another stack of files to match the one she dumped on her chaotic desk.

"Okay," she said, standing by her chair instead of sitting. She fished through a stack then grabbed a rather large folder and opened to the front page. "The simple explanation is this: Your grandmother just died and left everything to you, and now you're fabulously wealthy."

I waited for her to start laughing. When she didn't, I swallowed and tried to find the best way to tell her that she was wrong. "Both my grandmothers are dead," I said. They had been since before I was born.

The paralegal rolled her eyes. "Well *now* they are, but up until a month ago your maternal grandmother was alive and kicking."

"There has to be some mistake," I tried.

Sighing, she handed me the folder, though one glance told me I wouldn't understand any of it. "Look," she said, "Maria Alvarez was, up until she died, one of the most philanthropic people in the city, maybe even the state, and she claimed to have no family to inherit her legacy. Then she got sick and had a change of heart, and that meant a whole lot of paperwork we had to do so she could change her will to include the granddaughter she had ignored her whole life. She was filthy rich, so I don't see why you're fighting this as much as you are.

"And that's my cue," she finished, glancing at her watch and once again taking up a mountain of papers. "Talk to Mr. Davenport, and don't try to pretend you're not at least a little interested in the situation. Most people dream of long-lost relatives suddenly bequeathing them a fortune."

And then she was gone, and I sat there for I didn't even know how long trying to process what I'd just heard. The one thing I knew for sure was I really didn't like that paralegal.

"Miss Alvarez?" The receptionist had come to find me, and she gave me a gentle smile that calmed some of the jitters bouncing around inside me. "How are you feeling?"

Honestly, I didn't know *how* to feel. It was all too much to take in, and the paralegal hadn't exactly helped things by spewing all of that all at once. "It's a lot to take in," I said. *Understatement of the century.* "I'm not sure any of it feels real."

She patted my arm, which was at least a little reassuring. "Mr. Davenport is available to talk to you now," she said, "and I promise he is nothing like Clarissa. Unfortunately, she was the only one free to explain to you. If you'll follow me."

The instant I saw Mr. Davenport, I relaxed a little. He was an older man, somewhere in his fifties, and there was a sense of calm about him that filled his entire office, which was cluttered but not nearly as much as Clarissa's had been. He looked up when the receptionist showed me in, his eyes soft behind his glasses, and gestured one hand to a leather chair opposite him.

"Thank you, Stacy," he said. His voice was quiet, but there was an edge to it, like a sense of confidence and superiority that was most likely fully deserved, if my little research into the guy was to be believed. He was a formidable lawyer, but after looking at him a moment, I was pretty sure he didn't have the same intensity during his day-to-day life.

"I assume you have some questions," he said to start.

I nodded. My mouth felt dry, my tongue sticking to the roof, and I could barely breathe as I sat there still reeling. I asked the only question that was fully formed in my head: "My abuela was alive?" I didn't even know how to ask the million other questions I had.

Davenport nodded. "Maria Alvarez was a client of mine for many years, since her charities are a large part of this city."

That was a good place to start. "Charities?"

"Ms. Alvarez was of a rare breed, and she used her fortune to benefit the common man, unlike many of the, uh, elite."

If his office decor and lawyer fame were any indication, I would hazard a guess that he was among those supposed *elite*. "And she left everything to me?" I asked. I wanted to ask how much it amounted to, but I couldn't find the heart for that question yet.

Davenport reached his hand out, and I handed him the folder I'd been hugging for support. He flipped through some pages then pulled out a single sheet and gave it to me. The letter was short, written in a wavering handwriting, and my fingers shook as I read.

My darling frijolita,

There is no good way to say what I want to say, and I only hope I get a chance to see who you've become before I am gone. First, I am sorry. I left my Dalia because I was angry and ashamed, and I regretted that every moment. I did not approve of her choices, and I thought Dios was punishing me by giving me a daughter who did not walk the straight path I set for her.

I realized too late I was wrong, and when I tried to make things right, she would not let me back into her life. I cannot blame her for that. What I most regret is never knowing you, my frijolita. All those years I could have loved you. There is nothing that can make up for the way I acted, but I hope, in some way, this can ease the pain I have caused you and your mother.

I left Mexico with a daughter I cherished and a fortune I did not need, and because my focus was wrong, I lost the most important thing to me. All I could do was dedicate my life to what I had left, and I hope I have made up for my mistakes in some small way.

There is much good to do in the world, and I pray to the heavens you have grown up well and remember that. Keep my memory alive, if you can find it in your heart to do it. I will love you always, my frijolita.

Maria

I read the letter twice. A third time. And I still didn't understand. My mother had told me she had lost her own mother just before I was born. Had she really lied to me my whole life? Or had I just misunderstood her meaning?

"I can understand how overwhelmed you must feel," Davenport said when he decided I'd finished reading. "There is every reason you will want time to process. But I must impress one thing upon you, Miss Alvarez, something that is, quite frankly, crucial to the contents of the will."

I looked up at him, waiting.

He took a deep breath. "Ms. Alvarez requires that in order to inherit her fortune, you must also inherit her work."

What did that mean? "Her work?"

"The charities and other philanthropic ventures she was involved in. In simple terms, you can only claim the money if you head the charities."

I wasn't sure what it was, exactly, but that was enough to knock me out of my stupor and bring me back to awareness. "Wait," I said. "So if I don't run her charities for her, I don't get any of her money?"

Davenport nodded slightly. "That is the basic idea, yes."

"But I don't know anything about running charities."

"She was rather convinced you would be able to figure it out. Apparently Alvarez women are, uh, *resilient*, I believe she said."

Well that much was certainly true, at least for Mama and me. But there was so much to think about, and I still didn't know enough about what was happening. "What happens if I don't want to run the charities?" I asked. Just how knowledgeable was this guy?

Davenport gave me a soft smile, though it looked like something he wasn't used to doing. "Then Ms. Alvarez's fortune divides among other well-established organizations, and her own charities will either dissolve or be taken over by someone else."

"So either way, people are still being helped?"

"Essentially."

Huh. From where I stood at the moment, either option seemed like a good choice. Either I could give up on Rockwood and do good here in the city (and apparently become fabulously wealthy at the same time), or I could trust that that money would be put to good use, and I could go back to the life I was comfortable in, the life I loved.

But how was I supposed to choose?

He must have sensed my dilemma, because Davenport smiled again and said, "You don't have to make any decisions right away. In fact, Ms. Alvarez was adamant you be given sufficient time to make your choice."

"How long is sufficient?"

"Ninety days from the date you are informed of the bequeathal. During that time you can learn about her charities and gain whatever knowledge and resources you need to make an informed decision. She has an apartment set up for you here in the city with the rent paid in full up to the expiration date of her offer, as well as use of a car and driver, and any other staff you might feel necessary. You also have access to me, as Ms. Alvarez's legal counsel, though…" He cleared his throat. "That one I would prefer to be an emergency resource. You are, of course, welcome to counsel with any of the employees here at *Davenport and Iyer*, should you have questions."

I took a deep breath and let it out slowly while I let all that sink in. I had a place to stay, people to help me, and all I had to do was test out the gig for the next three months? That would put me up almost to December, long before I would have to go back to camp if I made that choice.

"If I may," Davenport continued and handed me what looked like a party invitation, "there is an event tomorrow night that Ms. Alvarez planned, and it would be a good opportunity to get a feel for the world you will be entering."

A charity event in San Francisco? I had a feeling that sort of thing would be a whole lot fancier than anything I'd ever been to before. I'd brought my whole wardrobe with me, all of it stuffed into a single duffel bag and dumped in my trunk, and I didn't even have a skirt in there. "What…" There had to be a way to word this that didn't make me sound useless. "What am I supposed to expect at something like that?"

A hint of fear passed across his face, and he coughed to cover it up. "I don't attend affairs like that if I can help it. My wife lives for those events, but…" He frowned, glancing around his desk as if hoping for some sort of lifeline he could use so he didn't have to involve himself in a party.

"I can't handle it anymore!" came a sudden voice from outside the office. "I can't." And in walked a man who, though he had none of the stiff demeanor of Mr. Davenport, had such similar features that I didn't have to hear Davenport's response to know they were father and son.

"Matthew," the lawyer said with just a hint of a growl, "son, I'm with a client."

Matthew froze, his grey-blue eyes locked on me and his face turning beet red. "Ah," he said and bit his lower lip. "I am so sorry. Stacy wasn't at her desk, so I assumed… I'll go wait outside."

"Actually," Mr. Davenport replied, "your arrival is…serendipitous."

Raising an eyebrow, Matthew glanced between his father and me. "Is it?" he asked and folded his arms. Where a moment ago he had been loose and almost frantic, now he stiffened into a stance I had only seen in army movies (on the rare occasions I actually watched movies). His gaze changed from apologetic to examining, and I felt like I was under a very bright spotlight.

"You don't look like a greedy corporate tyrant," he said to me.

"Matthew," Davenport censured.

But I found myself smiling. As intimidating as this guy looked, I had a feeling it was all a front. "I'm definitely not," I said.

Glancing at his dad, Matthew seemed to catch some hidden meaning in the older man's expression and nodded before he turned his attention back to me. "I'm Matthew," he said, and held his hand out for me to shake. "And I'm so sorry for interrupting. I'm… Well, I'm losing my mind at the moment. And you are?"

I wasn't sure if I should laugh or not. "Um, I'm Beck. Alvarez. Your dad was just explaining some things to me."

Though he was trying very hard to look interested, Matthew could barely stand still and looked like he either wanted to bolt or start smashing things. It wasn't anger that was bothering him, and if I had to guess, I would say he was nervous.

"Why are you losing your mind?" I asked.

He smiled, clearly grateful to share his apparent woes. "My wife is due to go into labor any day now," he said.

"And I don't know why you're coming to me with this," Mr. Davenport sighed.

Matthew barely spared him a glance as he replied, "You had three kids, Dad."

"And you know very well I wasn't part of the delivery for any of you. Can't you go bother Adam with this?"

This time Matthew rolled his eyes and clapped his hands on his father's desk. "*Dad*," he said with a huff. "You know what Adam's like. He's not exactly the right person to make me feel better when he was about ready to tear his hair out waiting for Benny to come. It was no different for Harry."

"Matthew."

"Boy or girl?" I asked.

Yet again Matthew smiled at me and almost looked ready to give me a hug. "Girl," he said, and he looked positively thrilled about the idea, though still terrified.

"I love girls!" I told him. "I work at a summer camp for girls, and they're all wonderful. You're a very lucky man, Matthew."

"Okay," he replied, "you're my new favorite person. Dad, you're fired."

Davenport looked ready to pound his head against his desk. "I'm volunteering you, son," he said. "Miss Alvarez needs your help."

I was about to argue, since I didn't want to inconvenience yet another person, especially one who was about to have a baby.

But before I could say a word, Matthew stood up straight and said, "Absolutely. I don't even care what it is, because I badly need the distraction. Wanna get out of here before my dad changes his mind about helping you?"

"Matthew."

I grinned. "Sure. Uh, was there anything else, Mr. Davenport?"

"Doesn't matter," Matthew said and took my hand, pulling me up to my feet and out of the office. "Put me to work, Miss Alvarez. Beck, was it? Give me something to do before I go crazy. What exactly do you need help with?"

He dressed well, as far as I could tell, and if he was related to Mr. Davenport, he probably fit into that elite group his father clearly was a part of. But he seemed too down-to-earth to be a rich snob. (I didn't know what the elites were like, but I imagined them as rich snobs in my head.) Maybe he could help me know how to fit in at a fancy party, maybe he couldn't, but it was worth a shot.

"Apparently I have to attend a fundraising event tomorrow," I said as we headed for the elevator.

Matthew's eyes went a little wide. "I'm sorry."

That's concerning. "And I don't know anything about that. What to wear, how to act, what to say."

We stepped into the elevator, and he blew air out of his mouth in a steady stream. "Not gonna lie, Beck, that's not really my scene. I grew up in this world, but I got out of it as soon as I possibly could."

I didn't realize how disappointed I would be by that answer, even though I'd expected something like it. I could tell he wanted to help, and I really wished I had a good way to distract him from his baby nerves, but I could only focus on so many things right now.

"But," he added with a crooked smile, "I happen to have a family chock full of the rich and powerful, so you can really take your pick of fairy godparent, assuming you don't get scared off when you realize we're all a bunch of strangers to you and could be after one of your kidneys."

My stomach twisted itself into a knot, not because of his joke or because I had any fear of this guy or any of his family, stranger or not.

I could take care of myself for the most part. But with his words, I was suddenly missing my mom so much that my heart ached, and I wanted to curl up in a ball and cry.

Why hadn't she told me about my grandmother? All my life she'd pretended Maria Alvarez was dead, and for the last seven years I'd been sure my family was all gone. I could have had a home, and instead I was more alone than ever because I'd never even had the chance to know her.

Matthew apparently took my sudden misery as apprehension, because he took a step away from me and grabbed his phone. "I have an idea," he said and lifted it to his ear. "I think this particular situation is going to require a gentler touch. Hey, it's Matthew. What are you doing right now? I need your help."

CHAPTER ELEVEN

"The thing I've learned being a part of this world is you have to breathe and let everything roll off you. People will think what they think, but you are who you are."

Breathe. I could do that. It wasn't like I was about to walk into the biggest, fanciest, gaudiest party I'd ever seen and pretend I actually belonged there. *Oh wait.* I looked at the man next to me and tried to find some strength in knowing he would be at my side all night if I asked him to. He had spent all day yesterday and most of today helping me get situated, and while I was afraid I wouldn't be able to walk in these heels, I actually felt like I might look the part thanks to his ministrations.

"I don't know what I would do without you, Brennon," I told him.

According to Matthew, Brennon Ashworth was his brother. According to Brennon, he was a neighbor who got adopted into the Davenport family sometime in the last year because that was what the Davenports did. I didn't care how he was related, because without him, I would have turned and run away from the city with my tail between my legs, and I would have hated myself because of it. I had never run from a challenge, and I didn't want to start now.

"Are you ready?" Brennon asked and held out his arm so we could walk up the stairs together.

I looped my arm through his and took a deep breath. "As ready as I'll ever be," I said. All thanks to him.

As I'd learned yesterday while trying on what felt like a million dresses, he had worked his way up into the wealthy world after an average middle-class childhood. He didn't often go to events like this, but he was well-versed in dealing with the elites. What also made him an ideal partner tonight was the fact that he'd gotten married to the love of his life only a month and a half earlier, and though his wife was off on some journalism job, the guy had not been able to stop smiling since the moment I met him. It was that trait that had endeared me to him almost immediately and why I felt completely safe trusting him to get me through this party.

Plus, he was smart enough to have deferred dress decisions to Matthew's cousin, Catherine. She had incredible taste, so I felt more beautiful than I'd ever felt in my life. That definitely helped give me a bit of confidence.

I looked the part, but that didn't mean I was going to be able to act it. I just hoped I didn't completely make a fool of myself. *You've got this, Beck.*

The moment we stepped through the huge glass doors together, an elegant woman greeted us and addressed me without preamble. "Miss Alvarez, if you'll follow me."

I gripped Brennon's arm tighter, partly because I wasn't sure if they would let him come with me, but mostly because I was seriously reconsidering attending this thing at all. But Brennon gave me a look that told me he wasn't going to abandon me, no matter what anyone tried to say. I gave him a grateful smile then followed the woman past the grand hall, where the bulk of the guests were milling around, and through a set of mahogany doors that were so beautifully decorated that I could only imagine how much they cost.

The doors led to a much smaller room, though just as brilliantly lit as the grand hall, and inside stood a couple dozen people, all of them sipping champagne and talking in a low buzz.

The woman paused and leaned close so she could murmur, "These are Ms. Alvarez's most prolific patrons, and all of them are loyal to the work she does. We thought it might be easier for you to meet them apart from the other patrons, so you don't get overwhelmed."

I could have hugged her, though based on her tight hairstyle and perfectly pressed suit, I had a feeling she wasn't a hugger. "Thank you," I said, and I meant it. "I'm really new to all of this, so it'll be nice to ease into it."

"Of course," she replied then held her arm out to the nearest guest. "This is Corbin Glass, head of Glass Industries. Mr. Glass, I am pleased to introduce Rebecka Alvarez, Maria's granddaughter who will be stepping in for her."

She introduced me to at least a dozen people before she decided I could do the rest on my own. Thankfully, no one seemed to expect me to have any real conversations with them, and most of them just expressed their condolences for my loss. Brennon was a godsend and was absolutely brilliant with small talk, so I let him take the lead. I wasn't even sure how he managed it so well, since he had told me more than once he wasn't big on talking to strangers.

Brennon did know a few of them, though, and after listening to them talk, I realized they were his clients. He'd told me he was a stock-broker, and most of his clients were elites, which was how he was qualified to help me prepare for the event. Most of the people he knew were gracious and understanding. One, however, I disliked almost immediately.

"Chandler Wixcomb," he said to me before Brennon had even started to introduce me. He said it as if I should already know the name, though he was maybe thirty-five and pretty much ignored by everyone else, so he probably wasn't as important as he thought. "I've been donating significant amounts to your grandmother's causes for years, and you have impossibly big shoes to fill."

Nice to meet you too. Are all of her patrons as conceited as you? I bit my tongue and counted to five before I said anything, but even then I barely managed a neutral tone. "I hope I can do the job properly," I said. "Did you know her well?"

Mr. Wixcomb stuck out his chest, though he only succeeded in making himself look awkwardly bent. In the strangest way, he reminded me a bit of a horse, and I had to fight against laughing at the image of his face on a skinny horse's body. "Ms. Alvarez and I were good friends," he said, and he nearly shouted it so the whole room would hear the proclamation.

Several people, including Brennon, rolled their eyes and continued their conversations.

"I'm so glad she had someone like you as her companion." I pulled my phone out of my fancy new clutch, pretending it was ringing. "Excuse me."

As I turned and distanced myself just enough that I could pretend to be listening to the phone, I heard Brennon say something to Wixcomb in a low voice. I couldn't make out what it was, but when I glanced back at them, neither seemed all that happy about their hushed little conversation.

A bit of heat blossomed in my face, because I was pretty sure Brennon was defending me. I'd never really had anyone do that before outside of Linda. Most of the time I made sure I didn't need it, but in a place like this, I was out of my element.

There weren't many more people I needed to meet in this room, but I hoped that would be it. I'd only been there for half an hour, and I was already exhausted.

"Hey, Ashworth," a man said behind me to Brennon, "does this mean I'm finally going to meet your wife?"

I turned to correct the assumption, but then I froze. So did the man who spoke.

And if Brennon noticed the sudden tension in front of him, he didn't say anything about it. "Molly's flying in tomorrow, but this is my new friend, Beck Alvarez. Beck, this is—"

"Colin Donovan," I whispered.

Colin maintained his composure impressively well, since I felt like my whole face was on fire and he just looked slightly inconvenienced. He was good at hiding his emotions, though, and I liked to think I had left more of an impression than that.

"Oh," Brennon said, "you've heard of him then?"

"We've met, actually," Colin replied. "It's, uh, it's good to see you, Beck."

"You too," I choked back, suddenly dizzy. Somehow, amidst all the inheritance chaos, I had forgotten about him. Or at least forgotten he was one of the rich and powerful San Franciscans who came to this sort of thing. "I think I need some air," I whispered.

And suddenly the ground flew up to meet me.

Next thing I knew, I was sitting on the steps outside the venue, and a beautiful face was taking up the majority of my view. "What happened?" I asked as he came into focus, though my body swayed a little.

Colin put both his hands on my shoulders. "You fainted for a second," he said.

No way. "I don't faint."

"Well now you do, apparently. And I don't blame you. That dress is…" He glanced at it then turned rather red in the light of the building behind me. "It looks like it's pretty tight."

He wasn't wrong. According to Matthew's cousin, who had been video chatting with Brennon most of the day yesterday, there was no way to fit in with the elites without some discomfort. "The price of beauty," I muttered.

"Yeah," he breathed.

I was pretty sure my face turned the same shade as his. "So," I said, hoping to change the topic, "do you come to these things often?"

Now that I wasn't in danger of passing out again, he got to his feet and stepped down a couple of steps, both adding some distance between us and bringing himself to eye level with me. "What are you doing here, Beck?" he asked instead of answering my question.

"That," I replied, "is a bit of a long story."

I had no idea how long I was expected to stay at that party, but I had lasted as long as I could. Besides, I badly needed someone I could tell all my troubles to now that Gabby was back home in Santa Rosa. Someone who knew me better than Brennon, and there really wasn't anyone I trusted more with something like this than Colin. So I texted Brennon and told him I wasn't coming back in, and then Colin and I took to walking the streets of San Francisco.

After I told him everything I knew about the inheritance and its strange stipulations, Colin whistled low and stuffed his hands into his pockets. "I know next to nothing about law," he said first. "Our lawyer at JayTech tries to tell me things, but he generally gives up after a minute or two. But this sounds like an incredible opportunity, Beck. What are you thinking?"

"Considering I found out about it yesterday?" I heaved a sigh, but it didn't lessen any of the tension building in my shoulders. "I have no idea. My entire adult life has been about Camp Rockwood, and I can't imagine a different way to live. Especially a way like this." I gestured to a house we passed that was so big, I felt like we'd left San Francisco entirely because it wasn't attached to anything else like the rest of the city seemed to be. "I don't know anything about this world."

Colin laughed a little. "I've been in this world my whole life," he said, "and I still haven't figured it out. You'll get better."

We walked a bit in silence, but I decided I didn't like just listening to the sounds of the city. It was too chaotic, and it made me miss the silence of the forest. "How's Macy?"

"She's doing great," he said, and he grinned at me, his eyes dancing. "She keeps telling me about all these friends she's making at this new school."

"That's amazing, Colin."

"And it's thanks to you." He took me by the hand and pulled me to a stop so he could look me in the eye. "I'm sorry I couldn't make it to the last day of camp. After everything... It shouldn't have happened that way, and I've been regretting it for the last two weeks because I never got a chance to say... To tell you..."

My hand felt weak inside his, and I just stared at him because there was something in his look that made me desperate to know what he was trying to say.

But he sighed and dropped my hand, stuffing his into his pockets again. "I miss having you as my friend, Beck."

Oh. "I miss that too," I said, and while I meant it, a little spark inside me seemed to go out. *Get a hold of yourself, Beck. It's not like anything was ever going to happen anyway.* "I was a little preoccupied the last couple of days, otherwise I would have reached out." *Or not.*

His smile was so full of relief that it almost made me feel a little better. "You'd think I would have friends here," he muttered, "but for years I didn't need anyone but Jada. And after she was gone, I threw myself into work. And Macy, of course." He gestured for us to keep walking.

I reached down and pulled my shoes off first, and though Colin winced at the idea of me walking barefoot through San Francisco, that sounded a whole lot better than staying in my ridiculously high heels. "I know how that goes," I said, hopping over a little pile of broken glass that Colin grimaced at. "Outside of camp, I don't have anyone."

"At the risk of making assumptions, what sad lives we live."

I grinned. "You're not wrong."

"So." As we crested a hill and came to a cross street, Colin glanced both directions then silently suggested we go right. "You have three months to try out this whole charity heiress thing, right?"

"That's what it sounded like."

"Have you figured out where you want to start? I can imagine it's a bit overwhelming."

I let out a dramatic sigh, but it wasn't all that much of an exaggeration. I had no idea what I was doing. "I guess I have to figure out what charities my abuela even had and see if there are any contacts I can get ahold of. There have to be people in charge, right?"

He shrugged. "Most likely. I can't imagine Ms. Alvarez was able to personally run them all."

As I thought for a moment, I watched Colin as he walked. There was an easiness in his step here that he hadn't had back at camp, though he'd gotten better by summer's end. But clearly he was comfortable in San Francisco, something I could barely even imagine. The city was loud, bright, smelly, and full of so many people that I was honestly amazed Colin and I had even been in the same room at the same time. He didn't seem to mind any of that, and I wished there were a way he could teach me how to be a city person.

Assuming I even stuck around.

But first, I had one problem I knew for sure he could solve. "I have a serious question," I told him. "Where does one get good food in this place?"

His smile grew quickly, and the sounds of the city faded a bit behind the warmth that spread through me. "One can go any number of places."

"Well, what if one wants to go somewhere that only exists in San Francisco?"

He thought for a moment. "One could go to The Globe. I haven't actually been there myself, mostly because eating out isn't very fun solo, but I've been told by about a hundred people that it's the place to be. The chef is blind, so they say, but that doesn't make him any less brilliant at his job."

I raised an eyebrow. "A blind chef? Is that even possible?"

He held out his arm, which I took easily. "Want to find out?"

The Globe was definitely the place to be, as evidenced by the wait time of over an hour (though Colin assured me that was a pretty short wait compared to some nights). I was starving, but my tired and incredibly dirty feet told me I had to stay put and just wait it out. Besides, we found a cozy little corner of the lobby to wait, and I couldn't complain about being squished up against Colin for the next hour.

"So the restaurant has food from all over the world," he said to start our conversation up again, since it had gone through a lull as we walked in search of the place. "From what I understand, the chef has traveled all over and learned from the locals wherever he's gone, so his dishes are completely unique with his own little spin on what he's learned."

My stomach rumbled at the thought. At that point, since I'd been too nervous about the party to eat much all day, I would have been happy with a cheeseburger and fries. "Sounds delicious," I said. "Then again, pretty much anything is better than Chuck's food at camp."

His grin was almost distracting enough to keep me from focusing on the gnawing sensation in my stomach. "You know," he said, "his food wasn't all that bad."

"I never actually saw you eat at camp." Outside of grapes thrown in the air, though I wasn't sure I could count that... "Are you actually a solar-powered robot?"

"It's wind turbines," he replied. "In my hair. But people make that mistake a lot, so don't feel too bad."

I snorted and got a few curious looks from some of the other people in the packed lobby. "Have you gotten weirder since I last saw you?"

He raised one perfect eyebrow. He'd gotten a haircut since coming back, I noticed, and he looked all the more distinguished because of it. If he wasn't hunched into the little space with me, he might have looked just as sharp as the day I first met him. "Have I gotten weirder," he replied, "or have you gotten more normal?"

"Are you saying I was weird before?"

"You act like a pirate on a daily basis, Beck."

I grinned. "So? In my world, that's perfectly normal."

"Well now you're in my world, and we don't have pirates." His smile faded a little, and I had to wonder why that comment would deflate him. Was it a result of his world, or was it because of me?

"So," he said, much softer now, "I know you brought Brennon to that party with you to help you learn the ways of the wealthy, but you can't exactly expect him to be by your side for everything. Especially if his wife is flying in. He barely gets to see her. Do you think you can do all of this on your own?"

He was right, but I hadn't really thought about it. According to Matthew, there was a whole crew of Davenports who were willing to help me out, but it had been hard enough to accept Brennon's assistance at the beginning. The thought of calling up random people and tearing them away from their lives because I had basically been raised outside made me queasy.

"Eventually I'll figure it out," I said. "Or I'll choose not to take the inheritance, and I'll go back home."

Colin looked down, a thoughtful expression on his face. I wasn't sure if he realized he did it, but he picked up one of my hands and rubbed his thumb across my knuckles. "I can't pretend I am an expert in charity events or anything," he said, and he almost sounded nervous, "but, if you wanted, you could use me as a resource. My company does a lot of work with the Alvarez Trust, so I've been to a lot of those. I mean, I don't want you to feel obligated or anything, but—"

Though I knew it wouldn't help me figure out how I felt about this guy, I swiftly kissed his cheek and gave his hand a squeeze. "Thank you," I said sincerely. "I know you're busy, so I didn't want to ask, but I think if I knew you would be at some of these things, I wouldn't be so terrified to show up. You make me feel confident."

His small smile lit up the whole room. "Beck Alvarez thinks she needs more confidence? Preposterous."

He had leaned closer, and I couldn't help but remember our moment on the boulder. I was so positive he'd been about to kiss me, and it almost felt like he was considering it now. While I wouldn't have complained if he did, I had to wonder why he would do something like that when he'd been so clear about us being friends.

"Mr. Donovan? Your table is ready for you." The cheery hostess broke us apart from just a few feet away, and I had to commend her professionalism. She didn't bat an eye at finding us in an almost personal situation and simply offered us a smile before leading us into the restaurant.

"That wasn't an hour, was it?" I asked as we followed, passing the jealous expressions of those who still had to wait.

Colin glanced at his watch then grinned. "I have connections," he said, trying and failing to sound mysterious.

The restaurant itself was just as packed at its lobby, though it was much quieter inside than out. My guess was that people were too busy enjoying their food to talk much, which said a lot about their supposedly blind chef. The hostess led us deep into the elegantly designed room, back to a dimly lit table slightly secluded from the rest.

I wasn't sure why, but Colin started laughing when he saw it. "This is perfect," he told the hostess when she grew concerned. Once we'd sat down, he leaned over the table to say, "Brennon comes here all the time, so I asked for his usual table. I'm not the least bit surprised his table is a bit remote."

I had no complaints, and I could picture Brennon spending hours here. He definitely seemed the sort to be content by himself, though from what I'd heard about his wife, he was infinitely happier now that she was in his life. Even if she couldn't always be around because of her journalist job.

"It has a pretty good view of the kitchen," I said and nodded in that direction. "I'm surprised they let the guests see them work."

From where we sat, we could see each of the cooks busy at their stoves or whatever else, and the chef was easy to spot. He was pretty handsome and younger than I would have expected, and there was a definite blankness to his gaze as he chopped something on the counter in front of him, like he wasn't all that focused on what he was doing.

"Like I said, one of the place's drawing features is their blind chef," Colin replied. "Guess it would make sense why…hang on." He stood, squinting at the head cook. "No way." Without explanation, he hurried closer to the kitchen and said, "Is that you, Steve?"

The chef froze, and his scowl was a bit menacing until it morphed into something closer to curiosity. "I know that voice," he said, just loud enough for me to hear from where I sat. He stabbed the knife into the cutting board and wiped his hands on his apron, trying to see who it was who'd spoken to him. "Why do I know that voice?"

Colin laughed again, and my stomach did a somersault. His laugh was just as musical as it had been back at camp, maybe even more so. Did he have any idea how many people—women, in particular— seemed drawn to that laugh? I had to fight the urge to glare at any of them who looked over.

"You actually started the restaurant," he said to Steve the chef. "I had a feeling you would do that sooner than later."

Steve's eyes went wide. "Colin Donovan," he concluded and held out his hand in amazement.

Colin shook it with enthusiasm. "Congrats, man. On the wedding, too," he added. "I'm glad things turned around for you after everything."

Though Steve shrugged, his little quirked smile at the mention of a wedding conveyed a lot more happiness than he probably knew. "Have you been keeping tabs on me?" he asked. He said something else, but he said it too quietly for me to hear. It definitely dimmed Colin's energy, though, and I had a pretty good idea what topic of conversation would make him look so suddenly miserable. When he immediately twisted the ring on his left hand, I knew for sure, and I was tempted to go over to that kitchen and tell Steve what a horrible human he was for bringing up Colin's dead wife.

"Hello," a soft voice said before I could get to my feet.

I looked up and with a quick glance guessed the woman standing nearby was our waitress. "We're going to need a minute," I said with a smile.

She matched it, her eyes wandering over to the kitchen where the two men seemed to be deep in conversation. "I'm guessing he belongs to you," she said, and to my surprise she sat down in Colin's vacant chair. "I keep telling Steve he can't chat with every long-lost friend because it prevents him from cooking, but he keeps ignoring me. That's what I get for marrying someone so stubborn, I guess."

You're Steve's wife? "Is he really blind?" I asked. I mentally kicked myself for asking the wrong question, but the woman didn't seem to mind my lack of manners.

"Most of the time," she replied. "Some days are better than others, and he's convinced it's been getting better over the last few months. So you're here with Colin?"

Instinct told me to claim him before she got any ideas. Reality reminded me that not everyone was a cheater like Kurt, and she was probably happily in love with her best friend and had no reason to stray. Besides, Colin wasn't like that anyway.

"Yeah," I said, which sounded simple enough while still answering the question. Honestly, I wasn't sure if I was here *with* Colin or if we were just here. He kept giving me mixed signals, and I was too overwhelmed and exhausted to try and decipher them right now. I was just happy to have a place to sit and food to eat if I ever got a hold of a menu. "He didn't realize he knew the chef, though."

"I'm surprised Brennon didn't make the connection," she replied.

I stared at her. Had I seen her before?

She caught on to my confusion and was kind enough to explain: "Brennon's table is Brennon's table. Anyone who sits here can only do so if he gives the say so. One of the perks of being Steve's brother."

I glanced at the chef again, and though I was pleased to see Colin was smiling again as they kept talking, I was a little too preoccupied by the conversation happening in front of me. "They don't look like brothers," I said.

Where Brennon was slim, Steve was bulkier, and Steve's head was more square where Brennon's was oval. Their eyes were two completely different colors, too, and Brennon had a sharper jawline. Not quite as sharp as Colin's, though I may have been a bit biased where he was concerned. Everything about him was better.

I gulped some water before my thoughts ran away with me on that point.

"They're not technically brothers," the woman said with a grin. "But spend enough time with us Davenports, and you start to forget who you're really related to."

I choked, accidentally inhaling some water and coughing as my lungs fought to get rid of it. "Sorry," I gasped between coughs. By the time I managed to breathe again, Colin was back at my side.

"You okay?" he asked and put his hand on my shoulder.

I'm okay, but my pride isn't. "Fine," I managed, though there was still a bit of a cough fighting to be free. *So much for acting all fancy.*

"Macy does that all the time," he said next, which wasn't as reassuring as he thought. Macy was nine years old, and she was allowed to accidentally inhale water. I was nearly twenty-eight. Plenty old to know how to use a glass.

I took a careful breath then smiled. "I think I'll live," I said, though my ego was a bit bruised.

"Looks like you found my wife," Steve said just behind Colin. Instead of heading straight for her, he reached out his hand, which she took and gently pulled to bring him to where she was sitting. It was such an easy motion that they'd probably done it without thinking, and I couldn't help but smile at the idea that everyone had someone out there who was perfect for them. Steve may have been blind, but his wife didn't seem to mind in the least.

Though Colin still looked a little worried I might break into coughing again, he nodded to Steve and said, "Beck, this is my good friend Steve. We used to work together."

"Back before Donovan decided he was too good for the daily grind and ran off to do his own thing," Steve added with mock indignance. "And now look at him. Filthy rich and getting more famous by the day. Such a waste. You know, Lyra Davenport was just talking about you the other day."

Colin shuddered. "I don't even know how many times she's tried to contact me in the last few months. But how do you know Lyra?"

I was just as curious about that question as Colin. I didn't have a clue who she was, but the name Davenport couldn't possibly be a coincidence.

Steve wrapped his arms around his wife from behind and planted a kiss on the top of her head. "She's… Lissa, what would the technical term be?"

She thought for a moment. "In relation to you? Something like second cousin once removed by marriage…twice."

"The wife of your lawyer, Harris Davenport," Colin said to me. He still had his hand on my shoulder, though I wasn't sure he knew it.

Steve and Lissa both brightened. "You're the girl Matthew sent the SOS about?" Lissa asked.

Apparently that was a good thing, though I wasn't so sure, so I shrugged. Mostly I was still trying to figure out how Steve and Lissa were related to the other Davenports since it seemed fairly distantly, if at all. The family seemed to have a rather loose definition of "related."

"Was I that much of a lost cause?" I asked.

"I think Matthew's the lost cause until that baby of his comes," Steve said. "Don't read much into his concern for you. This family tends to adopt strays."

I was about to make an indignant comment, but Colin leaned down and muttered, "Don't read too much into that either. It's not a bad thing." And while what he said made me feel a bit better, it was hard to concentrate when he was so close that all I could smell was his incredible cologne. How had I not noticed it in the lobby? Maybe there were too many people around us.

"Maybe we should let these two eat," Lissa said next. *Thank goodness.* "Steve, your cooks are wondering why you abandoned them."

Steve rolled his eyes, but he made his way back to the kitchen anyway, putting his hands on any obstacle that might have been in his way. Lissa smiled at the pair of us then waved to someone behind me, and to my relief a waiter came with menus. "It's on the house," she said then wandered off before I could argue.

Colin was still at my side, and though I may have imagined it, it was with reluctance that he retook his seat across from me. He did, however, slide his foot forward so his shoe touched mine. It was hard not to think there was something in that gesture, but I knew better than to get my hopes up. My stay in this city might be temporary, and if I left, any hope of keeping Colin in my life left with it.

Soon I was going to have a decision to make, and I had a feeling that decision was only going to get harder as time went on.

Dear Dalia,

Apparently Abuela really liked her parties, and I haven't managed to figure out how people can spend so much money in order to raise money. Someone tried to explain the math to me, but I think the rich people in this city just want the chance to appear philanthropic, so they throw their money around however they can. Luckily, it doesn't seem like Abuela was like that. So far most people have told me she was a wonderful, kindhearted woman who loved everyone.

Just not us, apparently. Not until it was too late.

I'm trying really hard to take over for her and do the job justice, since I feel like she deserves at least an honest attempt from me, but the longer I'm in this city, the more I'm starting to realize that this world is nothing like my world. I'm not sure if I fit in it. There's too much I don't know, and I don't like feeling like something could blindside me like what happened last week. Apparently I'm not supposed to start singing along with the band, even if they're playing one of my favorite songs. All that accomplished was a lot of stares and a whole lot of embarrassment on my part because it seems none of these rich people know how to sing or actually have some fun.

I don't want to let you and Abuela down, but this is turning out to be harder than I thought. And tomorrow I have to attend a dinner party in her honor, and I won't be able to hide behind people smarter than me this time.

Needing your strength,
Beck

P.S. Did you know Abuela was a millionaire? If you did, why did you never tell me? If you didn't, why should I try so hard to live up to her standards when we did just fine the way we were? So far, there's only one good reason for me to stay and keep trying.

P.P.S. I've learned that the secret to wearing high heels is to tape a couple of your toes together. I don't know why, but it really works.

P.P.P.S. I now own more dresses than I've collectively owned over my entire life. What's happening to me?

CHAPTER TWELVE

"The trick to these," said Colin as we meandered up the front steps of a house that looked like it could hold five or six of the one I grew up in, "is to smile and nod. These people like to think they're right about everything."

"You keep saying 'these people' like you're not one of them," I replied. But I gripped his arm tight, immensely glad he didn't act like most of the elites I had interacted with over the last several weeks. Especially tonight, I badly needed his confidence and calm.

Mckenna Foster was by far the most high and mighty person I'd ever met, and I was convinced she was trying to find a way to destroy me. She and the rest of the elite world. She'd already managed to elaborate, in detail, how little I knew about the charities I was trying to keep track of, and she liked to point out any flaw that presented itself. I had no idea what she would gain from me leaving, but she had become a strange sort of motivator for me to learn everything I could about fitting into this world.

But I was about to step through the door and into her home, and that was enemy territory. Anything could happen.

"It's one thing to be wealthy," Colin said. "It's another to want the world to know it. Do you remember what I told you about talking to everyone?"

I nodded, though doing so made me feel even more sick to my stomach than I already was. "Talk to the obnoxious first or they'll think

I'm ignoring them. Then the reserved ones, because they'll be grateful for being acknowledged. Everyone else won't mind waiting."

He pulled me in a little closer, which I'd come to realize was his way of reassuring me. I hadn't been able to spend tons of time with him the last few weeks, since he had been busy most nights with his company and I had been bogged down by charity research, but there had been enough lunches and evening strolls that we had settled into a sort of rhythm together, just like we had back at camp. Only now the roles were reversed, and he knew everything while I knew nothing at all.

"I hope you don't mind," he said as we paused near the front steps, "but I rallied the troops for this one. Not that I don't think you're capable, but Mckenna Foster can be particularly daunting to the best of us."

I furrowed my brow, trying to figure out what that meant. "The troops?"

He smiled. "You'll see. Brennon told me these four would be particularly helpful tonight." He rang the doorbell then put his hand over mine in an especially comforting gesture. With him there to act as a buffer against whatever Mckenna might try, I wasn't nearly as afraid as I could have been.

Mckenna Foster answered the door with a pleasant smile and gracious greetings, though there was an edge to her words when she spoke to me. "You're just in time," she said and held her arm out for us to come in. "Everyone is just in the drawing room. Mr. Donovan, you're looking particularly striking tonight."

Colin was wearing the same black suit I'd first seen him in, and Mckenna wasn't wrong. He looked every bit the part of an elite, and he stood with a confidence I hadn't yet been able to match in this kind of setting.

"You're very kind," he said. He was using his business voice, the voice he most often used on the phone and which seemed to go away any time I came close. Tonight, however, he must have thought the sharp edge in his words would be useful, because he sounded stiffer than ever. "And thank you for the invitation tonight. I am immensely grateful for the chance to honor Ms. Alvarez and her work." He nudged me ever so slightly, hinting that I should say something.

I took a shaky breath. "Thanks for putting this together, Mckenna," I said then winced when her expression turned sour. I'd forgotten how this selection of humans were against using first names. *Too late now.* "You have a lovely home."

"Yes," she replied. "I do. Just in here, Mr. Donovan. Miss Alvarez," she added, probably strictly for civility's sake.

Everyone in the drawing room glanced up as we came in from the hallway. I recognized most of them from the weeks I'd spent making small talk with them, but there were a few I didn't know. Four, specifically, though one of them had the same soft eyes as Matthew Davenport, as well as a similar chin and ears to Harris Davenport. Without even meeting her, I could guess she was Matthew's sister, whom I hadn't had a chance to meet yet. The man on her arm had to be her husband, Adam. Though he was talking to Davis McCreary, I had a feeling he would have much rather been at home than chatting with someone.

The other couple had what looked like an entourage surrounding them. I could name Matthew's cousin Catherine thanks to seeing her briefly on Brennon's phone while I was trying on dresses my first day in San Francisco, and she was even more beautiful in person. Everyone nearby seemed rapt in attention as she smiled her radiant smile and said something I couldn't hear. The guy next to her was just as beautiful, but he had a James Bond appeal to him, especially because he stood almost a foot taller than anyone else in the room and was probably mostly muscle. And I really couldn't understand why anyone would be trying so hard to talk to him when he scowled like he would attack the next person who tried to steal his attention away from the wine glass in his hand.

"The troops?" I guessed in a whisper and nodded toward the four of them. But before I got a chance to approach, I felt a claw-like hand on my shoulder.

"Dinner is served now that you're *finally* here," Mckenna said sharply, though according to the giant clock on the wall it was just striking seven now, so I was perfectly on time. "As the guest of honor, feel free to lead the way."

Lead the way in a house I've never been in? There were so many things I wanted to say to this woman, but I held my tongue. I could feel Colin's eyes on me and his fingers wrapping around mine, and the whole room waited for me to mess up because they probably knew I had no idea what I was doing.

"Actually, Mckenna," said a sweet voice, breaking the silence, "I was hoping to talk with Miss Alvarez for just a moment. If you don't mind me keeping her behind for a minute or two." Catherine Davenport glided forward from the back of the room and gave Mckenna a smile that could melt hearts, and she took my other hand as if we were the best of friends.

Mckenna seemed torn between the idea of humiliating me and pleasing Catherine, who apparently was some sort of celebrity to these people. What really made her decision for her, I was pretty sure, was Catherine's husband, who silently placed his wine glass on top of a rather tall bookshelf—where Mckenna would never be able to reach it—and approached as well, his jaw tight and his eyes full of irritation, as if he was daring Mckenna Foster to deny his wife, just to give him a chance to demolish something with his bare hands.

Mckenna took one look at his expression and paled a little. "Of course," she mumbled. "Mr. Donovan, let me show you the way." And she grabbed Colin's arm and practically tore him away from my hold, leaving me bare and exposed.

The rest of the guests followed her and Colin down the hall, all of them giving Catherine's man a large berth just in case, until it was just me and my four reinforcements. The very second we were alone, the air in the room suddenly seemed to get warmer, and I had a feeling it was because Catherine's giant relaxed and actually smiled, which changed his entire demeanor. So he wasn't entirely frightening after all.

"Uh, thanks?" I said, slightly tempted to sit down and let myself breathe again.

"I've never liked Mckenna Foster," said Matthew's sister. "She thinks she's so important."

"But her husband does all the work to keep her high in status," said Adam.

"That's Lanna Munroe," Catherine said, still holding my hand as if she knew how close I was to collapsing. "This monstrosity behind me is my husband, Seth Hastings."

"Hey," he complained, but he grinned at me.

"And that's Adam," she continued. "Not even Mckenna Foster can ignore the King of Art when he wants to attend something, but once upon a time she wanted Adam to marry her niece, so she's not fond of either of the Munroes."

I nodded, though I wasn't sure why Brennon would think Lanna and her husband would be the most qualified to help my situation. Maybe it was just how calming the two of them were. I'd barely heard them speak, but I could already tell they were pretty calm and even-keeled people, likely very much like the other Davenports who weren't keen on flaunting their money. Adam may have been called the King of Art, which I'd learned was his nickname after he became one of California's top art dealers alongside his now-retired father, but he certainly didn't act like a king.

Catherine and Seth, on the other hand, seemed perfectly content to let the world know how important they were, but I thought maybe that was why they were useful. Mckenna had to constantly make sure the world saw her value; these two probably didn't even have to try.

"Don't worry," Lanna told me with a gentle smile. "Mrs. Foster can try to tear you down as much as she wants, but if you're as likeable as Brennon tells us, she'll have a hard time turning everyone against you."

"Play to your strengths," Adam suggested and took his wife's hand, as if he could only go so long without touching her. "If you have something she envies, she won't be able to resist hoping she can exploit you for it."

I frowned. "And that's a good thing?" Besides, I wasn't sure what strengths I actually had. I could rally teenagers and climb mountains, but I didn't think any of my skills would benefit me in this elite world.

"We're here for moral and emotional support, if you need us," Catherine said. "But we should go find the dining room," she added, and the others nodded. She linked her arm with mine and led the way down the hall. "Word to the wise, try not to let her sink those claws of hers too deep into Colin Donovan unless you want to lose him. That niece of hers is still single, and Donovan's the hottest item on the shelf right now."

Was he? Sure, whenever we went somewhere together, he did draw a lot of gazes, but I had met plenty of men who were both rich and single. What was it about Colin that made him such a desirable match?

Everything, I thought to myself. *Everything about Colin makes him worth pursuing.*

When we reached the dining room, the five empty seats were all spread out individually across the table. Apparently Mckenna had decided to be strategic and use name cards. I was worried for a moment I would be stuck between Jocelyn Montague, who was so old she could barely hear anything anyone said, and Frank Lee, who in my limited experience only knew how to talk about insurance policies, while Colin was clear on the other end of the table next to Mckenna.

But Catherine, who still held to my arm, nudged me toward her husband, Seth, who took me without question. He led me around the table and to the seat on Colin's other side, which was currently occupied by the annoying Chandler Wixcomb.

Seth coughed once, and then Chandler was on his feet.

"So sorry," the horse-like man mumbled and was out of his chair so quickly that he nearly knocked it backwards into us. Seth caught it, though, and once Chandler had taken my assigned seat, he gently directed me into the chair.

My face was on fire, like it always was when I came to these things, and I refused to look at Mckenna because I knew she would be livid. So instead, I stared at my empty china plate and waited for Seth to use some more strategic glares to rearrange the seating and let the four of them all sit together near the other end of the huge mahogany table. I was positive that if Mckenna wasn't so afraid of Seth and enamored of Catherine, she wouldn't have been so compliant with the family's antics.

And to my horror, tears threatened to build in my eyes.

I didn't want my life to be like this. Letting other people fight battles for me, battles I didn't even need to have in the first place, made me feel like a kid again, like I was sitting in a hospital room waiting for my mom to take her last breath because there was nothing I could do to help her. Was this really what a life in this world would always be like? I knew I didn't belong, so I didn't need people like Mckenna Foster to ostracize me even more and make me realize more than ever that I had no family here. No home. If all that waited for me in this life, given to me by a grandmother I didn't know, was endless events like this with people who didn't care about me outside of my relation to someone they revered, why would I even stay?

A warm hand grabbed mine, and I looked at Colin next to me. No matter how much I told myself it couldn't be true, I could have sworn the emotion in his gaze was saying only one thing: *Stay.*

Overall, dinner could have been worse. Most of the conversation around the table was centered around my grandmother, since the night was meant to honor her legacy, and pretty much everyone in attendance had spoken to me enough over the last few weeks to know I hadn't even met her, so they didn't try to include me this time unless it was to compliment her and her work. The Davenports gave me occasional smiles, which really helped keep me from fading into the back of my chair and thinking no one actually wanted me there. Most important, though, was Colin, who never once let go of my hand beneath the table.

I hadn't noticed until then how convenient it was that he was left-handed, otherwise the constant contact would have been a lot more difficult.

Mckenna Foster pretty much ignored me. She ignored everyone, actually, and spoke only to Colin. To his credit, Colin reverted to his business persona and was all sharp and emotionless with her. He gave short answers to her questions and focused mainly on his food, which he described as "decent" when she asked him about it. I had to cough into my napkin to keep myself from laughing when I heard him.

I hardly talked to anyone, though I was okay with that. There was only so much small talk I could use, and I'd used it all up with most of the people around the table with me. I mainly just watched and listened while I nibbled at my food, which was actually pretty spectacular. And out of everyone at that dinner table, it was the man on Mckenna's other side that most intrigued me.

John Foster hadn't said a word all evening. It seemed he was content to let his wife do the talking and the hosting, but the longer I watched him, the more I wondered if he was simply used to being ignored. Being married to a woman like Mckenna couldn't have been easy, but even without hearing him talk, I could tell he genuinely loved her, given the way he sent soft smiles her way. That was as surprising as the fact that she could so easily ignore him.

I'd seen his type in girls at camp all the time, the ones who came from more difficult backgrounds and who had learned that the easiest way to exist was to keep quiet and roll with the punches. He was clearly a successful man, if Adam was to be believed about him being the breadwinner out of the two of them, but that didn't seem to be something he considered an accomplishment. Otherwise, he would stand tall next to his wife and not stay in the shadows.

"You have a wonderful home, Mr. Foster," I said just as the caterers were bringing in a dessert that looked like an upside-down pudding with gold flakes on top.

It took him an incredibly long time to realize I'd said *Mr.* instead of *Mrs.*, and even then he looked up from his plate with confusion. When he caught me looking at him, he coughed and muttered, "Thank you," before glancing at his wife, who was watching me with narrowed eyes.

That only made me want to talk to the guy even more. "I haven't had the pleasure of talking to you yet," I continued. "What is it you do for work?"

Yet again he glanced at his wife, but he seemed almost excited to know someone actually wanted to know about him. However, just as he opened his mouth, his piece of work wife butted in and said, "He's an executive. A very successful one."

I felt Colin's hand tighten around mine, but I told myself I had to ignore him for the time being. This was a battle I could fight myself. I kept my gaze on Mr. Foster, making sure he could see that I was waiting for his own response. I even smiled a little, and his cheeks pinked a bit as if he'd rarely received a kind gesture.

"I head one of Ms. Alvarez's charities, actually," he said quietly. "One of your charities now, I suppose."

I sat up a little straighter. I'd been visiting the many charities my grandmother had started, and while I hadn't been to all of them, I was surprised I hadn't met him before now. Had he always been present and simply shadowed by his wife? "Really?" I asked. "Which one? What does the charity do?"

"We supply funding to several programs around the Bay Area," he replied, and he'd gotten loud enough that the people nearest us had started listening with interest. Apparently they hadn't heard him speak much in the past. "For children with…less fortunate upbringings."

Now *that* was something I understood and could get behind. "Which programs?" I asked. "Any I might have heard of?"

"There are quite a few," he said, "but our largest donations go to the Hargrave School. It's a——"

"I know exactly what the Hargrave School is," I said, maybe a little too excitedly because the whole table glanced my way. Still, this was the first time I could actually contribute to a conversation, and I was not about to let that opportunity pass. "Several of my girls come from that school."

Foster furrowed his brow. "Uh, your girls?"

Oh right. No one had bothered to learn anything about me, so no one knew about Camp Rockwood. "I help run a summer camp," I explained. "Hargrave sends most of their girls to us every summer to give the program a bit of a break, and they're some of the sweetest girls I've ever met."

"A summer camp," Mckenna scoffed.

Mr. Foster, however, simply frowned. "I find that surprising," he said. "Hargrave is one of our more difficult programs, with some of the most troubled girls. We've had a hard time keeping the place staffed, even with the benefits the Alvarez Trust can offer."

That honestly wasn't surprising. "Camp is a place where they can be themselves without judgment," I explained. "They can feel like they're normal girls, which is harder to achieve when they're all together like that. What sort of staff do you generally hire?"

Foster puffed out his chest a bit. "I assure you, Miss Alvarez, that we hire only the most qualified of teachers, with the highest level of training."

"Well there's your problem."

"Excuse me?"

Mckenna put her hand on her husband's arm. "John, maybe you shouldn't have this discussion over dinner."

I smiled, and I was enjoying my position more than I should have. But John Foster was too intrigued by my argument to pay any attention to his wife. "Mr. Foster," I said, "those girls don't need to be treated like special cases who need highly trained teachers who think they know what's best for them. They need people who understand what it's like to grow up with single parents or no parents. People who know what it's like to live poor and underprivileged."

Though he lifted his eyebrows, likely intrigued, he sent another glance to his wife and said, "I don't see how that—"

"Let me fill the open staff positions," I said. "Give my people three months, and if they don't make a difference, you can find some more of those fancy specialists and replace them. At this point, what can you lose?"

Also at that point, if I had decided not to stay, which was still up for debate, I wouldn't be here to stop him from replacing them any-way.

Foster pursed his lips, still a little unsure, and I knew that whatever he decided, it would probably change the way the rest of the room saw me. So far I'd mostly just been an observer, trying to learn as much as I could about the way my grandmother had run things. This was my first step into actually taking charge, and for the first time I felt like I was taking a step in the right direction. I'd never liked standing still in the background.

"Technically," I added, "I'm not sure you have a choice. I could use that money somewhere else." And while I wasn't entirely sure if that was true, since Maria's charities were part of the stipulation of me even touching her money, I needed Foster to know this was important. So I stood my ground.

Mr. Foster took a deep breath, but for once his eyes didn't stray to his wife. He seemed just as ready to stand his ground as I was. "I think that is a solid idea, Miss Alvarez. Do you think you could stop by our offices in the morning to discuss this further?"

I couldn't stop myself from grinning. "Absolutely. I can see us doing a lot of work together, Mr. Foster."

He smiled, and in that moment he looked nothing like his wife, who was scowling at me as if I'd just suggested I meet up with her husband for a romantic liaison. He looked like the sort of person I actually wanted to run a charity, unlike most of the other people I'd met over the last several weeks. "I look forward to it," he said.

A moment later, conversation started back up among the other guests, and the dinner returned to its usual simplicity. I sat there in my chair feeling drained but triumphant, and I couldn't even bring myself to taste the ridiculously expensive dessert sitting in front of me. Yes, I had just experienced a win. But now I had to find teachers willing to work with troubled teens, and that wouldn't exactly be easy. It took a special kind of person to have the patience to help those girls who felt like they didn't deserve anything good in their lives. No matter how much money I could throw into the project, I worried it wouldn't be enough to attract the people who were probably already working hard in a similar place somewhere else.

"You," said a gentle voice in my ear, "were amazing."

I took a deep breath that was filled mainly with Colin's cologne, and I relaxed a little. "Was I?" I whispered back. "Thanks."

"You're also cutting off the circulation in my hand."

"Oh!" I released his fingers, which I'd apparently been crushing that whole time because my own were aching from the effort. "Sorry."

But though he stretched his fingers out with relief, he simply moved his hand to just above my knee and gave me a small smile. "It's nice to see some of the old Beck coming back," he said. "The one who wasn't afraid of a challenge. You've got this."

I really wanted to believe him, but I knew that no matter how many people I had on my side, there was no way I would have been able to get this far without him. And I had no idea how to tell him that. I valued his friendship more than I valued anything else in my life.

CHAPTER THIRTEEN

I enjoyed Halloween for the most part, but the wealthy world took it to the extreme. I had always imagined this sort of group to be the ones giving out king-size candy bars to the kids trick-or-treating, but I had learned pretty early in October that they didn't do trick-or-treaters. They didn't decorate their houses with cobwebs and skeletons. They didn't put on funny costumes and bob for apples.

No, they threw masquerades.

"It's the biggest night of the year," John Foster muttered to me as we sat in our weekly board meeting the week before Halloween.

Janice Achebe, our CFO, was up there spouting off facts about donation projections or something along those lines, and though I always tried to pay attention to her whenever she spoke, I had started doodling on my agenda. She generally knew what she was talking about and did her job well, so I wasn't too worried about listening to what she said. If it concerned me, she would address me directly.

I leaned a little closer to John and made sure no one else realized I was having a chat instead of taking notes like I probably should have been. "So what kind of masquerade are we talking here?" I asked him. The only thing I could picture was that one scene in *The Phantom of the Opera*, and suddenly I was envisioning Harold Watson, who sat across from me, in a cape and a half-mask to hide at least one of his jowls.

"The usual kind," John whispered back, which didn't help me at all. "Not to worry, Miss Alvarez. With an event this important, and you as the face of the Alvarez Trust, we won't leave anything up to chance."

In other words, he would hire someone to choose my outfit and do my hair so I didn't embarrass anyone. I'd gotten better at looking the part on my own, but my choice to wear my hair in a braid this morning, since I had been up too late at an event last night and had slept in, probably hadn't done me any favors.

"Who's invited to this one?" I asked next, though I was already slipping my phone out of my purse and typing a text:

You're coming to a masquerade ball with me.

John didn't answer, and he looked up instead because Janice had sat down and opened the floor up to the Trust's chief PR guy, Dustin Hewlett.

"We all know what happened at last year's masquerade," he said first, and the rest of the board chuckled. I would have to ask someone the story later. "But we're anticipating record attendance to this year's event. Ticket sales are higher than ever, and I'm sure many of our less prolific attendees are eager to meet Miss Alvarez."

I swallowed, though it did nothing to help the sudden buildup of nerves. I hated when the entire board looked at me, especially when it seemed like they expected me to say something. What did Colin say to do when I was at a loss for words? Smile and agree. "I'm looking forward to meeting them too," I said.

My phone buzzed, and I glanced down at Colin's texted reply: *I am, am I? The Halloween one?*

I quickly typed back a "yes" then returned my attention to the board, who were watching me with mixed expressions. Most of them seemed to like me for the most part, but a couple of them still weren't sure what my grandmother had been thinking when she passed operations over to me.

"That was a patron," I explained before Mr. Watson started judging me too harshly. "He was asking about the masquerade."

Dustin raised an eyebrow, probably because it seemed unlikely anyone would be asking me of all people for information. And though he was one of the ones who seemed to like me, he couldn't hold back his question: "Which patron?" To his credit, he did offer me an apologetic smile as soon as he said it.

"Colin Donovan," I said. Thank goodness he was one of them.

"Oh, will Mr. Donovan be attending this year?" Janice asked. "We missed him last October."

My phone buzzed again, and I deflated a bit when I read the text.

Macy will kill me if I miss trick-or-treating, Colin said. Thankfully, he added a second text before I could get too disappointed: *So I'll have to come a little late.*

"I think he is," I said with a small sigh of relief. "Sorry, I didn't mean to distract you, Dustin."

As Dustin jumped into the plan for last-minute promotions for the gala, I sat back in my chair and tried not to smile too wide. With an event this big, I badly needed Colin there next to me. It wasn't like we spent tons of time together, what with all the work I was doing with the Trust and Colin getting close to releasing a new app, but our small moments together reminded me, every time, how comfortable I could be when he was around, even when surrounded by the judgments of the elites I was supposed to be a part of. Colin had been my friend before I got suddenly rich, and nothing had changed since. Pretty much everyone else I knew (outside of the Davenport family, maybe) was only nice to me because of what my abuela had left me.

By the time the meeting ended twenty minutes later, John Foster had already arranged half a dozen appointments for me, with seamstresses and stylists and for some reason a nutritionist. Though it was only Tuesday, I knew the week was going to fly by and suddenly it would be Saturday. And while I was excited for a definite chance to see Colin, I wished I didn't have to wait until Halloween. I didn't spend nearly enough time with my friend, and it was starting to make me realize just how much I liked having him around.

And it was a whole lot more than was good for me.

I knew how to keep eighty preteen girls organized and happy, and I'd thought that was quite the accomplishment. Clearly, children were a whole lot easier to handle than a city's worth of the rich and famous, because the latter required the absolute best in all things and couldn't be placated by a candy bar.

When I arrived at the venue after being primped, polished, and altogether peacocked, I realized John Foster had been right to make sure I got the works when it came to a makeover. I would have assumed my driver would bring me to the event pretty early so I could get situated before the event began, but as I stepped onto a legitimate red carpet and the cameras started flashing, I quickly realized this thing was a bigger deal than I'd expected.

Reporters shouted questions at me while photographers called my name, and I forced myself to smile because that was what I was supposed to do. Smile and nod and act like I was meant to be here. Had they done this with my grandmother too? If I did decide to stay in the city, would there ever be a chance I could simply stay behind the scenes? Charity work should have been about the work, not the publicity, but the longer I was here, the harder it was to think I was actually making a difference.

"Can you tell us about the changes you made to the Hargrave School?" A voice cut through the rest as I made my way up the carpet, and I paused. The woman looked less pushy than the others, and she'd picked a topic I actually cared about over what shoes I was wearing.

So I gave her a real smile and said, "I'm trying to help those girls feel like they have a chance to make something of themselves," I said.

The reporter lifted an eyebrow, while everyone around her glared at her for getting a comment out of me. "And why this school? Why these girls?"

I shrugged. "Why not? They deserve love and attention as much as anyone." And while I wished I could say more, I could see John Foster up ahead, gesturing for me to continue inside. Probably before I said something I shouldn't.

But as I took a step, the reporter asked one more question: "Do you plan to make similar changes elsewhere?" she asked.

I paused. I would have loved nothing more than to take over the hiring for every low-income area and provide what orphaned and foster kids needed to be successful in life. But mostly I was just the face of the company and had no real power. I was pretty sure I could take the power if I wanted it—the Alvarez Trust was mine, after all—but was I really qualified?

"I hope so," I said, and then I picked up my giant skirts and hurried up the path to join John.

"Take a deep breath, Miss Alvarez," he said as two masked men pulled open the doors in front of us.

I was about to ask why, but my question died on my tongue.

The place was breathtaking. Literally. I gasped as I took my first look of what seemed to be another world, and I couldn't seem to find my breath again as I took it all in. I felt like I'd stumbled onto an old-time movie set where all the characters were royalty and everything was made of gold and electricity was still a thing because the whole giant room was so lit up by chandeliers and lights on strings that it looked like midday in the heat of summer. Everything sparkled. Everything shone. And I was so overwhelmed by the whole of it that I couldn't even focus on the details.

"It's beautiful," I said in a whisper.

"Like I said," Mr. Foster replied. "The biggest night of the year."

There were already a few dozen people milling about while an actual orchestra played in the corner, and each guest seemed more elaborately dressed than the last. They wore gowns so large they bumped into each other and suits so black and shiny that they seemed to glow, and each and every person in the room wore a mask, many of them far more intricate than I could have imagined. Golds and silvers and blues and burgundies and so many jewels that I was half-tempted to think they might actually be real gemstones.

The weird part was none of them looked happy. True, I couldn't see the top halves of most of their faces—some even wore full masks—but pretty much everyone seemed to scowl as if none of the majesty around them could possibly be good enough. They could dress me up like them all they wanted, but I was pretty sure I would never understand this world or the people who lived in it.

John took my arm and leaned close to me so I could hear him over the growing chatter of the gathering crowd. "It's ten minutes to eight," he told me. "Are you ready for your speech?"

I swallowed but nodded. I had only found out about the speech yesterday, when Dustin called me to ask how long it would be, but I figured I had been to enough of these to know what to say. Welcome everyone, thank them for their donations, tell them to have fun. If I couldn't manage this tiny little thing, what good was I? As long as I didn't forget what I was saying halfway through, it was no different from singing the National Anthem for my school. In fact, it was probably even easier, since none of these people sang so all they did was talk. I could talk.

No problem.

"What's important is the donations," John said next, which probably meant he didn't have much faith in me.

"I thought it was important to have fun," I mumbled. That was what I would tell my girls if this were a camp thing, though we'd never done anything at camp that made me nervous, and I'd definitely never worn anything this uncomfortable.

John gave my arm a squeeze, and then he spotted his wife stepping in through the doors and hurried off to greet her. She looked just as miserable as the rest of them, even if she was flawlessly beautiful. Mckenna Foster would likely never be happy.

A gentle cough behind me made me turn, and I smiled when I recognized Harris Davenport. Abuela's lawyer had chosen to go without a mask, and though the woman on his arm seemed exactly the sort to care that her husband wasn't following protocol, I had a feeling Mr. Davenport wasn't as easily persuaded by his wife as John Foster was.

"Miss Alvarez," he greeted. "Allow me to introduce my wife, Lyra."

She looked just like Lanna Munroe, blonde and beautiful, but there was an impishness to her expression that told me she wasn't nearly as gentle as her daughter. "Miss Alvarez," she cooed and took my hand. "What a pleasure."

And while I wanted to thank Mr. Davenport for having guided me just enough to get my foot in the door of this life, the door to the venue was slightly more interesting and pulled my full attention away.

Colin was sneaking in behind a couple in black and white-checkered clothing, dressed from head to toe as a pirate.

Not just any pirate, though. He was a full-blown Jack Sparrow-like pirate, down to a days-old beard and a sword—a real sword, I was pretty sure—at his hip and so many little details that I almost couldn't tell it was him because the whole outfit looked so authentic. And while

I was somewhat convinced no one would be able to recognize me after John's little minions dressed me up, Colin spotted me from a distance and gave me a smile before he navigated his way through the crowd.

"Hey, Beck," he said when he arrived. "You look amazing."

He said it so lightly, so easily, and I wished I could do the same when I opened my mouth and said, "You're a pirate."

He glanced down as if he'd forgotten. "Right."

"I did tell you this was a masquerade, not a costume party, didn't I?" Though I was pretty sure they were almost the same thing…

Laughing a little, Colin lifted a garment bag he was holding, which I hadn't noticed because the rest of him was so distracting. "I could have changed in the car," he explained, "but honestly, with this crowd, I'd feel less judged showing up as a pirate than having a button done wrong."

I couldn't stop staring at him, and it was becoming a bit distracting. His white shirt wasn't fully buttoned, and I was seeing a whole lot more of Colin than I'd seen before. "Uh." I coughed. "Macy's idea?" I guessed.

He grinned. "She loves Halloween. She always gets to choose the costumes, and she's pretty particular about the details."

"I wish I could have come trick-or-treating with you guys," I said.

"I'm going to go change," he replied and briefly touched my elbow before he slipped away through the crowd.

I tried not to let myself get too disappointed. I hadn't seen Macy since being in San Francisco, and for a while I figured that was because we were both so busy. But lately, it seemed like any time I brought up the idea of hanging out with her too, Colin managed to change the subject or disappear.

As soon as Colin was gone, I turned back to the Davenports because I wasn't entirely sure what to do with myself. Until it was time to give my little speech, I was probably supposed to mingle, but I highly doubted any of these attendees wanted to talk to the outsider who had infiltrated their favorite charity group.

Thank goodness for Mr. Davenport, who must have sensed how lost I was as he said, "How are you settling in, Miss Alvarez?"

Before I could answer that question, his wife took me by the hand as if we were the dearest of friends. "How long have you known Colin Donovan?" she said in a mock whisper that was plenty loud for anyone around us to hear.

I really didn't want to talk about Colin, not with the woman who supposedly had been trying to get in contact with him for a long time, but I knew better than to be rude to someone as high up the social ladder as Lyra Davenport. "We met a few months ago," I said and put on a smile. "He's been a lot of help while I've been figuring all of this out."

Her smile wide and fake, Lyra looked like a plastic version of her daughter as she took me in. "It's a pity I don't have any more daughters to throw at him, but at least my Lanna made a more than worthy match."

I hadn't seen Lanna or her husband since that dinner party at the Fosters', but they did seem happy together. I doubted that was what she meant, though. More likely she was referring to Adam Munroe's booming art trade business. Did this woman know anything outside of the surface level?

"I'm not sure Colin is looking for a wife," I said and tried not to grimace because that was probably true. How could anyone replace Jada?

"I'm not sure he would let you choose one for him if he was," Mr. Davenport muttered under his breath. Perhaps he was more like his son, Matthew, than I'd realized, and I suddenly liked him more than before.

Lyra waved both comments away as if she didn't have a care in the world. "Oh, *everyone* is looking for a partner, whether they know it or not," she said. "What about you, Miss Alvarez? Has anyone struck your fancy since coming here to San Francisco?" Perhaps it was my imagination, but her blue eyes seemed to flicker to the staircase where Colin had disappeared. "I hear there are quite a few dashing young men out there in the regular world."

"Lyra," said her husband with a frown.

She waved that admonition away as well. "Yes, I suppose you're technically one of us now," she said. "Though perhaps not for long?"

I stared at Mr. Davenport, trying to figure out how much he had told his wife about me. I would have thought there would be some sort of client confidentiality privilege, particularly in a case like this. The look he returned, though, was genuinely innocent and almost sympathetic, and that worried me more than the possibility of a chatty lawyer. How many people were discussing me and how long I would be able to last in this world?

What, had someone set up a betting pool?

"Miss Alvarez?" said John Foster behind me at the same time the enormous clock on one end of the ballroom struck eight. I had to stop worrying about what people were saying behind my back.

It was speech time.

Though the music stopped when I stepped up to the microphone in front of the orchestra, the chatter around the room didn't dim even a little. I had to cough into the mic, which sounded ridiculous, and even then I barely caught anyone's attention. I was tempted to start singing, just because I knew that would insult their sensibilities enough to get them to look outside themselves for one moment, but a ridiculously loud whistle broke through the buzz of conversation. I peered through the spotlights in search of who I had on my team, and even though I couldn't see his face, I was pretty sure the man towering over the rest of the crowd was Catherine's husband, Seth. I was even more positive when he gave me a thumbs up.

"Good evening," I said into the mic, and heads swiveled in my direction.

So many heads.

Relax, Beck. They're not going to eat you.

I took a deep breath. *Welcome* was done. Now for the *thank you.* Then to the *have fun* part. Easy. "On behalf of the Alvarez Trust, I want to thank each of you for coming out tonight with your wonderful donations. It is people like you who help us make the world a better place, and all of us here at Alvarez recognize your generosity. I…"

My words got lost on my tongue because I had looked up when I caught movement at the far end of the ballroom, where a set of stairs came down from the upper level of the venue. And though he wasn't exactly close by, the sight of Colin Donovan left me suddenly breath-less. The pirate had become a mask like everyone else, but I was pretty positive no one wore a black cape like Colin wore it. No one could have a simple black mask like him and look like he was the most important man in the room. No one could smile at me and make me feel like the rest of the world disappeared.

Not like he could.

It all came crashing back when John Foster coughed right in front of me.

"Have a wonderful time tonight," I stammered, and I knew I wasn't going to be capable of anything beyond that. When I nearly tripped stepping down from the platform where the orchestra sat, I grabbed John's arm and said, "Please tell me that's all I have to do tonight."

Though he was clearly confused, he nodded. "I mean, it would be best if you stayed for the full event, but there aren't any other duties for you to perform."

No wonder people were trying to decide when I would crack and run away from this life.

"Good," I breathed at the same time Colin appeared from the crowd.

He'd always been handsome, but this was something else. This was somehow a step above the sharp and pristine businessman I knew he was.

"You clean up nice," I managed to say when he came up to my side and slipped his hand into mine. "Though I'm not sure how I feel about the beard."

Some men really worked facial hair. Some didn't. And though Colin looked just as distinguished as always, he didn't look like himself.

He quickly shook John's hand and muttered a cold greeting to Mckenna, who had been actively pretending I wasn't even here, and then he grinned at me as if no one else existed in the room. "Like I said, Macy is a stickler about details. It'll be gone in the morning. Do you dance?"

I stared at him. "Do I what?"

"Dance."

"No."

"I bet you do." And before I could argue, he pulled me into the crowd, which had slowly started to shift and part for the few people who had also had the idea to dance.

For a man who was afraid of ziplines and good at overturning canoes, Colin was remarkably smooth. He slid me into position without ever letting go of my hand and began to waltz. Or whatever it was we were doing… And even if I had no idea how to dance like this, it didn't matter, because Colin knew how to lead. Every little touch and movement told me exactly what to do to stay in sync with him.

As if he knew how surprised I was, he grinned again. "I told you I went to a classy school, right?"

"I didn't think ballroom was a common thing anymore," I replied.

"It is when your parents spend their lives going to things like this." He spun me under his arm then deftly caught me, though he held me a whole lot closer than he had a moment ago. "You really do look amazing," he said into my ear.

A shiver ran through me, which made no sense because I could feel his warmth through his tux. Or maybe the whole room was warm. "I look ridiculous," I replied. "I'm not sure I'll ever get used to these things."

"If it's any consolation," he said as we spun together, "I think you're doing great."

It was a little hard to concentrate with his cologne filling my nose and his face so close to mine, but I tried to stay focused. "You've really only seen how good I am at eating," I said. "For all you know, I could be terrible at this whole charity thing and I'm only meant for counseling girls in a summer camp."

As soon as I said that out loud, it seemed to settle heavy in the pit of my stomach. What if that was actually true?

Catching onto my sudden anxiety, Colin paused our dancing and looked down at me with a slight frown. Even with the mask covering a third of his face, I could see every bit of emotion in his eyes. It was so different from his expressionless business face that I was riveted. He never seemed to use that mask with me anymore, and I very much liked that about him.

He let me see everything about him.

"Don't sell yourself short," he said softly, leaning even closer, though I hadn't thought that was possible. "I could name more people who have mentioned how much you've added to the Alvarez Trust than I could count who have complained. And believe me, people have an annoying habit of talking to me, so I've heard a lot."

He brushed his thumb across my cheek before shifting us back into the dance as if he hadn't just said something absolutely bolstering.

I felt so safe inside his hold, and he drowned out the rest of the ballroom, so it was just me and him. Resting my head against his chest, I closed my eyes and let him lead me in a gentle sway that made me feel like I was floating.

"Don't listen to those who aren't confident enough in themselves to give you a chance," he whispered.

And because it was Colin, I knew I should listen to him.

We danced together most of the night. Or wandered the top level where it was slightly cooler. Or sat on the steps and talked while we watched the guests get more and more drunk and more and more eager to pretend they were people they weren't. Eventually, we both lost our masks, and though I couldn't speak for him, it was so much easier to be myself instead of something mysterious. Colin always made it easy.

He made it easy to ignore the judgments of everyone around me and focus only on the one who mattered.

And when the night ended, it was hard to say goodnight as he helped me into my car and sent me home. I didn't want the night to end, because I was pretty sure something had changed between us. Something significant, though I couldn't quite place what it was. Outside of getting a little bit closer than he had in the past, Colin hadn't acted any differently than usual. Maybe, for him, our relationship was exactly the same.

But I knew it wasn't for me.

I was pretty sure I was falling in love with the man and had been for a long time.

That was going to be a problem.

Dear Dalia,

How has it already been more than two months since I came to San Francisco? I feel like I only just got here, but at the same time I feel like I haven't even had a chance to sit down and have a moment to myself. I don't know how Abuela did it all. There's always events and parties and board meetings and planning committees. It seems like every moment of the day someone needs my attention, and half the time I don't even know what they're talking about. I just took Colin's advice, and I've been smiling and nodding pretty much from day one.

At least the Hargrave School seems to be doing well. The two teachers I hired have had a lot of breakthroughs with some of the girls, and John is considering letting me bring on a couple more after the end of the semester, which is good because I had so many applicants that I could barely choose those first two! There are a lot of people in this city who want to do some good. It was also so nice to see some of my girls outside of camp, and they practically flipped out when I went to the school the first time. Part of me wonders if they've been behaving better because they know I'm involved, but that's probably just ego talking.

But if it isn't, and they're only good for me, what'll happen if I decide not to stay? I miss having my own schedule and being able to do things my way, and the longer I'm here, the more I miss my life.

But I'm really starting to love this new life too. There are parts of it that make me feel like I'm a part of something bigger than the camp will ever be, and there's one particular reason for me to want to stay. I'm just not sure he knows it.

I wish I knew what to do. I wish you could give me advice like you used to. I wish life were easy and I only had one good path to follow. I wish Abuela had brought me into all of this before she died so she could have shown me the ropes.

I wish you were still here.

Love,
   Beck

P.S. I wore a dress the other day because I wanted to, not because I had to. What is wrong with me?

CHAPTER FOURTEEN

I'd never been to Colin's office. It wasn't because he hadn't wanted me to, but I was generally so busy—and so was he—that we just met up somewhere in the middle most of the time. But for the first night in weeks, I didn't have an event or a meeting, and Colin had asked me to come meet him so he could take me somewhere. He wouldn't tell me where and said he wanted it to be a surprise.

I'd spent the whole day freaking out about what that might mean, and I had called up Brennon when he was on his lunch break to help calm me down.

"I know Colin," he'd told me. "Known him for years. He's not the sort to do anything crazy or out of the ordinary, so whatever you're thinking, it's probably not it. What did he tell you to wear?"

"Casual."

"See? Nothing to worry about," he'd said, and he sounded so convinced that I believed him.

But now that I was stepping through the doors of the rather large building where his company headquarters were, I was starting to sink back into freak-out. Brennon was right about Colin not being the sort to do anything crazy, but he'd never surprised me with anything before. It was one of the things I loved about him, the way he was always up front and direct about everything.

Well, almost everything.

I had no idea what his feelings for me were, and I wasn't sure if I would ever know.

"Excuse me," I said to the security guard who sat behind the desk in the lobby. "Could you tell me how to get to JayTech?"

He barely glanced away from his computer. "Ninth floor," he grunted.

"Uh, thanks." I followed his pointed finger to the elevators, of which there were many, and pushed the up button. Almost immediately, the door to my right opened to let me in, and I stepped inside, pushed the number nine, and told myself that I didn't need to be shaking as much as I was. Everything was fine, and Colin wasn't going to do anything crazy, and I was supposed to enjoy this night off I had. Colin had seemed excited on the phone when he realized I was free, and that should have been enough to keep me from freaking out.

I figured, since it was after six, most people would be out of the office by now, but when the elevator doors opened onto the ninth floor, several people rushed past me all at once, seemingly in different directions as if there was some sort of disaster they were trying to avert. They had a sort of rhythm, I realized a moment later, and were able to avoid colliding with each other as if they'd had a lot of practice. They twisted and spun as they flew across the open office space, flitting from desk to desk and shouting things to each other as they typed. The weirdest part was they all seemed to be enjoying the chaos. One girl grinned as she dumped an enormous stack of binders on another guy's desk, and a couple of men were tossing a baseball back and forth across the room as they shouted what seemed like random phrases at each other until, quite suddenly, one of them caught the ball and said, "That's it!" then started furiously typing away at his computer.

None of it felt like the Colin I knew, and for a moment I was pretty sure I'd ended up in the wrong office.

But then someone called my name, and I looked over to see Colin's assistant, Ramesh, navigating his way from the back of the office. I'd met him in passing a few times, and I was glad to see a familiar face amidst the chaos.

"Colin's just finishing up a phone call," he told me when he'd reached the elevators where I still stood. "I keep telling him he either needs to hire a receptionist or move my desk closer to the doors, but he won't do either. I think he likes to make me run, and he can't shout at me from far away. This way."

I stuck as close to him as I could. I'd gotten used to the slow and lazy way of the rich world, and it was nice to be back in an environment that reminded me of camp. Still, I was a bit out of practice.

"Is it always this chaotic?" I asked.

Ramesh ducked to avoid the baseball, which had started flying again. "Believe it or not, this is pretty tame compared to most days." When we reached the glass walls that separated Colin's office from the rest of the floor, he knocked sharply.

Colin, who was standing next to his desk with his shirt sleeves rolled up to his elbows and his tie loose, glanced up and flashed me a smile when he caught my eye. He said something, most likely to the speaker-phone on his desk, and then he waved me inside.

I glanced at Ramesh just in case I misinterpreted, and he smiled and opened the door for me.

Colin held up a finger as I approached then said to the phone, "I get what you're saying, Pete, but I don't think you're getting what I'm saying. I needed that done yesterday." He reached out his hand and gave mine a squeeze, but he kept his focus mainly on the phone call.

"We're doing the best we can," the guy on the other end said. "But I don't think you realize—"

"I've had my people working nonstop on this for weeks, Pete," Colin replied. "You took a four-day vacation to the Bahamas last week." He was using his business voice, and if I'd been on the other end of that conversation, I would have been sweating like a pig. Colin Donovan, as I'd learned the first day I met him, was not someone to cross. "Now," he continued, "if I were confident enough to leave a project this big, I would hope I was confident enough that it would also get done on time."

I moved to the wall of windows behind his desk and looked out over the city's twinkling lights. Now that November was here, it got dark much earlier than I liked, and I always felt like my days disappeared too fast. But if I had a view like this, instead of constantly having to travel back and forth across the city, I didn't think I would mind it as much.

Pete was mumbling some sort of excuse, but Colin wasn't about to take it. "You have until six a.m., Pete," he said. "Otherwise, our contract with you is done."

"But you can't—"

Colin hung up before Pete could argue, and then he let out a sigh before he turned to me. "Hi," he said, his voice suddenly so much gentler.

I grinned. "I feel bad for Pete."

"I should have fired Pete a year ago."

"Poor Pete."

"Are you going to stay over there, or are you going to come closer so I can greet you properly?"

That question surprised me, and I felt my stomach do a little flip like it always seemed to whenever Colin did something out of the ordinary. *Brennon, you liar.* I kept my feet planted where they were, curious to see what he would do.

"I'm admiring your view," I said as if that were a perfectly valid reason not to take the few steps it would take to bring myself to his side.

Colin clenched his jaw a bit. "I can see that." There was an intensity to him, both in his words and in his eyes that were so fixed on me it was making my head start to spin.

"You could always come over here and enjoy it with me," I replied with a smile. "It really is a spectacular view." And as soon as I said that, I caught a flash of fear in his expression, and I had a sudden recollection of him standing on a zipline platform, clearly afraid for his life. How had I forgotten Colin Donovan was afraid of heights?

"It makes more sense for you to come over here," he said.

I looked down at the street below, which really was a considerable distance down there. If I didn't have a window there, I'd be afraid as well. But I leaned my shoulder against the glass and said, "I can almost see the—"

Colin grabbed my hand, pulling me away from the window and into his arms at a safe distance from the windows. "Isn't this better?" he asked as he looked down at me. His eyes slid to my mouth.

I couldn't seem to find my words. Or my breath. Colin held my hand and wrapped the other around my waist, and I was pressed up against him with only a few inches between our faces. This couldn't possibly be how friends greeted each other, could it?

"Hi," he said again.

"Hi," I said back.

"It's almost six forty-five," Ramesh said in the doorway.

And while I was tempted to throw something at the assistant, Colin just laughed a little and touched his forehead to mine before he pulled away. "Time for us to go," he said and caught the suit jacket Ramesh tossed to him. "Ram, is the car ready?"

"When you are, boss."

"Great." He reached out, and I took his hand with only a minor bit of hesitation.

Brennon had said I didn't need to worry about whatever Colin had planned for tonight, but he was already acting strange, particularly because I was convinced he had been about to kiss me. Outside of our brief moment in his friend's restaurant, the last time he'd gotten that close was back at camp, and that hadn't ended well for anyone. So I really didn't expect it to happen again.

As much as I wanted it to.

But, as always, I fell into easy step beside him. This was how we were, and no matter how much I wanted more than that, I couldn't complain about what I did have.

"Where exactly are we going?" I asked as we navigated the chaos of his office, avoiding someone on a scooter of all things and that ever-flying baseball. "And I feel underdressed," I added when we stepped into the elevator. Though he often wore a suit like he was now, I was generally in more professional wear because I only got to see him in between charity things.

Colin took in my jeans and sweater and gave me a smile that made the elevator feel incredibly small all of a sudden. "You look beautiful," he told me. "As always." I noticed he didn't answer the question about where we were going, but it was hard to concentrate on that when he was looking at me the way he was. "I promise you'll enjoy this."

The intensity between us was almost uncomfortable, and yet I didn't want to lose it. Still, I couldn't really stop myself from reverting to our usual interaction and said, "Oh, and you know me so well?"

His hand tightened around mine. "I like to think I do."

I like to think so too.

Colin led me out to his car, where his driver Emil waited for us, and I climbed inside with my trepidation mounting. I generally loved surprises, but Brennon had said it well when he told me Colin wasn't the sort to do something so cryptic. That made me nervous, no matter how convinced he was that I would enjoy whatever the evening entailed.

Only a couple of blocks down the road, Colin's phone rang, and he spent most of the drive talking to Ramesh, who had apparently come across a scheduling problem. Ten minutes into the call, Colin started to get frustrated, and he took my hand again as if I offered some sort of comfort.

"Ram," he said, while I tried to pay attention to where we were going to try to find some clue, "you know I'm not about to budge on this one. I don't care if the whole board thinks I need to be there, but I am *not* skipping Thanksgiving. I won't do that to Macy."

I smiled as I gazed out the window. After my own father skipped out on us, and seeing so many broken families behind the girls I loved, it was nice to see a man who knew his priorities. But hearing him mention his daughter brought to my attention, yet again, the fact that I hadn't seen Macy since the last day of camp. Any time I had tried to bring up Macy and how much I wanted to see her, Colin had, albeit smoothly, steered the topic away to something else before I could get any traction.

After spending a whole summer trying to find ways to help her break out of her shell, it was hard knowing her father didn't want me around her. Had I done something to make him think I wasn't a good influence? I thought we were friends.

"I'm not discussing this anymore, Ramesh," Colin said and hung up with a little sigh. "Sorry," he said to me immediately after. "Sometimes work never ends. But now we're here, so…" He dropped his phone into the pocket of the seat in front of him and smiled in a way I hadn't really seen before, which was surprising, since he usually smiled when I was around him. This was a sort of smile that was a mixture of nerves and excitement, and it wasn't until Emil pulled the car into a narrow parking lot and up to the front doors of an elementary school that I started to understand.

"Talent show," I said, reading the school's marquee out loud. "Wait, *Macy?*"

And when Colin grinned, all of my anxiety dissolved.

"Come on," he said, slipping out of the car and pulling me with him. "I don't want to be late. Emil, did you bring the case by earlier?"

Emil nodded and gave us a salute before he drove off, leaving us to filter in with other excited parents.

"So what's Macy's talent?" I asked as we flitted in between the other attendees, since clearly Colin was worried about missing it. But either he didn't hear me or he didn't want to answer, because he said nothing until we found our way to the little auditorium, which was already pretty full. There were a couple of seats on the end of a row near the front, and Colin pulled me past a couple who were heading in that direction so we could get there first.

"Save me a seat, okay?" he said, and then he kissed me on the cheek before he vanished behind an elderly man with a walker.

I pretty much fell into the upholstered folding chair. As often as Colin held my hand and touched my shoulder and put his hand on the small of my back to offer support when I needed it, he'd never actually kissed me. And while it may have only been a quick peck on the cheek, it left me dizzy and hot and wishing I was wearing something fancier than jeans and a sweater I'd owned since I was seventeen.

Colin had *kissed* me.

I was so distracted that I didn't realize at first that he was still missing when the lights dimmed five minutes later and the curtain rose, revealing an older woman in a long black skirt and a red velvet button up. She looked so much like my old elementary principal that I grinned and turned to tell Colin that she must have become immortal at some point, only he wasn't there.

"Welcome," the woman said into the microphone, and the sound creaked out over the old speakers. "We're so excited to see so much support for our kids, and they've been practicing so hard for the last couple of months. Please enjoy tonight's performances, and don't forget we'll be having a cookie social afterwards."

I glanced around the auditorium, but I couldn't see Colin anywhere. For how quickly he'd rushed us in here so he wouldn't be late, he was really cutting things kind of close. My look around also gave me a good view of the school, and I was surprised to see how…not modern it was. When Colin said Macy was in a new school, I hadn't realized it would be something like this. I had always pictured Macy being in a state-of-the-art facility that was only a few years old and involved highly specialized teaching techniques that had been well-researched and proven to pump out smarter, more successful kids. But this school was probably built in at least the fifties and looked just like my school had, all of it traditional and simple and a place where kids could be kids. It was so unlike the world I'd been living in the last few months that I liked it immediately.

What I didn't like was the fact that Colin was missing.

"First up," said the woman on the stage, "is Macy Donovan, and she'll be singing us a song."

As the audience clapped politely, I pulled out my phone and opened the camera so I could record it in case Colin somehow didn't show up in the next few seconds. I still couldn't see him, and I craned my neck to see into the very back corners of the auditorium. But no Colin.

"Hi," said Macy's timid little voice into the microphone, and I turned with pounding heart to start recording.

Then I froze.

Colin was up there with her, a guitar in his hands and a microphone at his mouth.

"I'm going to sing a song in Spanish," Macy said, her hands shaking a little but her eyes glittering with excitement. "It's called 'La Adelita.'"

And Colin started to play.

I felt like I was going to explode, and I immediately lost sight of both of them because my eyes welled up with tears. Colin played his guitar with the ease of someone who had been playing for years. Macy sang the words I knew so well with the voice of an angel. And when Colin started to harmonize with her with a voice just as clear and beautiful, I could no longer breathe because they sang it just like I did, slow and thoughtful and with all the emotion it deserved.

Without any doubts left in my mind about how I felt, I listened to the man I desperately loved sing with his daughter the song that had been my personal anthem for as long as I could remember. The song that was the last piece I had of my mother.

And when they reached the end, Macy alone sang the last line, the one I still hadn't been able to remember since I'd last sung it at camp: "*Que por mí no vayas a llorar.*"

Or, in other words, *Don't cry for me.*

And I lost it. When the audience started to applaud, I bolted out of my chair and ran up the aisle, smashing through the back door and out into the hallway where I could breathe again. My whole body felt like it was about to shatter into a million pieces, like there was fire coursing through me, like all I had to do was take a breath and I would fly. It was good and bad and I wanted to sob and laugh and I had no idea how anyone could feel so many things at the same time.

"Beck?" Colin touched my shoulder, and I immediately fell into his arms before I fell apart. And he held me so tight, tighter than he'd ever held me, and for the first time I thought maybe there was hope for us, and we could finally be more than friends. "Beck, what's wrong?" He rested his head against mine as if we were made to fit together.

"Nothing's wrong," I said, though it was hard to make it sound believable when I was crying so hard. "I just…that song…"

"I shouldn't have let her sing it. I knew it was important to you, and—"

I pulled away, though I gripped the front of his suit coat to keep myself from melting in a pathetic mess on the floor. "No," I said. "No, it was beautiful. I… It made me think of my mom."

Nodding, he brushed the tears from my cheeks and still watched me with concern. He kept his hands at my cheeks, but he couldn't seem to find anything to say.

I had to explain better, but that meant I had to understand myself, which was slowly becoming easier now that I wasn't sobbing. I took a deep breath and lifted my hands up to his arms, finding strength in the contact.

"I've spent the last eight years crying over her," I said. "And I'm always going to miss her. But that song… She sang it to me the day she died and told me to remember it. And I don't think I paid attention to that last line until I heard Macy sing it. *Que por mí no vayas a llorar.*"

"Don't cry for me," Colin said, and he dropped his hands to my shoulders, his eyes distant as he thought about that. "She wanted you to move on."

"And I thought I had," I replied with a shrug. "But…" I waved my hand toward my face, where I still couldn't completely stop crying. "How do you let go of someone who was such a big part of your life?"

He leaned in closer, and one of his hands slid up to brush my cheek. "I have no idea."

The silence that followed his response was so unbearable that I had to fill it. "I thought you said you didn't sing," I said.

He touched his forehead to mine, and our noses brushed. "I didn't have a reason to before. And now I do."

"Because of Macy?"

"Because of you."

And our lips met in a soft kiss that felt like a promise. A conviction that right now he needed me as much as I needed him. And while that was all it was, it was a promise that I clung to as we slowly made our way back into the auditorium to watch the rest of the show.

Macy screamed when she saw me at the cookie social after the performance (a social that, to my utter happiness, consisted of homemade cookies brought in Tupperware with masking tape labels). She bolted across the gymnasium where Colin and I waited and barreled into me, knocking me into her dad. "What are you doing here?" she shrieked, and I was infinitely glad to know she was happy to see me. "How long have you been in San Francisco? Did you hear me sing your song?"

My emotions, which had been riding pretty high, did a loop-the-loop as I internalized her other questions. She hadn't even known I was in the city? "Of course I heard you sing," I said and bent down to give her a proper hug (and to hide my disappointment). "You were amazing!"

"Dad, why didn't you tell me she was coming to S.F.?" Macy asked next.

Colin simply shrugged and avoided that question altogether, choosing instead to stuff a cookie into his mouth.

Macy gave him a quick scowl then returned her attention to me. "How long are you going to be here?"

Well that's a loaded question. "I'm not sure."

"Are you gonna be here for Thanksgiving?"

I felt the blood drain from my face, and though I wasn't looking at him, I was pretty sure Colin grew tense too. "Um, probably," I said, though I was worried what my answer would lead to.

As I expected, Macy lit up. "Do you want to come with us? Since you don't have your mom to do it with. Oh please come. It's usually just Nana and Gramps and Dad and me, and it gets so boring."

"Mace," Colin muttered, but he seemed to have lost his voice. Did he want me there, or did he not? He'd put on his emotionless business mask, so it was impossible to tell.

"What?" Macy said, looking between us. "Everyone should have somewhere to go for Thanksgiving."

Thanksgiving was still over two weeks away, and a lot could happen in that time. I hadn't figured out my calendar well enough to know what my schedule looked like that far away, and there was a high chance there would be some sort of charity thing going on that day. But mostly, I had no idea what things would be like with Colin after that time. After almost three months of things staying pretty much the same, something had changed between us tonight. But was it enough to make a lasting change? I still couldn't read anything in Colin's face, and it wasn't like I could ask him with Macy standing right there and a whole bunch of parents milling around pretending not to pay attention to the woman Colin Donovan had brought with him.

Catherine was right; even among the middle class, maybe *especially* among the middle class, Colin was a hot commodity.

I put on my best smile and tucked one of Macy's dark curls behind her ear. "I'm not sure what I'm doing for Thanksgiving," I told her, "but I promise I'll keep you guys as an option. How does that sound?"

Thankfully, it was enough of a compromise that she smiled and nodded, and then she rushed to hug her dad. "Mrs. Pratt said we sounded so good!"

With his daughter's eyes closed as she hugged him, Colin met my eye and saw my question—*Why didn't you tell her I was here?*—and though there still wasn't much to his expression, he showed me enough for his message to come out clear: *Not now. Not here.*

"Ready to go home, kiddo?" he asked when Macy pulled away.

"I'll go get your guitar," she said and skipped off.

And while it might have been a good moment to talk, I could still feel a number of eyes on me, so I kept my mouth shut. It was amazing how being surrounded by adults made me feel more out of place than hanging out with a bunch of teenagers for weeks on end.

CHAPTER FIFTEEN

Two days after the talent show, I woke to my phone ringing in the kitchen. It wasn't even that early, but I had the full day to myself and had planned to sleep until the sun was high in the sky. I didn't generally get grumpy, but today was special.

I wasn't much for celebrating birthdays.

It didn't help that I hadn't heard a word from Colin since he and Macy dropped me off after we left the school. If I had ever thought I knew Colin pretty well, I was really starting to think otherwise. After a kiss like that, why would he just go radio silent? What had I done wrong?

By the time I finally stumbled out of my bedroom and picked up my phone, it had nearly gone to voicemail. And though I had no idea why the Rockwood camp director would be calling me, I answered anyway.

"Hey, Linda," I said, and thankfully I didn't sound like I'd just woken up.

"Beck! I just wanted to call and wish you a happy birthday."

I glanced at the clock on the microwave. It was barely eight o'clock, and Linda wasn't exactly a morning person. But she sounded so awake and alert that I was pretty sure she'd been up for a while. "Uh, thanks."

"Do you have any fun plans today?"

"No."

"Oh. Well, I hope you find something to do. How was your little trip to San Francisco?"

I sat on one of the bar stools beneath the kitchen counter, trying to figure out why Linda would be so determined to make small talk. She always called me on my birthday, but usually it was just a quick call and an excitement for the upcoming summer. Something was different.

"I'm still here, actually. That letter was a bit bigger than I expected it to be."

She took a moment to answer, probably trying to figure out what I meant by that. "Oh," she said again.

"Linda, was there another reason you called?"

"I, well, maybe it can wait. I don't want to bother you on your birthday, after all."

"Just tell me." I felt bad for being short with her, but I didn't have my usual pep and energy today. I just needed her to give me whatever bad news she had so I could get on with moping.

I heard her take a breath, and then she said, "I… Oh, I might as well just come out and say it, huh? I'm stepping down as camp director."

My stomach flopped, and I had to grip the countertop as I processed that. "What? But why?"

"I've given enough time to Rockwood, and it's too hard to spend the whole summer away from Mark."

I tried to picture the camp without Linda there to organize everything, and it just made me feel queasy. I'd always thought her husband didn't mind lending her out to us every year, but apparently I was wrong. "Linda," I said, though I couldn't form any more words than that.

"I want you to know I put a lot of thought into this, Beck, and it hasn't been an easy decision. I'm going to miss those girls more than I can say. But I hope they'll be in good hands after I'm gone."

I highly doubted anyone could have the same passion for the work as she did. "I don't really have the words," I said, because I felt like I had to say *something*. "What are we supposed to do without you?"

"That's why I'm telling *you*, Beck. I can't think of anyone who would be better suited to my job than you."

I nearly dropped my phone. Take over Camp Rockwood? While it had never really crossed my mind, the whole idea brought an actual smile to my face, which I'd thought would be impossible on a day like today. "I…"

She laughed. "Obviously you can have some time to think it over. But the job's yours if you want it. Just let me know by February, in case I need to hire someone else instead. Happy birthday, Beck."

And she was gone.

How could she just spring something like that on me and expect it to be okay? Ideas started sprouting in my head, ways the camp could be better, things we could do for the girls that would give them better skills for their future lives, and I felt sick as it started to overwhelm me. And then my eyes caught sight of a flyer for an event in a couple of weeks that I was eager to have go well because it involved the Hargrave School.

I'd never felt more torn in my life.

I'm going back to bed. Leaving my phone on the counter, I trudged into my bedroom, flopped onto the mattress, and promptly fell asleep, wishing I could just sleep the whole day away.

Two hours later, I knew I needed to get out of the house before my thoughts made me go crazy, so I put on an outfit that made me feel beautiful and called up someone who I hoped would be able to find a way to make the day a happier one.

"This is Matthew."

"Matthew," I said, and I smiled when I heard how tired he was. "It's Beck Alvarez. I met you a few months ago, at your dad's office."

"Alvarez. I remember," he replied. "What's up?"

I took a deep breath and hoped I hadn't read the guy wrong. "I know this is going to sound presumptuous," I said slowly, "but I was wondering if I could come meet your baby."

I'd heard through the grapevine (aka Colin through Brennon) that Matthew's wife had given birth only two days after my arrival in the city. Any interaction I'd had with the Davenport family, few though they were, had almost always included at least a brief mention of baby Artemis, and I'd been dying to see her, since every one of them thought she was the cutest thing to have ever existed.

Matthew took a moment to respond, and when he did, his voice was friendly but cautious. "You're right," he said. "That's pretty presumptuous."

I wilted. I didn't have any other plans to cheer myself up, so it was looking like a day of rom-coms and ice cream in my apartment that still felt like a stranger's home, even though I'd been living there since the end of August. I only had one play left, and it was a pretty weak one.

"I've had a miserable day so far," I told him, "and that's no way to spend a birthday. And your entire family has been raving to me about how darling your little one is."

There was another pause, during which I held my breath. "Tell you what," he said finally. "If you can convince that lazy Brennon Ashworth to get his butt over here with that wife of his, you can tag along. Artie is over two months old, and I'm offended they haven't been here yet to tell me how perfect my daughter is. Deal?"

I breathed a sigh of relief. "Deal."

Within an hour, I was knocking on Matthew Davenport's door with Brennon and his wife, Molly, right behind me.

When Matthew answered my knock, he looked like he had just rolled out of bed, which honestly could have been true. He wore plaid pajama bottoms and a milk-stained t-shirt, and his hair, which was considerably longer than the last time I'd seen him, stuck out at odd angles as if he hadn't bothered brushing it in a while.

Brennon muttered something under his breath, and Molly snorted a laugh that she quickly tried to hide with a cough.

Matthew just blinked with exhaustion and jerked his head for us to follow him inside, though I had a feeling he knew exactly what Brennon had said.

For a Davenport, Matthew had a tiny house. We passed a little living room and a set of stairs that probably led up to two, maybe three bedrooms, and the kitchen was small enough that I couldn't imagine him hosting many dinner parties like Mckenna Foster. He led us down to a little sitting room with only a couch and a loveseat, and only the enormous TV hanging on the wall above a whole lot of movies would have hinted at the fact that he came from a massively wealthy family. And while the rest of the house was pretty clean, this room looked like a tornado had come through and tossed everything onto the floor and any other surface.

"Take a seat," Matthew muttered before collapsing onto the couch. "If you can find one." I sat on the other end of the couch, while Molly and Brennon took the loveseat, and Matthew seemed overjoyed to relax a moment. "And now is not the time for your sassy little comments, Bren," he added as he closed his eyes. "I'm worried she'll hear the sarcasm and think it's a great time to—" A shrill baby's cry from the bassinet in the corner interrupted him, and he let out the smallest of moans. "And that's my cue."

Before I could offer to help, he rolled himself off the couch and approached the baby, murmuring little words to her as he lifted her out of the bassinet and cradled her against his chest. And while he looked beyond exhausted, there was so much love in his eyes as he gazed down at his baby that I was more glad than ever that he had let me come, even though I was pretty much a stranger.

"That's a good girl," he said as she started to quiet. "That's right. You never cry if you have an audience. Just for Daddy." And without preamble, he handed her over to Molly, who took her eagerly.

"Oh, she is so precious, Matthew," she breathed as she looked down at the little two-month-old. "She looks just like Indie."

Once again on the couch, Matthew smiled, clearly agreeing. "Her eyes seem to be getting greener every day, so I'm hoping that trait passed on."

"She's going to break hearts," Brennon said as he smiled down at little Artemis.

Matthew groaned. "I have at least thirteen years before I have to start worrying about her dating anyone, Brennon. Eighteen if I'm lucky. Don't even bring that up."

"She's so even-tempered," said Molly.

"Like I said," Matthew replied with a sigh. "She's good for an audience. At least she cries just as much when Indie is home as when she's at the shop, so it's not just me."

"Do you know what she does when you're not in the room?" Brennon asked with a smirk. "'Cause it still might be you."

Matthew grabbed a nearby diaper and tossed it at him, though it caught the air and fluttered to the ground halfway. "Sometimes I think I liked you better when you didn't talk," he grumbled.

I should have felt awkward sitting here in the middle of a family conversation. I had never met Matthew's wife, Indie, even though I was sitting on her couch and grinning at her baby, and I'd only just met Molly during the car ride over. And while I had no idea what kind of shop Indie worked at or how well Brennon and Matthew knew each other or if Brennon and Molly wanted kids sooner or later or even at all, I felt so comfortable sitting there being witness to this little family introduction. The Davenports had a way of making people feel like they were a part of the family, and I hadn't felt that way in a long time.

"So why has your birthday been so miserable?" Matthew asked suddenly, turning his head to me as he slumped even deeper into the couch.

"It's your birthday?" Brennon asked in alarm. "Why didn't you say something?"

I smiled and shrugged. "I don't really care about my birthdays." *Not since Mom died.* And to Matthew I said, "It's complicated."

"Well," he replied, "my baby is currently occupied, and you have no idea how much I would love a conversation that doesn't involve poop and feeding times."

"How is that any different from life before the baby?" Brennon asked under his breath, though not quietly enough to keep from being heard.

"You better shut it, Ashworth," Matthew warned, though Molly and I both laughed. Even Artemis almost managed a smile, and Matthew let out another sigh. "Trust me," he said to me, "I've learned the hard way that it helps to talk about your problems before they become something bigger. We may be strangers, but strangers can save your life if you let them."

I bit my lip, debating, but Matthew was probably right. As much as I'd gotten through hard times by writing letters to my mom, this particular problem seemed too big for that. Besides, I was trying to do what she wanted now that I understood her song. I was trying to let go. Move on. I wanted my letters to be happy.

"So I've been in San Francisco for a few months now," I began and looked at Brennon, wondering how far back my tale of woe needed to go.

When I turned back to Matthew, he'd somehow produced a bowl of popcorn—literally—and popped a few pieces into his mouth. "I'm already riveted," he said with mock attention.

I wanted to be annoyed, but it was exactly the sort of thing I would do in the same position. He was making the situation feel lighter, making it easier to say. *Yeah, I'm definitely glad I came here.* "And I've been trying to take over my grandmother's legacy," I continued.

Matthew glanced at Brennon, who probably knew more about his involvement in the elite world and knew how much to explain.

"Alvarez Trust," Brennon said.

Matthew whistled. "Right. Alvarez. I should have known. My mom has been trying to get her hands into that machine for years. Now that she doesn't have any kids to marry off, she's been trying to find ways to get herself more attention, and the Alvarez Trust is the biggest nonprofit for miles. That's…well, I applaud your tenacity for even attempting to take those reins. Well done."

I winced. "I mean, I've done okay, and half of that is thanks to your family. The other half…" I didn't even know how to say it.

"Is Colin," Brennon finished for me.

Matthew sat up just a little. "Colin Donovan?"

Did everyone in this ridiculous city know everyone? "You know him?" I asked.

"Only by name," he replied. "Mom talks about him constantly." *Creepy.* "So I've heard."

Laughing, Matthew put a hand on my arm. "Like I said, she's after influence. Not his love. Don't go thinking she's one of *those* rich people. So, what's your connection to Donovan?"

I frowned. *Might as well just say it.* "That's the problem," I said. "I don't know."

If there had suddenly been crickets in the room, I wouldn't have been surprised. All three of them looked at me as if I'd just said a password that unlocked a super-secret side of their personalities that was both mysterious and powerful. It might not have been too weird if Matthew and Brennon hadn't grinned at each other, though it was nice to see Molly roll her eyes, as if the two of them were being ridiculous.

"I feel like I should be concerned right about now," I said, glancing between the two men.

"Here's the thing," Brennon said and leaned onto his knees so he was closer to me. "The Davenports have a sort of…pattern."

"I like to call it a superpower," Matthew muttered.

"And I call it life," Molly added in a baby voice to Artemis.

"Anyway," Brennon continued, "we've all experienced rocky paths on our way to happiness."

"I keep saying someone should make a movie about us," Matthew said. "Though Seth would have to play himself, because no one can measure up to the guy."

"He is large," I agreed. I had yet to meet anyone quite as big as Catherine's husband.

"I meant measure up to his idiocy, but yeah, I guess there's that too."

Brennon grinned. "You seriously have a death wish, Matt."

Matthew waved the comment away and sat up too, so now I felt like they had almost cornered me on the couch. "What Brennon means," he said, "is we've had a little bit of everything in our family. Love triangles, kidnappings, near death experiences, heartbreak—you name it. Whatever your lovesickness, we probably know the cure."

"And what makes you think I'm in love?" I asked, though my face immediately burned at the word.

"So I'm guessing you don't know how he feels?" Matthew said, ignoring my question since the answer was probably obvious.

I shook my head.

"Have you asked him?" Brennon said.

It sounded like such an obvious solution when he said it like that, but it was more complicated than that. "I've known him for almost six months, Brennon, and we've only ever been friends. What makes you think that would change now?"

"Donovan has a kid, doesn't he?" Matthew asked while Brennon frowned as he searched for a response.

I nodded. "She's nine."

"That's old enough to make things complicated. He can't only think about himself anymore."

I'd thought about that. "But she really seems to like me," I argued. "She was in my cabin at summer camp, and she practically blew my eardrums when she saw me for the first time the other day."

"Wait," said Brennon, sitting up. "Had you not seen her before now?"

I shook my head. "Not since the last day of camp."

"So Colin has been spending all this time with you, but he hasn't brought Macy back into the picture?"

I shrugged, mostly because I worried that if I said something, it would break my fragile calm.

"Now that's interesting," Matthew muttered.

Before I could ask him why, my phone buzzed in my pocket. I glanced at the ID then sighed. John Foster was calling, which meant my day of leisure was probably over. "Excuse me," I said and wandered up to the living room. "Hello?"

"I've had an idea," John said without greeting. That was pretty much how he started every conversation now, as if he worried anything beyond "Hi, how are you" would get lost like it used to before he figured out he could have conversations without his wife leading the way.

I sighed. "An idea?"

"Hargrave School has been doing so well, and I'm thinking we could implement your hiring process elsewhere, and…"

I knew I shouldn't, but I sort of stopped listening. He would probably send it all in an email anyway, but he had to call because he was excited about whatever his idea was. As annoying as he could be sometimes, I actually did like John. He was so unlike his wife that I still hadn't figured out how they were so clearly in love with each other, and for the most part he let me speak my ideas, even if they were bad ones. I had started giving him more responsibility outside of the charities he already worked with, and he seemed to thrive on the challenge.

"How does that sound?" he finished with a flourish.

I tried to sound excited. "I'm sure when you run that by the board on Tuesday they'll be thrilled." That was my standard response whenever John had a new idea, and so far it had treated me well.

"Oh, yes, that's a great idea. I'll start working on my presentation right away, Miss Alvarez. Have a lovely day."

Not likely. As I hung up and made to go back downstairs, Brennon and Molly were on their way up, Matthew right behind them.

"Hey, Beck," Brennon said with a little frown, "I had something come up at work, so I need to cut my lunch break short. I'd be happy to give you a ride back home, or…"

I glanced at Matthew, just to make sure he wouldn't mind if I stayed a bit, and he gave me a smile. So I shook my head and said, "I can get myself home, but thanks. I still need my baby time."

At the front door, Molly hugged Artemis just a little tighter when Brennon gave her a look that said a lot. But clearly it didn't say enough, because he had to put his hand on her shoulder and say it out loud too: "Give the baby back, Molly."

"Nah," she replied with a content sigh. "I think I'll just keep her."

"She's not yours to keep."

"Matthew won't mind, will he?"

"I'll get you your own baby," Brennon muttered, and then he went red.

But Molly just smiled and kissed his cheek. "Only if you promise," she said then carefully placed Artemis back in her father's arms and skipped out the door.

Matthew chuckled. "You dug yourself into that hole, my friend."

And to my surprise, Brennon smiled just as wide as Molly, even if he was still very red. "Who said that was an accident? See you around, Matt." Just before he hurried off after his wife, he gave me a sheepish smile and said, "Don't be mad at me, Beck."

"What is that supposed to mean?" I asked in alarm.

But he was already slipping into his car, the door closing behind him.

I groaned and held my arms out to Matthew. "Give me the baby," I said in a tone that left little room for argument. "I need her magic powers to fix me."

But Matthew bit his lip and lifted her up just enough to give her rear end a sniff. "She has magic powers alright," he said, "but I'm not sure you want these ones to get on you. I'll be back, and I promise you can hold her then."

If my phone hadn't buzzed again just then, I would have offered to change her diaper for him and give him a break, but instead I pulled my phone from my pocket and opened the text without looking at who it was from, since most likely it was just John repeating what he'd said on the phone.

But instead it was a text from Colin: *Why didn't you tell me it was your birthday?* And before I could reply, he sent another: *I'm taking you out tonight. You don't have a choice. Wear something fancy.*

"Why are you so confusing?" I muttered out loud. One day he was kissing me, the next ignoring me, and now he was taking me on a fancy date as if nothing was weird between us. The man could be straightforward about everything but the things that mattered most.

"Good as new!" Matthew announced, coming down the stairs and holding out his beautiful, smiling child.

As I wrapped her up in my arms, I prayed to the heavens that she would find love in the simplest way when she grew up. I figured someone should.

Colin showed up to my apartment later that afternoon in a limo and wearing a tux. I had debated what he meant by "fancy," and when I opened the door and saw him, I was immensely glad my gut had told me to put on the most gaudy evening gown I owned, one that was long enough to trip me and low enough on my back to make me feel uncomfortable. Catherine Davenport had picked it out for me at some point over the last couple of months, but I had never been able to bring myself to wear it.

Tonight, though, I wanted to prove to myself—and maybe to Colin—that I was capable of being a part of this world. Of *his* world.

And when Colin saw me standing in my doorway, he froze, his eyes wide and his mouth partly open. "Beck," he said.

"Thanks," I replied, clutching my bag a little tighter. "You're…"

"Thanks. Uh…" He held out his arm.

The moment I touched him, I felt an electric spark zoom through me. I had seriously considered telling Colin I didn't want to go out, no matter what he said, and now I had no idea why. Would I really pass up a night like this, with him, just because I was confused?

He led me down to the waiting limo and helped me climb inside. When he slipped in after me, he sat close enough to take my hand, as usual, but at enough of a distance that I felt like we were heading to prom and he was a nervous teen going on his first date.

We sat in awkward silence for about two minutes, which was longer than I could stand.

"I'm sorry I didn't tell you it was my birthday," I said at the exact same time he said, "I want to explain about Macy."

He coughed and pulled his hand away, as if he'd only just realized he'd even taken mine. Maybe he really hadn't noticed. "Why didn't you tell me?" he asked quietly.

I sighed. Which answer did I want to give him? "Birthdays were always a big deal for my mom," I said. "They've never felt the same without her."

"Oh. I thought maybe…" But he didn't finish that thought.

"Why didn't you tell Macy I was here?" I asked.

As he leaned forward and dropped his face into his hands, he clearly *didn't* want to talk about this. But I knew him well enough to know he wouldn't keep it to himself now that he'd brought it up. "Macy was so young when we lost Jada," he said. "But she remembers her mom as if it happened yesterday. I don't know how she does it, but she remembers little things about her that even I've forgotten, and…"

He sighed. "These last three years have been hard on everyone, but I think they've been hardest on Macy. At the beginning, she spent months barely able to sleep because she kept dreaming about the car accident, even though she wasn't there. I lost count of the nights I had to hold her until she fell asleep, and most of the time I couldn't bring myself to put her back in her bed, so I would just sit there all night listening to her breathe in my arms. And she was so shy, even though she hadn't been before. It was like… It was like she was afraid to connect with anyone in case they left her too. At one point she wouldn't even talk to me, and I was so scared. I took her to a therapist, and even then… I nearly fell apart when she finally spoke again.

"But I can't stop imagining the worst, that one of these days she's going to lose someone else, and she'll never come back to me. I want so badly for her to have a good, normal life, but she's so delicate. What if I let her get attached to someone, and they eventually leave?"

At that point, he looked at me, and I understood. I still had no idea if I was staying in San Francisco. Especially after that phone call from Linda offering me Camp Rockwood. And while a large part of that decision hung on Colin, how could I possibly tell him that when he was already carrying such a heavy burden?

I had never been prone to hesitate in my life, but this time I did. If I made my intentions clearer than they ever had been, if I told him how I felt, how would he respond? I had no idea, and that fear was too strong for me to ignore. So I kept my mouth shut and settled with reaching for his hand, making that move first instead of letting him do it, like he usually did.

And Colin smiled through his pain, slowly shifting closer so he could rest his temple against mine. "You're radiant tonight," he whispered.

I love you, I wished I could reply.

"This is a bit of a step up from a wobbly canoe," I muttered as I leaned over the rail and watched the waves roll past. "I've never been on a yacht before." I'd never even been on the ocean, and suddenly I understood the appeal. Especially with the sun just touching the horizon and casting a golden glow over the Bay.

Colin wrapped his arm around my waist and held me close to keep me warm, and I wasn't sure if he was even aware of the sunset. "This is one of my favorite places in the world," he said into my neck. "The only place I'm okay with the silence."

It wasn't exactly silent, with the boat's purring motor and the splash of the water and the sea breeze whispering in my ears. But I understood what he meant. For him, this was his lake in the forest.

"Did you do this with Jada a lot?" I asked, though I knew I wouldn't want to hear the answer.

Somehow, Colin managed to nuzzle even closer, making my heart pound in my ears. "Only on special occasions," he said, which was a pretty good answer, in my opinion.

We passed Alcatraz Island, where the last tour was returning to the ferry, and the yacht continued on toward the Golden Gate Bridge across unbelievably smooth water. It was as if the ocean had decided to be calmer than ever just for me. I'd never seen a more beautiful sight, and I'd never been more hopeful about a future with Colin.

I turned in his arms, and he adjusted his hold so I could look up at him. He looked happy. Not just happy—peaceful. As I brushed my fingers against a wave of his hair that fell onto his forehead, he closed his eyes and smiled.

"About Thanksgiving," he said, as if that was something I wanted to talk about right this second. There were so many other things I would much rather do at the moment.

But I nodded, waiting to hear what he would say. And when he didn't say anything, I sighed and slid out of his hold. "You don't have to worry," I said. "Matthew Davenport invited me over to his sister's house, so—"

He grabbed my hand, his expression pained. "That isn't what I was going to say."

"I'm not sure you were going to say anything." I didn't mean to be angry, but I was getting tired of the confusion this man gave me every other moment. Why couldn't he just pick a side?

Love me or don't, but stop making me wonder.

Please.

Groaning a little, Colin looked down at our hands instead of at me. "Beck, it's complicated."

"Why?" I asked. "Either you want me to come, or you don't."

He looked up, and his expression shifted to frustration to match mine. "Of course I want you to come."

"So why is it so hard to say that?"

"Because it's Jada's parents." He dropped my hand and moved to the other side of the deck, gripping the metal railing as if he thought he might fly away if he let go. "Not mine. And I just… She was their only child, and…" His shoulders drooped, making him look so weary.

I still didn't know if that meant he wanted this thing between us to become something more. Maybe he just thought that any woman in his life, friend or beyond, would hurt Jada's parents because it was like Colin was replacing her. And as much as I understood his reasoning, it didn't help anything.

"I'm sorry," Colin said, looking over at me. Whatever peace he'd had was gone, and now he was simply miserable. "I meant for tonight to be fun. Less…"

"Dramatic?" I suggested with a sigh.

He managed a small smile. "Something like that."

There was something seriously wrong with me, because no matter how much I was hurting at the moment, I hated more knowing that he was hurting too. I couldn't imagine how hard it must have been to even consider filling a void left by a spouse, and even if Colin only saw us as friends—incredibly close friends—it was still brewing a conflict inside him. He kissed me at the talent show, but did that even mean anything for him? Maybe he wasn't capable of moving on and making this thing between us something more, and I worried what would happen if I tried to push him. I didn't want to lose him as my friend, and even if that meant I had to go the rest of my life aching for more, I would rather have that relationship with him than none at all.

So I smiled and said, "You're kinda far away over there. You're getting dangerously close to lurking territory."

The smile that broke through his pain almost made my own pain worth it. "Well, we can't have that," he replied and came back to my side, slowly entwining his fingers with mine. "I want your birthday to be special," he said and tucked some hair behind my ear, "so the rest of the evening is up to you. If you were celebrating with your mom, what would you do?"

"Outside of going to our waterfall?"

"You have a waterfall?"

I grinned. "Doesn't everyone? No, it's where we used to go for every birthday, but it isn't exactly close. So I have a better idea."

Touching his forehead to mine, he breathed me in then said, "Name it."

There was something freeing about doing an activity that felt more like me, and while it had been a challenge bowling in my obnoxious dress, the whole notion had gotten us laughing like I hadn't laughed in a long time, especially when Colin made a particularly flourished throw and ended up in a heap on the floor with a hole high in his tux leg. He had had to tie his jacket around his waist to keep himself decent, and I was pretty sure I hadn't seen anything more ridiculous…except maybe his technique, which looked more like a flamenco dance than a bowling approach.

My final score was a whopping seventy-two, one of my lowest in a long time. Colin bowled a twelve.

"I didn't even know it was possible to bowl that low," I laughed as we sat squished next to each other in a tiny little booth at some corner diner we'd found near the bowling alley.

He slid his arm around my shoulders and rolled his eyes. "Be nice," he said. "I haven't been bowling since I was eight."

"You had a sad childhood," I sighed.

"The rich always do."

"You poor thing."

"I think you missed the point there."

I dug my elbow into his side, and he laughed.

"Be nice," he groaned again. "I'm pretty sure I tore a muscle along with my pants. That's what I get for leaving the house on Friday the Thirteenth."

I grinned. "Are you superstitious, Colin?"

"The Irish always are."

"You're not Irish."

Chuckling, he shook his head and said, "But my parents are *very* Irish, and they rubbed off on me in this one instance. Are you not superstitious at all?"

"Not at all. I happen to think thirteen is very lucky. Besides, I'm not afraid of a silly number."

"Yeah, well, you're not afraid of anything."

Six months ago that would have been true, but from the moment I met Colin Donovan, I discovered a fear that would probably never go away. I was terrified of losing him.

But I smiled and pulled the cherry off the top of his milkshake, popping it into my mouth before he could protest.

"Hey!" he said. "Eat your own cherry!"

"I already did."

"So why'd you have to go and eat mine?"

"Because I like cherries."

"I know you do, which is why I was nice and let you eat your own. You know what?" He grabbed hold of my milkshake and slid it out of reach. "No more ice cream for you."

And while I knew anyone else in the little diner probably thought we were acting like children, I dug my spoon into *his* shake and shoved an enormous helping into my mouth. "Yours tastes better anyway," I said once I'd managed to swallow, though not without giving myself a brain freeze. And then I laughed, because Colin was looking at me like he couldn't comprehend how I could be so problematic. "In my defense," I added, "my mom always let me eat her cherry, so it's pretty much habit at this point."

"In other words, I'm doomed to never eat a cherry ever again."

As soon as he said those words, both of us froze, and the room seemed to spin a bit as we looked at each other. It wasn't like he'd said anything specific, but it was impossible not to read into the subconscious thought behind what he said, whether or not he really meant it. And I couldn't help but imagine what life would be like if I knew Colin was always going to be there with cherries to steal.

Before I could say anything, though I had no idea what I would say anyway, Colin grimaced and pulled his phone out of his pocket. "It's the nanny," he muttered, reading the text he'd gotten. "She says Macy's got a fever. I should probably…"

I wasn't sure how much longer I could handle the emotional roller coaster of the night, so I smiled and said, "It's fine. You should go take care of her. I'm exhausted from beating you in bowling anyway."

His gratitude warmed the air around us, and he silently took my hand and slid out of the booth. He led me back to the waiting limo, which was quite the spectacle for some of the neighborhood residents who must not have seen one on their street before, and before I knew it, we were at my apartment door.

I turned without putting my key in the lock, and I was pleased to see how close Colin stood. "Thank you," I told him. "It's been a long time since I had a good birthday celebration like that."

He lifted one of my hands and pressed my palm to his lips. "You deserve to be celebrated, Beck." He kissed my wrist next, and my whole body felt electrified. This was different from a couple of days ago in the school hallway. There were no tears this time, no daughters who might catch us. This was just me and him.

And I could see the moment he realized that, when something sparked in his eyes, and it was as if whatever had been holding him back all this time just snapped.

I'd never been kissed the way Colin kissed me. Sliding his hands around my back and pulling me against him, he put everything into that kiss, and the world around me disappeared as I became lost in his embrace. I had never felt like I needed to be protected, and yet everything about his kiss told me I was safe. I was wanted. I was *home*. And I desperately wanted to stay there because nothing else would ever compare to this. No one could fit against me like he could. Months of dreaming of a moment like this hadn't come anywhere close to the real thing, and I knew without a doubt that I loved this man more than I thought I could love anyone.

I knew it eventually had to come to an end, but I wasn't prepared for what Colin whispered before he'd even pulled away: "Come to Thanksgiving with me," he said against my mouth.

My heart skipped a beat. "What? But I thought—"

"I don't care," he said and looked at me, something close to desperation in his eyes. "I mean, I do care, but I hate the thought of you not being there with me. Please come." And, as if I needed persuading, he kissed me again, long and slow until my head spun.

"Yeah," I breathed. "Okay." And I lost myself in his kiss again, knowing this was by far the best birthday of my entire life.

Dear Dalia,

I really hate my job. Okay, so the job part isn't that bad, but with the holidays coming up (aka a million events for me to oversee) and Colin's company launching their app, I haven't seen him since my birthday, which was almost two weeks ago. And it's killing me. A phone call a day isn't the same as actually being with him, and I didn't know how much I looked forward to seeing him as often as I do until suddenly I was missing him. I still don't know what we are or how he actually feels, and I've been so swamped with Abuela's charities that I've barely even had time to think about it.

I know I promised myself I wouldn't write so many letters to you. I'm trying to do what you told me and move on, but when I don't have Colin to give me strength, it's harder to keep myself from missing you. I think you would have really liked him. He's sweet and thoughtful and confident, and he's not afraid to show his emotions, which seems like a rare trait among men nowadays. And he makes me feel like I belong somewhere, which is the only reason I've stuck it out this long here in the city. If I didn't know I could turn to Colin, I would have given up a long time ago.

I'm still not sure if I can live this life. Really, truly live it. I can do all the work and say all the right things, but I don't feel like myself most of the time. The only time I do is when I'm with Colin.

It's Thanksgiving today. Colin should be here in about an hour. I'm nervous. I don't know why, but I am. If we were actually a couple, if I knew for sure we were dating, maybe it would make more sense to be nervous, but they aren't even his parents. So why do I want them to like me? And maybe it's Macy I'm nervous about. She was excited to see me at her talent show, but she definitely wasn't happy to see me getting close to her dad on the hike. I haven't been around her enough to know if she's changed her mind.

Whatever I decide, it feels like today is the day I have to choose. My ninety days is up next week. Maybe I just need to be grateful for my life, which means I need to figure out what my life actually is.

What would you do if you were me? I don't want to make Colin's life harder, but I think I'm too far gone. I love him, Mama. I wasn't supposed to fall in love with him. And if he doesn't want me...

I wish you were here.

Love,
    Beck

P.S. I promise that the next time I write to you, it will be because something really good happened. Like, "can't hold it in and have to tell the world" kind of good. I can't stay stuck in the past and expect you to somehow magically fix all my problems for me. So the next time you hear from me, I will be impossibly happy, whenever that may be.

P.P.S. I miss you. I always will.

CHAPTER SIXTEEN

I paced back and forth across the front room of my apartment while I waited for Colin to pick me up. I still couldn't figure out why I was so nervous to see him again, especially because the last time—my birthday—had ended on such a high note. Maybe it was because I had no idea how he was going to be. Was he going to continue his pattern of confusing back and forth, or had we finally crossed a threshold into something new?

When we'd talked last night, after I got back from our Thanksgiving fundraising event with the Hargrave School, Colin had sounded excited to finally get to spend some time with me, though he warned me that Macy was looking forward to me joining them and would probably talk my ear off during the entire drive to Healdsburg, where his in-laws lived. I had told him I would like nothing better, and the rest of our conversation had been light and easy, the way I liked it best. So at least we were still friends, no matter what else we might be.

I glanced in the floor length mirror in the hall and wondered—for the third time—if I should change. Brennon had told me not to worry about what I wore, since I had almost frantically posed the question to him a couple of days ago. Though I trusted my friend who had yet to steer me wrong, I felt like this was a special case.

"Just be you," he'd said.

And as I stared at my reflection in the mirror, I suddenly found myself wondering who that was.

For my entire life, I had unapologetically been Beck. I was loud and stubborn, adventurous and sometimes ridiculous, and I had never cared what others thought of me. But now I was *Miss Alvarez*, and maybe I had a strong opinion about certain things, but more often than not I followed the advice of others, even if I thought something could be better a different way.

If I had been the old Beck, I would have let the Hargrave girls plan last night's event instead of turning to the Trust's regular event coordinator, who hadn't even picked a venue where the girls could attend. If I was the old Beck, I wouldn't even care what I was wearing, and I would probably show up to Thanksgiving dinner in jeans and an old camp t-shirt because then I would actually be comfortable, instead of wearing dress slacks and a sweater that had cost more than my car was worth. Assuming my car hadn't been sent to the junkyard by some parking attendant who thought it had been abandoned months ago…

If I was the old Beck, I probably would have told Colin that I loved him long before now because I would have known that nothing he could do or say at this point would change that, so why should I keep it to myself?

"I miss old Beck," I muttered to my reflection. I missed how content I had been with my life.

And before I could talk myself out of it, I hurried into my giant closet and peeled off the clothing that still didn't feel like mine. I put on my favorite pair of jeans, even though they had a hole in the knee, and I slipped into a comfy green sweatshirt with pine trees painted on the front. I had just pulled my hair out of its intricate bun and left it hanging down my back in loose curls when my phone began ringing, so I hurried out into the hall and picked it up from the table near the door.

The moment I saw who was calling, however, I instantly perked up. "Gabby!" I shrieked as I answered.

She laughed, and I'd forgotten how much I missed laughing with her during the summer months. "Okay, so you do remember I exist. That's nice to know. I was almost tempted to go to your waterfall to see if you'd permanently retreated there." She didn't sound angry, but she certainly had a right to be. She had tried calling more than once over the last few months, but I had been so preoccupied with…everything.

How did she remember my waterfall, though? I'd told her about it years ago, just after my mom died, and I hadn't been back there in a long time. Maybe I should have kept in better touch with her, since she was clearly a better friend than I was.

"I'm so sorry I haven't had the time to call you back," I said. "I've missed my late-night therapy sessions."

"Hmm," she said, sounding worried. "Have you been needing those therapy sessions?"

Yes. "Not really. What's up? How've you been? What's new?"

She laughed again. "I was calling to wish you happy Thanksgiving. And I've been great. And I'm engaged."

I nearly dropped my phone. "What?"

"Kyle proposed last night!"

I had to sit down on my hideous fancy couch before I fell over. For as long as I had known Gabby, she'd never kept a boyfriend longer than a couple of months. "Gabs, that's…" *What is wrong with me?* "That's amazing!" I really was happy for her, and I hated that it was so hard to get that into my voice. "So when's the big day? Will it interfere with camp?"

"That's the other reason I called."

My heart sank. "Gabs, I don't like that tone of voice you're using."

It took her a while to be able to respond, and when she did, it made me feel even worse. "Kyle just got offered a job in Rhode Island. We're moving just before Christmas."

Put on a happy face. "Well," I breathed, "you have no idea how much I'm going to miss you, but that sounds amazing. I'm going to have to convince Sofie to be my new rival."

There was another pause. "Didn't she tell you about helping her parents with their grocery store?"

I took a deep breath. "Yasmine then."

"She's heading off to med school after she graduates in May."

Had I really been so distracted at the end of camp that I hadn't bothered to check in with any of my fellow counselors? Was *anyone* staying at Rockwood with me?

"Hey," Gabby said, and she was using the same voice she used on the girls when they were near tears. "Linda told me she's giving you her job. That'll be amazing, Beck!"

I spoke before I could stop myself: "I don't know if I'll take it."

"Why not? You were born for that job."

Why wouldn't I spend the rest of my life doing something I loved? The only reason I could even think about turning Linda down was because there was something here in the city worth staying for. But now my fallback was missing some of its key players, and suddenly I felt more alone than I had in a long time. If I didn't have Camp Rockwood as I knew it waiting for me, what did that mean for my options for the future?

There was a knock on the door, and I forced myself out of a spiral of what-ifs. "Hey, I have to go, but I'm so happy for you, Gabs. Don't you dare leave the state before I have a chance to see you, okay?"

"Wouldn't dream of it," she replied. "Love you, Becks."

I hung up and took another deep breath, forcing my emotions down so I was mostly just numb. That was the best I could do at the moment, though Colin deserved more.

When I answered the door, his smile stole the breath out of my lungs, and to my surprise, it only grew when he took in what I was wearing.

"Do I look okay?" I asked, my face burning with heat and my fingers shaking enough that I hid them behind folded arms.

He was wearing dark jeans and an emerald sweater that made his eyes more green than I'd ever seen them, and he still looked more sharply dressed than the average person, which made me feel like I'd made a poor decision in changing my outfit.

"You look like you," Colin said, his eyes roaming me from head to foot.

I cocked my head. "And is that good or bad?"

His answer came with a lingering kiss on my cheek: "It's perfect. You ready?"

"As I'll ever be."

As Colin predicted, I spent most of the hour-long drive turned in my seat so I could chat with Macy, who felt the need to tell me every single detail about her friends at school and the art project she'd done and the annoying boy who always wanted to hold her hand at recess when all she wanted to do was play kickball. Colin kept his eyes on the road, but he listened just as intently as I did, laughing when Macy and I sang a silly a cappella duet I had taught her at camp and grinning the rest of the time. There was nothing awkward or uncertain about the trip, and I found myself getting annoyed with myself for ever thinking things would be weird.

When we pulled up to a quaint little house nestled in some oak and walnut trees, Macy bolted from the car and went running into the house.

I was about to follow her, but Colin took my hand and pulled me close. He pressed his forehead to mine, his eyes closed, and he seemed to breathe me in before placing a gentle kiss against my lips. "I'm glad you're here," he whispered.

If this is your version of gratitude, I think you need to tell me again. I ran a hand through his wavy hair, which had gotten fairly long again since the end of the summer. "So am I," I said, and I was definitely feeling better about things than I had been after Gabby's phone call. Maybe my choice would be easy.

"I suppose we should go inside before Macy thinks we've gotten lost," he said softly, turning the end of his comment into another electrifying kiss.

I closed my eyes. "Do we have to?"

But Colin pulled away and tugged at a curl of my hair. "Don't let Hannah and Caleb overwhelm you," he said as he took my hand and pulled me toward the house. "They are every bit Judd's parents, and they don't really understand the concept of killing with kindness."

"Got it," I said, though my nerves had suddenly come back in full force. Would it be strange if I spent all of Thanksgiving out on the rainy porch instead of going inside?

Colin glanced at me then laughed. "You handled Mckenna Foster at her worst, Beck. I think you can handle a couple of suburban grandparents."

I told myself he was right just as we stepped through the front door, but then again I didn't expect a scream and a hug so tight that I couldn't breathe. Hannah Miller was surprisingly strong for how slender she was. She even managed to lift me into the air.

"You must be Beck," she said into my ear. "Col told us he was bringing a friend this year, and I can't tell you how excited that made me."

I felt fortunate to stay on my feet when she set me down, since I was still struggling to get air in my lungs, but I couldn't help but grin as I took her in. In the weirdest way, she reminded me of my own mother, in the way she wore her black hair in a thick braid and had a flowery apron over her clothes (which, I noted with delight, were the epitome of what I expected a suburban grandmother to wear: khaki slacks, a knit orange sweater with a giant turkey on the front, and a bit of flour streaked across her dark forehead). And maybe it was her smile, the kind of smile that said a person didn't have to be her blood to be her child.

"Thank you so much for having me, Mrs. Miller," I said.

"It's Hannah, please. Oh, Col, it's been way too long." She wrapped him in a similar hug, though she was much too short to lift him like she had me.

Colin held her just as tightly as she did him and closed his eyes as he drank in the greeting. "Hey, Mom," he said. "Work has been crazy, but I promise to be better for the rest of the year." Hannah slapped his shoulder, and he laughed, the sound filling the little entryway. "You know I'm kidding," he added and kissed her on the cheek. "I'll be better forever. Where's Pops?"

A shriek of happiness from Macy, followed by a deep and booming laugh, answered the question for him.

"Sounds like he gave her the surprise," Hannah said with a sigh. "He was supposed to wait until Christmas."

His eyes wary, Colin hung up his jacket then made his way down the hall, which led to a wide open room that contained both a quaint little kitchen and a modest sitting room, where Macy sat on the couch cradling a guitar as if she'd never seen anything more beautiful. From where I stood, I wasn't sure if Colin was pleased, mad, or just overwhelmed as he locked eyes with his father-in-law, who tried very hard to look innocent but came up rather short.

Caleb was a tall man, strongly built and with the kindest brown eyes I'd ever seen. His short, curly hair was only partially gray, and if not for the walking cane resting against his knee, I might have thought him just as spry as Colin. He looked like the sort of man who would give up everything he owned if he thought it would make someone happy, and I instantly adored him.

"You really shouldn't have," Colin muttered to both his in-laws, but then Macy leapt to her feet and came to his side.

"Can you teach me, Dad?" she asked, bouncing on the balls of her feet. "Gramps says now that I have my own guitar you don't have any excuses not to."

"What's a man supposed to do if not spoil his only grandbaby?" Caleb added with a chuckle.

Colin put his hand on Macy's head and gave her a weary smile. "Of course, kiddo," he said. "But after dinner, okay?"

"Macy," said Hannah, "why don't you come help me with these potatoes?"

"Okay!" Macy said, though she gave her guitar one last little stroke before setting it back in its case and hurrying over to the kitchen.

"Now that you're here, son," Caleb grunted, struggling up to his feet, "I was hoping you could help me with a little problem I've got."

"Of course," Colin replied and followed his father-in-law back down the hall toward the door.

I stood in the middle of the room by myself but smiling like an idiot because I had had no idea this was what family was supposed to be like. My whole life it had been just mom and me, and for the last eight years just me by myself. It had never really bothered me, but then again I hadn't known what I was missing.

"Beck!" Macy called and waved me over. "Nana says you can help with the rolls."

"Perfect," I replied.

If this was what I could have if I stayed in San Francisco, that choice was looking easier and easier.

"Has anyone seen Colin?"

I paused in the middle of setting the table and looked up at Hannah's question. According to my watch, it had been almost an hour since he and Caleb had gone outside, but Caleb had come back in within ten minutes of leaving. I'd been having so much fun cooking with Macy and her grandma that I hadn't even noticed how much time had passed.

Caleb was reading the paper, and he seemed surprised to see Colin wasn't in the room with us. "I only asked him to check on a leak because I couldn't get to it," he said, his thick eyebrows pulled together. "Shouldn't have taken him more than a couple minutes."

I glanced at Macy and Hannah, who both had their hands full of food to bring over to the table. "I'll go see where he is," I offered.

Though I had no idea where else he could have gone, I figured it wouldn't take too long to search the house for him, since it wasn't a large one. I would start in the last place Caleb had seen him, somewhere outside, and go from there. It didn't seem like Colin to just disappear for such a long time, and as I stepped onto the porch and into the light drizzle that had started falling, I had a slight moment of panic. Had something bad happened to him out in the rain?

But the moment I saw the ladder leaning against the house, my fear faded. Maybe the answer was a little simpler than an accident befalling him. Grabbing hold of the ladder, I pulled myself up just high enough for my head to poke out above the roof.

And there he was. Lying on his back, soaking wet with an arm over his eyes.

I bit back a laugh. "Whatcha doing?"

He didn't move. "I live here now," he said.

"Is that so?"

He simply nodded, apparently resigned to his fate to be trapped on the roof forever.

I climbed the rest of the way up and sat myself next to him, and when I took his arm from off his face so I could clutch his cold fingers between my palms, he kept his eyes shut tight. "You know," I said as I rubbed his hand, "this is a pretty spectacular view." And I wasn't lying. From this vantage point, I could look out over a vast vineyard thick with rain and mist.

"I'll take your word for it," Colin mumbled.

I grabbed his other hand so I could try to warm that one up too. "You know you can't stay up here forever, right? Your dinner will miss you."

"I'll live on fallen leaves and wind from now on."

"Who will teach Macy how to play the guitar?"

"You can do it. You're good at everything."

"And what if I really *really* want you to come down?"

He opened one eye, then the other, and I honestly couldn't tell what his expression was telling me. There was a bit too much anxiety in it to get a good read on his reaction to my question. "Really *really*?" he asked.

I kissed his cold palm. "I can throw in another 'really' if you think it would help."

"Three reallys? Wow." He sat up so slowly that I worried he was too cold to move, and then he slid himself closer to me and hooked one arm around my bent leg as if I would make a good anchor if he fell. "I was starting to think no one would come rescue me," he said, his lips quirking in a smile.

"Yeah, well, apparently you're the only one who likes pumpkin pie, so it would have been a waste if you—"

His kiss cut me off completely, and I felt like I was suddenly very much in danger of falling off the house myself because the roof seemed to vanish beneath me. His lips were cold, like the rest of him, but they sent a wave of heat through me that made the chill of the rain disappear.

"Maybe I should live up here too," I whispered without meaning to.

Colin let out the smallest of laughs, and then he said, "Okay, but could you really help me get down? I'm freezing."

After five minutes of coaching him over the edge and promising to catch him if he fell, we made it back inside the house just before the drizzle turned into a downpour.

"Did you get yourself lost again, Colin?" Hannah called from the kitchen.

Colin's cheeks were already red from the warm house, but I was pretty sure he blushed as we entered the back room. "Just got myself a little stuck," he muttered. "Did I leave some clothes the last time I was here? These are soaked."

I could tell Hannah wanted to ask why he was sopping wet, but she swallowed her questions and nodded down the hall that led deeper into the house. "I found them in a pile at the foot of your bed like you were some teenager. I washed them for you, and they're in the dresser."

Rolling his eyes, Colin muttered, "I'm going to take a shower," then quickly kissed my cheek before hurrying off down the hall.

As if I felt her gaze, I turned just as Macy looked away, and I couldn't tell if her neutral expression was real or if she'd put it there when I noticed her watching me. I wanted so badly to ask her what she would think if something happened between Colin and me, but that was something I needed to ask Colin first. If I wanted to choose whether I was staying or going, if I really wanted to make a commitment, I had to know if he would be willing to make one too.

I should have asked him while he was stuck on the roof, I thought bitterly. Then he wouldn't have been able to run away if my wonderings scared him off somehow.

"Beck," Hannah said brightly, "if you would be a dear and finish up this gravy…"

The day was far from over, and I had plenty of time before I had to make a decision. *Just enjoy the day,* I told myself. *You deserve this.*

Hannah was an amazing cook, and I ate more than I'd eaten in months, which was surprising, considering I hadn't stopped laughing since the start of the meal. Hannah and Caleb were somehow both impeccably polite to each other while still managing to throw in veiled teasing insults that were a clear indication they had been happily married for a long time, like when Hannah managed to tell Caleb he smelled bad while mentioning his musical talents, though he got her back when he hinted that she snored.

I'd never felt the warmth that I felt in the Millers' home, and I drank it in as the day went by. This was a family full of so much love that it spilled out of them and into the house around them. Macy was happier than I'd ever seen her and seemed to adore her grandparents, even when Caleb smashed a glob of pie in her face, and Caleb laughed so loud it echoed off the walls. Hannah got embarrassed anytime someone complimented her food and flat out said the only reason she loved cooking it was because it brought everyone together. And Colin?

He sat across from me with his foot touching mine, and any time I met his eye, I felt like I exploded into a million little stars. Could a man look at me like that and not be in love? I really hoped not, because somehow I had fallen so far for this man that the thought of leaving him couldn't even form in my head anymore.

I love you, I tried to tell him in every stolen glance.

After dinner was over, Macy dragged Colin into the sitting room to force him to teach her some chords on her guitar. Caleb limped over to join them, and as much as I wanted to witness the heart-bursting scene, I insisted Hannah let me help her with the dishes.

"Oh no, dear," she tried.

"I guarantee I'm more stubborn than you," I replied and moved into the kitchen, grabbing a scrub brush before she could stop me.

When all the dishes were clean and drying, I wandered over to the living room where Macy was now curled up in Colin's arms while Caleb told them some sort of story. There was a seat next to Colin on the couch, but as tempted as I was to fill up that space at his side, I found myself drawn to the hallway, where the wall was lined with photographs. I'd only been here a few hours, but I felt like I was a part of this family, and I wanted to know everything about them that I could.

The photos spanned the length of the wall, starting with what I guessed was Hannah and Caleb's wedding day. They looked amazingly happy and beautiful and in love, and my chest burned with warmth as I slowly made my way through their early married years and to when they had Jada.

Jada was the most adorable child I'd ever seen. Even as a kid, she was just like Colin described, and she had this glow about her that somehow came out of the old film pictures. Most of her teenage photos were with many other people, so I could tell she'd been well-loved. I wished I could have known her.

Without knowing anything about this family, they were clearly wealthier than I would have guessed knowing them as they were now, but that hadn't defined their lifestyles. They were a lot like Colin.

Speaking of Colin…

At the end of the wall, he joined in on photos, much younger than he was now but just as handsome. Macy was in most of the photos with him, somehow even more adorable than her mother, but as much as I wanted to linger on her, I couldn't really bring myself past a picture of Colin and Jada on their wedding day.

They were so young. At eighteen, they were barely older than some of my girls at camp. Colin was baby-faced and seemed to be in a daze, as if he couldn't understand how he had been so lucky to get himself there. Jada was radiant and obviously happy beyond her wildest dreams. I wondered what it felt like to be so utterly and completely content.

"I always thought they got married too young," said a soft voice behind me.

I turned and saw Hannah looking at the same wedding photo with a sad smile. I really didn't know what I could say to that.

Luckily, she felt the need to fill the silence that I couldn't. "I worried about Colin at first," she said. "We lived in a wealthy area, and most of the boys at that school came from a world where they were superior and could have anything they wanted. I worried about my sweet Jada and how they might treat her. But Colin was different."

I glanced into the living room, where Colin sat with his eyes closed and a small smile on his lips. Macy seemed to be falling asleep against his shoulder. "He's still different," I said, almost in a whisper, as if saying it too loud would somehow make it not true.

Hannah's smile warmed. "He's such a good boy," she said. "Once I met him, I realized he and Jada were good for each other. And if I had pressured them into waiting until they were a little older, until they had dated a while longer, they wouldn't have had much time together.

I think maybe Jada knew, and she didn't want to waste what little she had."

"I'm so sorry about your daughter," I said.

"I'm sorry about your mother," she replied and patted my shoulder. "None of us want to lose the people we love, but I think we just need to learn to hold to the ones we still have while we have them. If that makes any sense."

I glanced at Colin again. "Yeah," I replied. "It does." Now, more than ever, I knew my life was a million times better if it had Colin in it, and my choice was easy. I wanted to be wherever he was, because whether with the camp or with the Alvarez Trust, I could still help my girls. The only variable was him.

"You've been good for him, you know," Hannah said. She gazed at Colin, little worried lines wrinkling her forehead. "He's been so alone, and he's starting to smile again. Thank you for being such a good friend to my boy." Giving my shoulder a squeeze, she wandered back into the kitchen, probably to start putting the clean dishes away.

And while I would have loved to help, Colin was getting to his feet with Macy held tight in his arms, and I couldn't help but watch him with his daughter.

She mumbled something, and Colin frowned, saying something to her just as softly. When she spoke again, he looked over at me with an expression of curiosity then headed my way with Macy in tow.

My face blossomed with heat, and I stuffed my hands into my pockets to hide my sudden, unfounded nerves. "What's up?" I asked, keeping my voice low.

"Sing me a story," Macy replied, gazing at me with drooping eyes.

My heart seemed to do a flip in my chest. "Of course!" I said and followed Colin as he carried her down the hall and into a little bedroom that was clearly Macy's, since it was decorated in pinks and purples and a dozen stuffed animals on every open surface.

Colin gently laid her on the bed, and though he seemed to hesitate, he touched my shoulder, backed away, and slipped through the door, leaving us alone.

Macy immediately grabbed my hand and pulled me down onto the bed next to her so we were lying there facing each other. "Will you sing 'La Adelita' for me? You do it so much better than me."

"Well that's just not true," I replied. "I think you're going to have to teach all the other girls at camp next year."

"Dad said I can go every year until I'm sixteen. I wish I could go every year forever."

I smiled and pushed some curls out of her face. "I know how you feel," I said, and an ache settled in my soul. If I stayed here to run Abuela's charities, like I was mostly likely going to do, I wasn't sure if I would be able to go back to camp. Most of the Trust's biggest events were in the summer. "How about you sing the song with me, okay?"

She nodded. "You start."

So I did, and even though I hadn't sung the song since the start of summer, the words came back to me as easily as they always did. When Macy joined in, I switched to the same harmony Colin had done in the talent show, and I had to fight back tears. But they were happy tears. I'd barely seen her for months, and yet I loved this little girl almost as much as I loved her dad.

Macy was pretty much asleep when we sang the last line, and though I could have gone back to join the other adults, I stayed where I was, lying there on her bed and running my fingers through her dark curls. I felt so peaceful here. And yes, I would miss camp, but Colin and Macy would make it worth it. I could be happy here.

I closed my eyes with contentment and just listened to her breathe for a while, and I might have fallen asleep, I wasn't sure. But soft voices stirred me from my thoughtless silence, and I opened my eyes to a dark room.

"Macy seems to like her," Hannah said.

"Beck was her counselor at camp," Colin replied.

Though I had my back to the door, I was pretty sure they were standing in the hallway just outside.

"You seem to like her too."

My stomach twisted.

Colin sighed. "Don't do that, Hannah."

"What? It's clear as day."

"It doesn't matter if I like her."

My mouth felt dry. Why didn't it matter?

"Col, it's been three years. You love her, don't you?"

I held my breath, and I could have sworn time stopped as I waited for him to answer that question. If ever there was a time for the man to be straightforward, it was now. Was it really so hard to say yes or no?

What if he said no?

I could hear Colin breathe, could imagine him running a hand through that wavy hair of his. Did he even know how much I needed him to answer that question? I wished I could just see his face and prepare myself for what he was about to say. Did I have to tell myself he would always be my friend and nothing more? Or would his answer be infinitely happier than that?

"You need to do what's best for your family, Colin," Hannah said.

"I know." His voice was strained. "But Macy..."

"She's stronger than you think."

"It's not that simple."

"Do you love her?"

"Hannah, I can't—"

"*Do you love her?*"

"I don't know."

Something broke inside me.

I thought I had buoyed myself up to handle a no. His friendship was worth more than losing him. But somehow this was worse. This was knowing I wasn't enough to be a yes but I was more than simply wrong for him. This was months of secretly wishing and suddenly knowing he hadn't given it enough thought to have a real answer. This was a man who wasn't willing to give this thing between us a chance, who wasn't brave enough to even try.

And I knew what my decision was.

I had to leave.

CHAPTER SEVENTEEN

I stole Colin's car. It was a terrible thing to do, but it was the easiest way—maybe the only way—to put as much distance between us as I could before he realized I was gone. As soon as he and Hannah left the doorway, I crept down the hall and slipped his keys from his jacket by the door, and I drove as fast as my nerves would let me.

I parked his car outside his office building and dropped the keys in the company mailbox, and then I took a cab to the garage where I'd left my car so many months ago. Though it took a little coaxing, my little tin can started up and seemed almost happy to see me.

It didn't take long to pack up my stuff when I got to my apartment. Most of it had been paid for with my abuela's money anyway, and I didn't deserve to keep any of it. Not since I was choosing to leave.

I almost called Harris Davenport on my way out the door, but I figured a call like that could wait until Monday, since he was probably with his family for the holiday.

At least he had one.

It seemed like everything tried to hold me back. Stop lights, my gas tank on empty, my powered-down phone sitting on the seat next to me because I couldn't bear to see Colin's name light up the screen if he called. But eventually I made it across the Bay Bridge, where the lights lit up the dark water in a mesmerizing pattern as if to tell me I was making a huge mistake.

Maybe I was.

But I didn't have the heart to stay.

I should have seen this coming. People had a habit of leaving me behind. Why would Colin be any different?

I drove away from the place where I'd fallen in love with a man who likely wouldn't ever love me back, knowing I had lied to myself about how I would be fine if we were just friends.

I only made it to Yuba City before I had to stop because I was too tired. And then I curled up in the backseat as the tears came.

I thought about calling Gabby and begging her to tell me what to do. But would she understand? She had a huge family, and now she had Kyle and was moving on with her life. She was happy. I couldn't burden her with my sadness, no matter how much I wanted to talk to someone who knew me. I couldn't call any of the Davenports for the same reason. They had been kind to me, and Matthew's words rang in my head—*it helps to talk about your problems before they become something bigger*—but no matter what that family thought, I was pretty sure none of them had ever experienced something like this. None of them had had their heart ripped out, so how could they possibly understand?

"You're alone, Beck," I whispered out loud and curled into a tighter ball. "You're always alone."

And cried myself to restless sleep in a crowded Home Depot parking lot, wishing I knew what to do.

I was up and driving again before the sun rose, a half-hearted idea in my head, but at least it was a direction. I didn't have any tears left, but an ache had settled deep in my chest that probably wasn't going to go away anytime soon. It kept me heavy in my seat as I drove.

And two hours later, I parked my car, grabbed a bottle of water from the trunk, and started walking.

I hadn't been here in ages, but the little trail still felt familiar, like it had only been a few days since the last time I was here. I'd come so many times as a kid with my mom that it felt like our trail, and I was desperate to get as close to her as I could. I badly needed her wisdom, but I would keep my promise: no more letters until I was unbelievably happy. No matter how long that took.

It was time to figure out how to fix my own problems and face the unknown future.

"Eventually," I said to myself.

For now, I needed the peace of Feather Falls.

By the time I reached the waterfall, it was late morning. The sun was high and warm, though there was still a chill in the air, and the place was remarkably empty. Resting my water against a rock, I slowly made my way out to the edge of the fall and sat down, sticking my feet over the ledge. I remembered the first time I had seen someone sitting here, back when I was seven or eight, and I'd thought they were crazy. Mom said they weren't afraid to live, and the next time we came, I vowed to see what I was missing by being too scared to try.

The view was unbeatable. With the roar of the falls as a soundtrack, I could look out across what felt like the entire world. Maybe I would be okay. There was so much out there, and as hard as it was to think about, I could find somewhere new to go if I really wanted.

It wasn't like I had much waiting for me. I didn't even have my own apartment, since I always slept in cabins or dorms wherever I was working, and all of my possessions fit in the back of my run-down car. I had never liked city life, and the only reason I had lasted as long as I had was Colin. Now that I knew where he stood, I no longer had that tie to this fancy life I'd been thrown into.

Neither could I go back to the way things were before all of this. As much as I loved Camp Rockwood, now it would only make me think of Colin.

Yeah, a clean break would be easier.

I just had to let everything go.

First, I needed to make a plan. I couldn't just quit everything without somewhere to live or a way to make money. My skill set was pretty limited, but with all the work I had been doing with the Hargrave school, I was pretty sure I could get a decent job as a teacher. Just not in the Bay Area... Maybe I would make my way farther down the state, or even go up to Oregon and find a liberal school willing to take an unorthodox approach to helping kids like that succeed.

Yeah, Oregon would be nice. I could take on an hourly job until the next school year started up and save everything I could so I could start to build a future for myself. It was abundantly clear that I would be spending the rest of my life on my own, so I couldn't rely on anyone else anymore. Everyone inevitably left, anyway. I knew that, and I would just have to accept that.

And no matter how hard this new plan of mine was going to be, I had to follow through. I owed my mom a letter of utter happiness, and I refused to let anyone else decide when I would be able to write it.

I wasn't sure how long I'd been sitting there among the rocks and listening to the rush of water, but eventually I caught the sounds of a jogger on the trail, and I knew my time alone was up. It had done what I hoped, though, and I was starting to feel at peace about what had happened over the last few months. I had learned and grown so much that if I really thought about it, the future was bright. There was so much possibility, and I didn't have to be scared of what might come.

You've got this, Beck.

The jogger came around the corner, and I turned to get up and give them a chance to enjoy the view like I had. Only, as soon as I caught sight of him coming out of the trees, my body shut down.

Colin looked awful. Sweaty, exhausted, a patch of dirt down the side of his jeans as if he'd fallen at some point on the trail. And yet he was just as handsome as he always was, and I was half-convinced it was all a dream.

But why would I dream up something this painful?

Panting, he looked ready to fall over, as if it had been a long time since he'd run anywhere. "You are a hard woman to find," he said finally, sounding very real.

I stared at him. "What?"

"It was, like, four miles of trail to get out here."

I must have fallen asleep at the wheel and died, because I couldn't understand how he could possibly be here. "Colin, how did…"

He shook his head, dropping the jacket he held on the rock next to him. "Do you have to sit so close to the edge?" His eyes flitted to the waterfall below me, but he mainly focused on me. "Beck, I need…" Some of the color drained from his face when he glanced at the edge again, and he took a step back.

I didn't move. It was hard enough seeing him; I didn't need to get close enough to touch him. "How did you find me?" I asked.

He swallowed. "Because I know you, Beck. And I know you miss your mom. I had to call Gabby to figure out which waterfall was yours, but I knew if you were going to run anywhere, it would be here. Why did you run, Beck?"

My words seemed stuck in my throat. I didn't have the strength to say any of the thoughts that had been running through my mind, but I knew I had to say something. So I asked him, "Why did you come after me?"

No one had ever come back after they left.

His eyebrows furrowed and his hands shaking, he stared at me as if I should have already known the answer to that question. "Do you have any idea how in love with you I am?" he said.

I stared at him as my whole body seemed to freeze in time. "What?"

"And it scares the hell out of me." He tried to take a step closer, but his face turned so white that he looked like he might faint if he got any nearer the edge, and he retreated back several feet. "Beck, I loved Jada more than I ever thought I could love anyone."

If he was trying to explain things, he was doing a horrible job. "Colin, what—"

"And when I lost her," he continued, "I thought I would never be able to open my heart again because it had broken so completely." He glanced down, shuddered, and then he set his jaw and stood up straight. "Then I met you," he said and stepped forward. "And suddenly it was like all those little cracks in my shattered heart started to fill in." Another step. "You made me whole again, Beck. And it nearly killed me when I had to leave the camp at the end of the summer because I couldn't comprehend my life without that brightness that you bring to it. But I had to leave, and I was absolutely miserable until I showed up to a party and there you were, more beautiful than I'd remembered, and I thought to myself there was no way you could be real." He had reached the edge of the rock ledge now and could barely breathe through his fear.

I got to my feet, ready to put some distance between us if listening to him got too hard.

"These last few months have felt like a dream," he said, and his fingers found mine as if he needed to touch me to know I was real now. A shudder ran through me at his touch, but I couldn't move. "I kept waiting for the moment I woke up and realized it was all just a fantasy. I mean it when I say I am terrified of how much I love you, because if you don't love me back, I can't... I need you, Beck."

I didn't know what to feel. The last twenty-four hours had left me in such a state of disarray that I could barely tell what was real anymore. "You told Hannah you didn't know if you loved me," I said.

He paled even more. "You heard...?" He shook his head. "That doesn't matter. I told Hannah I didn't know because I was so scared of all of this. And then you were gone, and I realized... I don't want to be scared anymore. I don't want to spend my whole life alone just because there's a chance I could lose you. Loving you and risking the small chance that I could lose you is worth so much more than keeping my heart safe, and I can't imagine being apart from you for even the smallest of moments. You're everything to me, Beck."

I took a step back, trying to distance myself so I could breathe and think. But my foot met nothing but air, and for one horrifying second I thought I would plunge off the edge of the waterfall and cease to exist. But Colin pulled me back to solid ground and into his arms, where he wrapped me in an embrace that felt like it shut the whole world out so it was just me and him.

"Beck," he said as I shook in his hold and realized what had almost just happened. "Please forgive me. I wish I could be brave like you, and I wish I had told you how I felt months ago. Tell me I'm not too late."

I clung to his shirt as my thoughts slowly settled around me until I could think again. Breathe again. "You love me?" I whispered. No matter how much I wanted to hear that, it felt too impossible.

He somehow managed to hold me even tighter. "More than I have words to say," he whispered.

But it wasn't that simple. He'd said so himself. I pulled away, keeping myself a safe distance from the waterfall, which he seemed to appreciate. "What about Macy?" I asked. As much as I loved her, as much as she might like me, she could never be okay with me replacing her mom's spot in her dad's life.

Colin managed a small smile and pulled a piece of paper from his back pocket. "She gave this to me last night after you left," he said, carefully unfolding it and looking down at whatever was written on there. "Most of it is just camp stuff, but…" He held it out, and when I took the paper, he pointed to the last few lines, which must have been written by Macy.

> *…and you were right about this place. Camp Rockwood really is magical, just like you said it would be. I didn't notice at first because I think I was wishing for the wrong thing, but now I know that it can make anything come true because it brought me someone for Dad. I think he's finally happy again now that he loves Beck, and that makes me happy. Anyway, I hope you like Heaven. I miss you, but I know you're kind of still here because Beck says you can read these letters if I write them to you. When you read this, can you make sure Beck and Dad find each other again? I think they need all the help they can get. Thanks.*
>
> *Love, Macy*

Tears filling my eyes, I looked up at Colin and found him half-smiling as he rubbed his ring finger on his left hand. His *empty* ring finger. He had taken his wedding ring off?

"Clearly Macy knew my heart before I did," he said with a little shrug.

I swallowed. "I mean," I said carefully, "you are a little slow sometimes. Not the sharpest tool in the shed."

"Definitely not," he replied and took a step closer. "You'd think, having been through this before, I would be better prepared."

My heart stopped. "What?"

And my stomach dropped at the same time he did.

"Marry me," he said as he knelt on one knee and held up his ring. "I guarantee this won't fit, but one of the perks of owning a ridiculously successful tech company is having the means to buy new things, and I can fix the problem as soon as we get somewhere with a little more Wi-Fi. And maybe a credit card machine."

I thought I might fall over as I stared at the little circle of silver between his thumb and forefinger. "Are you serious?"

"I'm kneeling in the dirt at the top of the sixteenth tallest waterfall in California. And yes, I looked it up because I knew you would be crazy enough to think a four hundred-foot cliff was a relaxing place to hang out. So yeah, I'm serious."

"But what about Rockwood?" I whispered, knowing very well it was a terrible argument.

Colin's gaze sharpened just a little. "You mean the camp you were offered to run, something you conveniently forgot to tell me about?"

I nodded, at a loss for words.

"I think you'd be perfect for the camp."

"But the Alvarez Trust—"

"Can spare you for a few months out of the year, Beck. You promoted John Foster for a reason."

"But—"

"I'm still kneeling here," he said, and though he was going for an impatient tone, his growing smile gave him away. He was coming out the victor, and he knew it. "Beck Alvarez," he said, "I can guarantee that if you marry me, I will do everything in my power to make sure you will be happy for the rest of your life."

I cocked my head. "That's quite a bet," I said and couldn't help but smile. "I'm afraid it might not be worth the risk."

"You're not afraid of anything," he replied, and in the next second he was on his feet, my head in his hands and our mouths only a hairbreadth apart. "Marry me," he said again and gave me the softest of kisses.

"Will you sing songs with me?" I asked as my heart threatened to explode.

He smiled. "All the time."

"And would you go skydiving with me?"

He kissed me again. "If you asked me to."

"Do you promise to stop lurking?"

"No. I will always be right behind you."

"Good." And though it was absolutely terrifying to admit something like this out loud, I said it anyway. I had been wanting to say it for so long: "I love you, Colin Donovan."

His smile, though small, could have outshined the sun. "Is that a yes?"

I laughed, and I had never been happier than I was in that moment. It was the kind of happiness I wanted to shout to the heavens because I couldn't keep it to myself. "Yes," I told him.

Absolutely yes.

Dear Dalia,

Another summer come and gone. I can't believe how quickly time flies by when you're having fun, no matter how many times people say it. Maybe this year was worse, though, because I have never had so much fun in my life. Taking over the camp meant I didn't have to look out for my one cabin of girls, AKA I got to look out for all of the girls, and I have never loved them more. All of them were so supportive of me taking Linda's spot, and I'm pretty sure all the Hargrave girls were even better behaved than usual, which is saying something. We had so many girls apply for camp that I built three more cabins and an extra wing on the mess hall just to make sure we had enough space, and I'm already planning for more next year.

Who would have thought Rockwood would become so popular?

You were wrong, you know. You probably don't know that I remember, but when I was eleven, you told me about a day that would come in my life that felt like a dream because I was so happy. You said for you it was the day I was born and that I would recognize it when I saw it. You were wrong, because I swear every time I think I've hit that day, the next one is even better. I...

CHAPTER EIGHTEEN

I paused writing and looked up, though nothing had caught my attention, really. Not a sound or movement. It was just a feeling.

A good feeling.

All of the girls had left this morning, so Camp Rockwood was strangely silent after two months of constant noise. I couldn't help but close my eyes as I sat on my little bench by the lake, soaking in the silence and reminding myself how nice it was to slow down and take a moment to just breathe. Before I knew it, I would be back in the city, and John Foster would have a million ideas to run by me because a phone call a week definitely didn't give him enough time to tell me how great I was at leading the Alvarez Trust as well as offer up new ideas for me to play with.

I couldn't wait to get back into the pomp and circumstance and try to keep turning the elite world on its head.

For now, though, everything was simply peaceful.

But where had Colin run off to? Leaving my half-finished letter on the bench, I started wandering the lake's edge, tempted to start singing, since he would most likely join in as soon as he heard me. But I didn't want to break the silence. Not yet. I would find him eventually.

For the most part, he had holed himself up in my office all summer and focused on work, since his company had somehow gotten even more chaotic over the last several months. He occasionally made his appearances—a highlight for some of the girls, apparently—but he recognized the need to give Macy some independence while she was here at camp and did his best to keep himself scarce.

At least from the girls. I had never let him stay hidden from me for long.

There he is.

Grinning, I paused at the edge of the dock and watched him for a moment, since a year ago I wouldn't have been able to imagine him in this spot let alone actually witness it. He had stretched out on the far end of the dock, his face in the sun and his legs hanging over the edge so he could stick his bare feet in the cool water. He looked so at ease that I was tempted to leave him and come back later.

It was his t-shirt that pulled me closer, though.

Colin didn't generally wear t-shirts, so that by itself was quite an accomplishment. But the thing looked ridiculous. It looked like a hundred girls had taken a pack of sharpies to it, and when I got closer, I realized that was exactly what it was. Notes and pictures and several hearts and XOXOs had turned the white shirt multi-colored, and I could only just see the word "McDreamy" printed across the front in black.

They must have given it to him at the farewell ceremony this morning.

"Starting a new fashion trend?" I said, kicking off my sandals before I sat and dipped my toes in the lake.

He opened his eyes, and in the sunlight they were more gold than green as he looked up at me. "I promised I would wear it the whole day," he said, his face turning red.

It took every ounce of strength I had not to laugh. "You, Mr. Donovan, are quite the distraction."

He sat up so quickly that I barely had time to flinch before he had me wrapped up in his arms. "And you, Mrs. Donovan," he said against my mouth, "have no idea what distracting is."

I fell into his kiss, warm from the sun and his touch and the pounding of my heart because how could anything possibly get better than this?

Two and a half months of marriage, and he still managed to make me love him more with every passing moment.

Eventually, we settled next to each other on the dock, hip-to-hip with our feet in the water. Colin played with my fingers, and I rested my head against his shoulder, and I wished I could stay there forever.

"How was Macy today?" I asked quietly. The lake was so peaceful that I felt like anything above a whisper would break the calm.

Colin took a slow, deep breath. "She couldn't wait to leave me behind," he said, and his voice carried both relief and worry.

"She'll only be gone a week, Colin. And Zoey's family won't let anything happen to her."

"I know."

He did know. I knew he did. But the last time he had left his daughter for more than a day, she had lost her mom, and that would always stay with him.

"Hey," I said and twisted, pulling one leg up beneath me so I could sit facing him. I smiled when he wrapped an arm around my back, just in case I fell. He was good about that, making sure I didn't fall. "I know you're scared," I told him, pressing a hand to his cheek. "And you have a right to be. But do you remember what you said to me on that waterfall?"

Turning his head so he could kiss my palm, he nodded.

"Love comes with risks," I said. "And I know how much you love Macy. I love her too. But she's been looking forward to this all summer. This is a big step for her, spending a week with a friend, and she's grown so much. You need to let her heal."

Colin took his time examining my face, reading every emotion I tried to show him, and when he did speak, he did it so softly that I had to lean even closer to him to hear. I was pretty sure he did that on purpose. "What would I have ever done without you, Beck?" he said. "You saved me."

He looked way too kissable in that moment, and I couldn't help myself despite the seriousness of his comment. Kissing my husband was one of my favorite pastimes, particularly when he went a while before making the time to get a haircut. I would run my hands through that hair of his for hours if he let me.

"You saved me back," I said, though it took me a moment to find my breath again. "I never would have survived those first few months in the city."

"And now you're everyone's favorite charity queen," he replied.

That was over-exaggerating, but I had had a lot more people interacting with me after the elite world saw how much success we'd had with the Hargrave School. With that on top of everything John and I had been doing with the Trust, I couldn't go two days without some new wealthy so-and-so wanting my help running their next charity event.

But no matter how good things had been in May, I'd been away for more than two months. Things could have changed.

Colin must have seen my apprehension, because he tucked my hair behind my ear and kissed my forehead. "Relax," he said. "You're as much a part of that world as you are this one, and you've made sure they know it. You'll be fine, and you'll hit the ground running like you do with everything. You're not scared of anything, remember?"

I was scared of finding out none of this life I'd made for myself was real. But if that was my only fear, I was pretty sure I would be fine.

Before I started freaking myself out more, I figured it would be a good idea to change the subject.

"So we have a whole week without Macy," I said and moved myself onto his lap. We hadn't even gotten a week for our honeymoon, which had been a day and a half squeezed in between two Alvarez Trust events just before summer started and I had to get ready for camp.

Colin grinned. "I can't remember the last time I had a week without a kid to worry about. What do adults do when they have free time like this? Eat ice cream for dinner and stay in their pajamas all day?"

That sounded pretty fantastic, actually, and I would definitely suggest it later in the week. But for now… "I can think of one thing we can do," I said and teased a kiss against his lips.

He clearly liked whatever he thought I was going to say, because he pulled me closer. "What's that? If you're with me, I'll do anything."

I glanced across the lake, where a large platform stood high in the air with a cable stretching over the water. I hadn't been ziplining yet this summer, and I wanted to fly before my feet touched the ground again. But I couldn't do it alone.

Oh, he was going to regret those words.

The End

Special sneak peek of Book 7 in the Simple Love Series,

Let Go

EXCERPT FROM *LET GO*

I was okay with the divorce. Honestly, I'd seen it coming for a while, and Jordan was nice about the whole thing. Yes, he got the house and the furniture and the dog, but I got to keep my car. He worked hard, so it only made sense that he got most of the things. And I could handle losing my job. I was the newest on the team, and the company was struggling. Logically, if they had to get rid of anyone, I was the best choice. I was even fine with my parents moving to Denmark on a whim. I might not have seen that one coming, but I would still be able to video chat with them, even if the hours were a little off. They deserved to do what made them happy, and I couldn't argue with their decision. They promised to come back for Christmas in a couple of years, at least, so it was fine. I was okay with all of that happening over the last week.

But the flat tire was too much.

It happened just outside of Kansas City. The car suddenly jerked away from me, and I might have screamed a bit as I pulled over to the side and thankfully managed to get to the curb without too much careening back and forth like I always saw in the movies. It was late in the afternoon, and clouds were building overhead, and I sat there for a minute just trying to catch my breath.

"This is what happens when you aren't paying attention," I told myself and unbuckled my seatbelt with shaking fingers. At least there wasn't a lot of traffic going past, so I didn't feel like a complete idiot when I got to the passenger side of the car and frowned at the completely mangled front tire.

What had I hit? A chainsaw?

I took a deep breath and shivered as a bit of wind cut through my sweatshirt. I just had to think this through. My dad had taught me how to change a tire when I learned to drive, and yeah, okay, that might have been fifteen years ago, but how hard could it be? I had a spare in the trunk, and Dad had drilled it into me to always be prepared for this kind of thing, no matter what.

My first instinct was to call Jordan, and thankfully my phone was still in the car or I might have actually done it. Never mind he was way back in Chicago—calling my ex-husband was a terrible idea no matter what. I knew better than to bother him with something I should be able to handle myself. So instead of crawling into the car to get my phone, I rolled up my sleeves and pulled open the trunk.

"Well," I huffed and stared down at the complete mess of junk inside.

That was the problem with moving across the country without renting a van; I had a lot more stuff than I realized, and I wasn't so great at the whole block puzzle game thing, so it was all just piled in there and shoved into every little nook and cranny, wherever stuff could fit. It would all have to move if I wanted to get to the tire.

"We'll be smarter this time around," I told myself and started digging.

Half an hour later, I managed to clear out the trunk just enough to hoist open the floor mat and hold it up with my shoulder so I could grab the spare tire. Dang, were tires always that heavy, or was it just this particular one? I needed to go to the gym more often, apparently. Though, now that I didn't have a fancy one down the street from my house—the house that I no longer had—that wasn't likely to happen.

If I was being honest, it hadn't happened anyway.

"New Year's Resolution," I muttered then heaved the tire out with a grunt. "Never mind it's July."

By the time the tire was out and waiting, and I had grabbed the thingy to lift the car up, I was exhausted, and I hadn't even gotten to the fixing part of all this. I had no reason to be tired just from moving things around.

"Don't lie to yourself," I said, frowning down at the mess of tools I didn't know how to use. "You were exhausted to begin with. At least it can't get worse."

I should have known not to say those words out loud.

Kansas rainstorms were a whole lot worse than Illinois storms. Or maybe it was just this particular storm. It didn't matter which was true, because I was still soaked within minutes, and the second I bent down to try to lift up the lifter thingy, my feet slid in the mud and sent me sprawling.

And I cried.

I hadn't even cried the night Jordan handed me the divorce papers, but I sat there in the mud, huddling against my pathetic little car, and sobbed as the rain kept pouring buckets down. I missed my job, even if I hadn't been doing much marketing despite that being my job title. I missed my parents, even though I had just barely spent a day and a half with them.

I missed Jordan.

His little good morning kisses and the way he smiled when I gave him his coffee in the morning and the way he breathed when he was deep asleep. I really hadn't been able to sleep over the last week without him next to me, which was why I was so tired.

I wanted my life back.

I wasn't sure how long I sat there and cried in the rain, but it was long enough that I was starting to feel a little ridiculous. I was thirty years old, for goodness's sake. I was crying over a *flat tire*, and there were people out in the world who would kill to have a car at all. People probably *had* killed for a car like mine.

I gulped. "Don't think about that, Amelia," I said and brushed my wet sleeve over my face to dry my tears. Metaphorically. "You've had your cry, and now you can get back up and get to work. A pity party won't do anyone any good, and Amelia Blake does not sit in the mud and wait for Prince Charming to come to her rescue."

I would probably have to change my name, wouldn't I? Jordan was pretty clear about wanting everything that was his, and that included his last name.

What would I change it to? Go back to being Amelia Cartier? That felt like a step backward, a return to the girl I used to be. There was a letter sitting on my dashboard that had another suggestion, but even thinking that one made me shudder. No, I wasn't brave enough for that name. At least not yet. I would have to look somewhere else, because it wasn't like people just walked around offering up names to share.

"Do you need some help?"

I shrieked and slipped in the mud again, sliding onto my backside and giving myself a pretty thorough view of the man who stood over me with concern. I hadn't heard a car pull up, but then again the rain was loud enough that I probably wouldn't have. But given the guy's level of soaking, I was pretty sure he'd been walking down the road, not driving it.

"Oh," I said, struggling to my feet, though the mud made it difficult. He was a pretty young guy, and by the looks of him he had been walking this road for a long time. Days, probably. "No, I'm…" I glanced at the tire and the lifter thingy that was still just sitting next to the car because I hadn't even gotten it underneath. "I'm fine."

His lips quirked on his thin face as he took me in. I must have looked terrible, covered in mud and soaking wet. Then again, he was just as soaked, so I was only half terrible. "You sure?" he asked, and one of his black eyebrows rose higher up his forehead than the other. His eyes were such a bright, icy blue that they seemed to glow through the storm, and I couldn't look away.

"Oh yeah," I said and tried to sound confident as I smiled at him. "I don't want to bother you, and I'll figure it out. How hard can changing a tire be, right?"

The quirk turned into a smile to match mine, and he glanced up the empty road, as if waiting for someone else to come along so he could be off the hook. But then he slid his shoulders out of what I realized was a guitar case and held it out to me. "Hold this," he said, and the moment my hands grasped the guitar, he dropped down to his knees and slid the lifter a few inches deeper under the car.

I stood there somewhat dumbstruck as he worked, maneuvering the thingy and twisting the x-shaped tool until the car started to rise on one side. He didn't have the problem of sliding around in the mud like I had, though I wasn't sure why it was so easy for him when he wasn't exactly a big guy. His black t-shirt did nothing to hide how slim he was, and though he was taller than me, that wasn't saying much. I was average at most, so this guy couldn't have been more than five foot nine. And yet he worked the tire off without much issue and was already lifting the spare into place before I was even aware he was doing it.

That was when I realized what I was holding. And that it was getting completely wet. The hard guitar case was old enough that I had a feeling it wasn't exactly waterproof, so while the stranger fixed my tire for me, even though I hadn't asked him to, I hurried to my pile of stuff behind the car and dug through it until I found a blue tarp that had sat in my trunk for years. It wasn't the prettiest solution, but at least it would keep the guitar dry. Drier than it was at the moment.

By the time I came back to the side of the car to see if he needed help, he was on his feet with the lifter thing in one hand and the ruined tire in the other. "You'll probably want to buy a new one," he said, lifting the tire a little before tossing it into the trunk. He was nicer with the lifter, holding it out to me so I could put it where it belonged. "Jack."

"Oh yeah!" I said. "*That's* what it's called."

He laughed, and water dripped from his dark, too-long hair as he shook his head. "No. I mean, yeah, that's what it's called, but I meant… I'm Jack." And he held out his greased and muddied hand.

Suddenly the rain didn't feel quite so cold as my face burned with heat. "Oh."

He pulled his hand back, apparently thinking I didn't want to shake it, which wasn't at all the truth. I was about to, but now he probably thought I was both pathetic and rude. I liked to think at least the latter wasn't true.

"Thanks," he said and nodded to the tarp covering his guitar. "I've been meaning to get one of those."

"You can keep it," I replied before he tried to give it back.

Smiling again, he tucked the tarp a little more securely around the case then lifted it up and slipped it back over his shoulders. "Well, don't drive too fast on that spare. You should be able to make it back to Kansas City to get yourself a new tire. Ideally you should get four, but the others don't look too bad, so you might be okay."

My heart seemed to sink into my stomach. Needing to buy one new tire let alone four was going to be bad enough, but I hated the idea of backtracking, even if it was only twenty or thirty miles. This drive was pushing my bank account's limits as it was, and gas wasn't exactly cheap.

"Thanks," I said and started running through my budget again, trying to see where I had some extra money. I stared at the spare tire that looked so innocent but wasn't as helpful as it wanted me to believe.

Jack was already a good thirty feet down the road before I realized he'd started walking again.

"Wait!" I shouted and nearly slipped in the mud again when I dashed forward to stop him. "You're going to walk in this rain?"

He glanced up at the sky as if he hadn't even noticed the water pouring down. How could he smile at a time like this? I was legitimately waiting for the floods to come, and he didn't seem bothered in the least. "You know, it's not too bad," he said and grinned. "At least it's summer, right?"

Looking back at my repaired car, I knew I couldn't just let him wander off into the storm looking like a drowned rat. The man had fixed my tire, for crying out loud, and I was taught better than to let him go without something to repay him. "Come with me back to Kansas City," I said. "Let me buy you lunch."

My budget screamed a little.

But Jack smiled again, and the expression was so warm that I knew I couldn't rescind my offer. "I can't argue against free food," he said and wandered back to the car. And before I could stop him, he slid the guitar off his shoulders again and began reloading my trunk.

I thought about arguing, but I was too tired for that and simply joined him, handing off my little possessions as he placed them with a lot more care and deliberation than I had. Clearly this guy was a lot better at that one game with the falling cube shapes than I was. Within ten minutes, everything I owned was back in the car, and Jack was squished in the front seat with his guitar between his legs as we drove in the opposite direction of where I wanted to go.

Weirdly, it felt almost normal to have him sitting next to me as I drove, and at first I chalked it up to familiarity. I'd been married for several years, so it wasn't like I spent a lot of time in the car by myself. But then I considered the fact that Jordan was always the one who drove, and I couldn't remember the last time I had had a passenger when I was behind the wheel.

Something about having Jack in the car with me after my little breakdown made all of this feel better somehow. In the middle of the worst rainstorm I'd ever seen, Jack was almost like his own source of calm as he looked out the window and silently watched the plains go by. Sure, I'd hit rock bottom. When it rains, it pours, all of that. But I had a feeling everything would be okay.

I had no idea what it was, but something about Jack felt important. Like we were meant to cross paths on this highway in Kansas.

I wondered if I would ever figure out why.

ABOUT THE AUTHOR

Dana LeCheminant has been telling stories since she was old enough to know what stories were. After spending most of her childhood reading everything she could get her hands on, she eventually realized she could write her own books too, and since then she always has plots brewing and characters clamoring to be next to have their stories told. A lover of all things outdoors, she finds inspiration while hiking the remote Utah backcountry and cruising down rivers. Until her endless imagination runs dry, she will always have another story to tell.